Praise for Bi

"Bite Somebody is the Pretty in Pink consciously retro, and not afraid to be goofy. Sara Dobie Bauer knows how to keep a reader smiling."

—Christopher Buehlman, author of *Those Across the River*

"I devoured this book (no pun intended) in one greedy sitting. It is gripping, it is funny, and OH MY GOD, it is sexy. Celia Merkin is a fabulous heroine, vulnerable and steely in equal measure, and Ian is a proper dreamboat. I just loved this. Sara Dobie Bauer's next book will be on my must-read list."

—Lucy Holliday, author of *A Night in with Audrey Hepburn*

"Bite Somebody is sexy, funny, and A-positively alive with colorful characters. Celia is perfectly imperfect and insecure; adorable sexy human, Ian, sparkles more than any undead ever could; and Imogene is the kind of bad-influence friend we all need in our lives. Bursting with tasty giggles, devilish guffaws, and swoony sighs, Bite Somebody is an absolute pleasure to sink your teeth into."

—Jennifer Scott, author of *The Accidental Book Club*

"Witty banter and hot sexy-times make Bite Somebody sparkle in all the right ways!"

—Beth Cato, author of *The Clockwork Dagger* series

"Often side-splittingly hilarious, at times poignant and overwhelmingly relatable, Sara Dobie Bauer takes us on a journey of self-discovery, friendship, and first love—with a dash of A-positive, surfer dude charm. Bite Somebody is a fresh, witty, rum-soaked take on the modern vampire story that you'll want to shamelessly sink your teeth into."

—Tiffany Michelle Brown, author of *Spin* and *Give it Back*

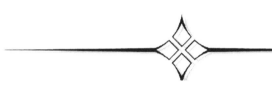

6/2/18

To Ryan—
Only bite the people
you love !!

Bite Somebody

❖

Sara Dobie Bauer

signature Sara D Bauer

World Weaver Press

WW

Published by World Weaver Press, LLC
Albuquerque, NM
www.WorldWeaverPress.com
Editor: Trysh Thompson
Cover layout and design by Amanda C Davis. Cover images used under license
from Shutterstock.com.

First edition: June 2016
ISBN-13: 978-0692661833
ISBN-10: 0692661832

Also available as an ebook

For Sam, who's still looking for her surfer boy

ACKNOWLEDGMENTS

What began as a short story turned into *Bite Somebody*, thanks to *Shimmer Magazine* editor and author, E. Catherine Tobler, who thought Celia's voice was too good for a mere 5000 words.

Fellow romance author and Twitter friend, Megan Gaudino, referred me to World Weaver Press, for which I owe her several martinis. My editor at WWP, Trysh Thompson, has consistently geeked out over how much she loves my characters, and without her, this book wouldn't have happened.

HELLO! to the entire city of Longboat Key, Florida (Drift Inn, too), because, if you hadn't noticed, my silly vampires took over your town.

Thanks to writer Tiffany Michelle Brown, my creative Gemini twin who operates as a sexy red balloon that consistently manages to lift me from rejection funks.

Thanks to my Sami who read *Bite Somebody* in one afternoon, texting off and on about how she was laughing…crying…laughing because of how much she related to Celia. Sam was the first person who made me realize *Bite Somebody* was more than just rom-com and that the book might actually affect people's lives.

My parents accidentally raised two artists. (The horror!) Yet, they have persevered and supported me with their love and loud cheerleading—along with Aunt Susie, my SOMOH (Sexy Old Maid of Honor), more friend than relative.

I'd be nowhere without my gorgeous husband, Jake, who supports his wife's crazy career and supports his wife's, oh, *general craziness*. I love you, babe, always. Thanks for loving me back, no matter what.

God gets a shout out, too. (Sometimes, buddy, I don't know what You're thinking, but You never let me down.)

Finally, to everyone who's ever had a fat day, a sad day, or a maybe-I-don't-want-to-live-anymore day: Remember to find the funny, because even when blood hunters are after your boyfriend, there's still Bob Marley. There's still the ocean. There is still love.

BITE SOMEBODY

"Immortality is just living longer with more embarrassment."
Dracula (paraphrased)

CHAPTER ONE

Celia Merkin rode her powder blue beach cruiser down the humid length of Admiral Key, past darkened palm trees swinging in the nighttime breeze—and one hissing goose. She arrived to work at the gas station just as her boss, Omar, was leaving. He looked like he should have been a bouncer—the size of the Incredible Hulk, but less green.

"Where's your apron?" he said.

She held up her orange "Happy Gas" apron, sucking air from her hurried ride.

"Why aren't you wearing it?"

"I just got here."

He rubbed his bald head, maybe for good luck. "You ride your bike here, Celia, right?"

"Yes."

"Then, wear your apron the whole way here. That way, people see 'Happy Gas' and think they should come here, too. Capisce?"

Omar was not Italian. Celia had no idea why he said things like "capisce." She nodded, thinking, *Why not? Not like wearing an ugly orange apron is going to ruin my image.* Not like she had an image at all.

"Enjoy your night," Omar said. "Gun's under the counter." He winked.

The bell above the door clacked when he left. The bell had been broken for months. It was now just an empty piece of metal that clacked when customers arrived: *clack, clack, clonk.*

Ralph was behind the counter, closing out his drawer. He was seventeen and read surfer magazines. "Hey, Red," he said in reference to her mess of hair.

"Please don't call me Red. You know I don't like it."

"Okay, Ceeeeeeelia." He put extra emphasis on her name and shook his tan hands in the air like flapping seagulls.

Celia had been with Happy Gas for three years, ever since she dropped out of college and sold her parents' house in the nearby city of Lazaret. She only recently switched to the night shift. She didn't have to talk to half as many people that way. Her therapist suggested she should meet more people, make some connections. However, the more interactions she had with others, the less she liked people.

"Tonight is gonna be tight," Ralph said, slamming the drawer shut on the cash register.

Celia put her apron over her head and loosely tied the strings.

"Don't you wanna know why?"

She sighed.

"There's gonna be this sick party at a club in Lazaret. Totally sick."

"You can't go to clubs," Celia said. "You're seventeen."

"Duh, Celia, I have a fake ID. Everyone cool has a fake ID."

Celia did not think Ralph was cool. Freddie Mercury was cool. Ralph was...a *tool.*

She wasn't surprised about the fake, though. Her gas station co-worker was all about illegal activities. Since she worked the night shift, he once asked how she slept through the day, what with the sun and all. She told him she put tin foil on her bedroom window, but

Ralph told her that was a bad idea. "Cops look for tin foil in windows as a sign of hydroponic pot growing."

Ever since he told her that, Celia had been paranoid and looking for a tin foil replacement. She didn't really believe Ralph, but she also didn't want to take a chance. Although she was not growing weed, she didn't know how she would explain a fridge filled with bags of blood.

Celia Merkin was a vampire, and it wasn't all it was cracked up to be. In movies, vampires were all super good-looking and confident and mysterious. Celia had seen *Interview with a Vampire*. She had seen all the vampire movies ever made, and every bloodsucker was always hot and suave. She expected to wake up one morning looking like Kate Beckinsale. Instead, she woke up with bed head and dry drool on the outside of her mouth wondering what the hell went wrong.

Ralph slapped a tan hand on her shoulder. "Do you ever hit the clubs, Celia?"

She shivered him off her shoulder. *Annoying little boy.* "No."

She wanted to tell him, *Yeah, I went to a club once and got turned into a vampire.* She even considered going all Bela Lugosi, "I vant to suck your blood huh huh huh." Celia had several such fantasies every day that she never went through with. Her therapist told her she was "repressed."

Ralph just shrugged. "Yeah. I guess cool guys don't usually go for girls like you."

Some of her red hair escaped her ponytail. She shoved it behind her ears and started paying attention to the cash register.

"Do you have a boyfriend, Ceee-leee-uh?" Ralph leaned close to her again. He smelled like Cheetos.

Celia didn't have a boyfriend, but *he* had walked by her apartment that day—the guy who made her nose tingle. She didn't know what he looked like, but he smelled like men's deodorant half worn off—sweaty, athletic male.

Woodsy BO.

Celia didn't cop to having a crush on the smell of her neighbor. Instead, she ignored stupid Ralph and pushed a button on the register that made the drawer open. She opened the drawer; she closed the drawer. She just wanted Ralph to leave so she could start reading her newest piece of research—a series about vampires called *Twilight*.

Since her change, she'd been doing all sorts of vampire "research." She'd gotten through *Interview with a Vampire*, book and film versions, which basically made her suicidal. In Anne Rice's opinion, vampires obviously were all super hot and wanted to bang each other, regardless of sexual orientation—just bang, bang, bang. Plus, they were all classy and confident. They were basically exactly what Celia expected to become when Danny's teeth popped through her skin, but her expectations were far from reality.

Ralph smacked her on the shoulder. "Of course you don't have a boyfriend!" He laughed like she'd done something hilarious, and Celia knew she wasn't funny unless it was accidental. He held onto his stomach and laughed and laughed. Maybe she should talk to her therapist about why a seventeen-year-old high school kid made her feel like the hunchback of Notre Dame.

He finally left.

She had a couple customers—mostly guys buying beer after day shift, other guys buying coffee for the night. There were some pretty girls, beachy girls, who bought cigarettes and bubble gum. Some tourists bought Tums.

Finally, about eleven, Celia got to settle in with her new book.

She sighed and started into *Twilight*.

She was just to the part where Bella first sees Edward when the empty bell *clank-clanked*, and she looked up to see a girl in the doorway. She was actually a woman, probably Celia's age, although at twenty-three, she still had trouble calling herself an adult.

The woman had wild, curly, purple hair, outlined by the lights above the gas pumps outside. Half her hair was pulled up in a purple plastic clip on the side of her head. She wore sunglasses—retro ones with red plastic rims—and a tight black t-shirt, tight jeans, and big combat boots. She carried a cassette player on her hip, attached to white earbuds that hung around her neck.

The woman let go of the door like it disgusted her and clomped right past Celia at the register. She stomped up and down the aisles, not looking at anything. Finally, she ended up at the beer cooler, which she passed up in exchange for juice—peach juice.

As she walked to the counter, Celia buried her nose in her book and pretended she hadn't been staring.

The strange creature pounded her peach juice against the counter. "Got any rum?"

"No, sorry, we don't sell hard liquor here," Celia said.

"Bummer." She reached into the pocket of her tight jeans and pulled out a black leather wallet.

"Three-fifty, please."

Purple-head planted a five between them, and as Celia toyed with the register, she felt like she was being watched. When she looked up to give the woman her change, her sunglasses were tilted down. Dark blue eyes bored into Celia. She was reminded of Dr. Savage, her therapist, the way she always looked over her glasses before making some deep, spiritual assessment.

"You're new," the stranger said.

"I've worked here for three years."

The stranger coughed out a chuckle. "No. *New.*" She smiled at Celia, only not really a smile. She flashed a gleaming set of white fangs at her.

"Oh! Yeah!" Celia shouted.

Holy shit! This was the first vampire she'd met since her turn three months before, outside of her blood dealer and her therapist. She wanted to hug the woman across the counter, but fearing possible death by humiliation, she hugged herself instead.

"How did you know?" Celia asked.

"You smell funny." She sniffed like she was making a point. "You haven't even had your first bite yet."

"N-no."

The woman stared at Celia some more. Based on the little twitch on the outside of her mouth, she was either amused or appalled. Celia could never tell the difference. Then, her new vampire friend (ish) took her change and shoved her wallet back into her tight jeans. "Okay, then. Good luck." She made a weird little noise like Butthead, only quieter, and turned for the door.

Celia was blowing it! Blowing it! "Wait!" She rounded the counter and stopped with her hand on the exit. "Could we hang out sometime?"

"You're fucking kidding me."

"No." Celia scratched her scalp. "See, I don't know anyone in the, in the...anyone else like me. Well, I mean, I guess I know two vampires, but I don't really like them. So I'd like to meet more vampire people. Maybe you could—I could hang out with you sometime?"

"Newbie, you gotta pull your shit together. You sound like Rain Man."

"I'm sorry."

"You're not my kind of people." The purple-headed vamp chick pushed the door open, past Celia. The air smelled like salt, fish, and gasoline.

"If you could just show me around a little or introduce me to some other vampires?" Celia followed her out into the night. "My therapist says I need to meet people, or, I mean, vampires, and make connections to help with my integration into my new lifestyle. I journal a little bit, too, but you know..."

"Why are you following me?" She headed out toward the street. Her boot clomps resounded like a car backfire through the quiet night.

"Because I need—I need help." Ten points for honesty.

The vamp in sunglasses turned to face Celia. She hid behind her shades. "I'm not helpful." She reached for one of the white earbuds on her shoulder and shoved it in her ear the way Celia imagined someone might shove an icepick in the head of their arch enemy.

"You could just let me go out with you some time. Once."

"I'm not into chicks."

"No, no!" Celia waved her hands in the air. "Not like that. A place where vampires go. You could take me, and maybe I could, you know, meet other vampires?" Celia paused. "You look like you know other vampires."

"I don't hang out with geeks." She popped in the other earbud.

"I'm not a geek. I'm a nerd."

The stranger slowly removed the newly placed earbud. "There's a difference?"

"Duh."

She did that weird, low Butthead chuckle thing again. "What's your name?"

"Celia Merkin."

"You know merkin is slang for a pubic wig."

"I know," Celia said. "It's not what my name means, though." She raised her eyebrows haughtily and looked at the pavement.

"Look, Merk." She adjusted her stance so one of her thin hips protruded out toward the street. "Find some guy. Have your first bite. Then, you know, pick people up at bars, take 'em home, and feed." She shrugged.

"I'm not good at picking up guys," Celia said.

"No shit?"

"I'm serious."

"I know you're serious." The woman pushed her dark sunglasses up on her nose and reinserted her earbud. "Just...bite somebody." She turned and started clomping away.

Celia was about to walk back inside Happy Gas when the mean vampire stopped walking.

"Hey, Merk."

"Yeah?"

She took off her sunglasses. She had on dark purple eye makeup that made the whites of her eyes glow like icebergs. "If you haven't bitten anyone yet, how are you…" She gestured with her sunglasses. "How are you walking around right now?"

"What do you mean?"

"You should be dead, desiccated, like, dried up." She indicated a choking gesture at her neck.

"Oh, I have a dealer," Celia said.

The purple-headed oddball stomped toward Celia, which made Celia step back until her ass hit the ice cooler out front. "You have a dealer? How the fuck do you have a dealer?"

Celia stuttered.

"Merk. English."

"I have a connection."

"What connection?" She stuck her chin out at Celia.

"I'm not supposed to say!"

The woman's dark eyes looked up and down the main drag of Admiral Key, and she sniffed the air. "You got blood at your house right now?"

"Yeah, I keep a weekly supply."

"When do you get off work?" The woman was so close, Celia could hear synth music from the lonely earbud that hung over her shoulder.

"Not until close to sunrise." Celia frowned. "But I don't work tomorrow night."

"Cool. Let's hang out."

"Really?"

"Totally." The stranger tried to smile. It looked kind of like a cheerful sneer. "I'm Imogene."

◈

Woodsy BO Guy walked by her apartment twice during the day

while Celia slept on and off, awakened by the itchy twitch in her nose. He lived right next door. The place was empty for a while, because Celia was on one side and her crazy landlady, Heidi, was on the other. No one wanted to live right next to their landlady, especially since Heidi had ears like a bat and obsessively watched this show about real-life murderers called *True Crime* at the volume of the hearing impaired.

Heidi's husband died under mysterious circumstances fifteen years ago in Iowa. Celia liked to pretend Heidi did it.

Celia had been spending a lot of time in her kitchen as of late, because the kitchen wall was the only wall shared with Woodsy BO Guy. She could smell him best from there. She'd never seen Woodsy, but for some reason, young Bruce Willis came to mind, circa *Die Hard*.

She'd also noticed a new bike at the apartment complex rack. For the longest time, it was just Celia's powder blue beauty. Now, there was this sleek, sexy black number. Most of her neighbors were either semi-chubby retirees from the north or alcoholic beach bums. They wouldn't own a bike that that. That bike belonged to Woodsy BO Guy; she could smell him on it.

Sniff. Sniff.

CHAPTER TWO

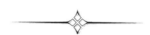

Imogene said she'd be over at eleven, which was perfect, since Celia had an appointment with her shrink at nine o'clock that night. Celia's parents died in a freak hurricane accident three years earlier and left her everything. Otherwise, she never would have been able to afford Dr. Rayna Savage.

She sounded like a comic book character, like lightning should shoot from her fingers—and maybe it did. Celia wasn't sure. Dr. Savage was hot with long, silky brown hair. She had an angular face with perfect bone structure. She was like those women in advertisements at Bloomingdale's, only she was a vampire.

Dr. Savage's office always smelled like lavender because she said lavender was calming. She kept the shades drawn, even though it was night.

She asked if Celia had been journaling, which Dr. Savage thought was super powerful for self-actualization.

"Yes!" Celia said. *Victorious!*

"Every day?"

"Well, twice," she said. *Less victorious!*

Dr. Savage tried to iron over the disappointed crinkle between her eyes by giving Celia a glittering grin. "Good. Twice is good. You should try journaling every night."

Celia sank further into the leather couch cushions, which evicted the sound of a fabric fart from deep within its pillows. "But something doesn't happen every night," she whined.

"Yes, Celia, something happens every night."

She wanted to argue with her doctor, because Celia didn't think hours spent watching her favorite 80s movies constituted "something."

"Just write what you're feeling," Dr. Savage said. "What are you feeling, Celia?"

She pulled a piece of lint from her yoga pants to avoid Dr. Savage's probing brown eyes. When her therapist was trying to probe, she tilted her chin down and looked at Celia over her spectacles. It was very unnerving.

But honestly, Celia had been feeling a lot, ever since the arrival of Woodsy BO Guy. He'd moved in to the Sleeping Gull Apartments seven days earlier, and Celia had been avoiding actually meeting him ever since.

She didn't bring up Woodsy. She wasn't ready. She didn't even bring up the strange girl named Imogene who would be at her apartment that very night. Instead, she said, "I'm feeling disappointed."

"Disappointed about what, Celia?"

"Well. Danny said becoming a vampire would make me more special."

Dr. Savage's voice went all sing-song. "You *are* special. We're *all* special."

Celia wasn't buying it. "Danny said I would be different and prettier and men would like me, but I'm just the same, only more pale." She threw her hands in the air. "I mean, it's been three months, I haven't bitten anyone, and I spend all my time drinking blood from hospital donation bags when I'm not working the night shift at a gas station. Being a newbie sucks."

Dr. Savage went probing again. "I think your problem isn't being a newborn vampire, Celia. I think your problem goes further back."

Like when she was the fat kid in high school? Like when she only had one friend, Layla, and she was only Celia's friend because she lived next-door growing up? Or like when she woke up the morning she was turned to find a note from Danny that just said, "See ya," along with phone numbers for Dr. Rayna Savage and a blood dealer named Steve.

Dr. Savage then announced, "I think you have a fear of your first bite."

Celia pouted. "I just haven't met the right person."

"Celia. You never meet anyone."

She pulled another piece of lint from her yoga pants and begrudgingly agreed to see Dr. Savage twice a week.

She came home from therapy to the smell of Woodsy BO Guy and the sound of his blender through the kitchen wall. Then, she straightened her house like her great-grandmother was about to show up with a white glove to test for dust. She hid her dirty laundry under the bed. She arranged her extensive VHS collection in perfect rows beneath her TV. She checked the fridge three times for blood as if some blood goblin was going to come steal it. She stood and appraised her obsessive reordering.

Celia had come to realize her apartment looked nothing like a vampire lair. Maybe if she had more candles. *Yes, definitely more candles.*

She put in a movie to await Imogene's arrival. She chose something that would calm her down: *Star Wars: Return of the Jedi.* She spent the next hour pacing between her living room and the kitchen. On one side, she was comforted by the sound of light sabers. In her kitchen, she was comforted by the scent of Woodsy BO Guy.

She only relegated herself to the living room when she noticed she'd pressed her entire body against the wall between apartments and scratched little claw marks in the off-white paint.

By 11:30, Celia gave up on Imogene, so she pulled out her copy of *Labyrinth*. David Bowie in spandex was very soothing. Then, there was a shattering knock on her front door. Celia thought the hinges were going to give way, which of course, scared the hell out of her landlady and possibly woke Woodsy BO Guy, who'd been sleeping for the past hour. Celia wasn't stalking him. It was just…he had a loud snore that she could sometimes hear through the cheap apartment plaster.

By the time Celia got to the front door, she could already hear Heidi screaming at Imogene from two doors down.

"Do you know what time it is?"

Celia opened the door in time to see Imogene say, "Whoa," and take a step backwards like Celia did every time she saw a palmetto bug.

Celia supposed Heidi was sort of shocking. She looked like she'd lived on the beach her whole life, since her skin closely resembled an antique baseball mitt. She wore a white-blonde wig. Even at that hour, wrapped in a robe the color of fluorescent yellow cat puke, she had on The Wig. The Wig was shaped like a huge, upside-down bowl.

Heidi shook her fist. "Do you know what time it is, Celia?"

"Yes, Heidi, I'm sorry. We'll be quiet."

"You better." She pursed her old lady lips together. Heidi had to be at least eighty, but it didn't stop her from walking the beach in a bikini every day. She turned and slammed her front door.

Imogene flicked a thumb at her absence. "What the fuck was that?"

"My landlady," Celia said.

"She looks like a fake person." Imogene nodded toward Heidi's front door.

"You think she's a robot?"

"I don't know, Merk. She's scary as shit, though." Imogene clomped inside. *Clomp, clomp.* She wore another tight t-shirt, same tight jeans, same combat boots, and red plastic sunglasses, complete with cassette player on her hip. Her crazed, curly hair was held in a clip on top of her head. She smelled like fruit punch. She pointed at Celia's poster of David Bowie.

"You like Bowie?"

"Um, yeah, he's okay."

"What do you mean he's okay?" Imogene seemed offended.

"I mean he's awesome."

Imogene poked at Celia's TV, then her VCR. "What's this, an antique? Why don't you get a damn DVD player?"

"Oh, well, all my movies are from when I was a kid," she said.

Imogene didn't say anything.

"It just seems a waste to update, you know?"

"I get it. I mean..." She gestured to the small cassette player at her hip. Then, Imogene stuck her nose in the air and sniffed. She continued sniffing as she moved through the living room and into Celia's kitchen. She planted her body right where Celia had been a couple hours earlier. She took a deep, deep sniff. "Who lives next door?"

Celia stood in the doorway and played with her hands. "I don't know."

Imogene took a breath that would have filled a pair of elephant lungs. "He smells good."

"Blood in the fridge!" Celia spat.

"Oh, right." Imogene moved away from the wall, which made Celia feel better. Maybe she *was* stalking Woodsy BO Guy. She felt ownership over his scent, and she didn't want Imogene anywhere near him.

Quickly diverting her attention, Celia opened the fridge, and Imogene made an impressed "heh" noise. "Wow, that's a lot of blood." She reached around Celia and grabbed a bag. "A-positive? Got any B-neg?" She dug through the bags.

"I only drink A-positive."

Imogene pulled out a single bag, popped the top, and jumped on the countertop, where she sat and commenced to consume. "Why?" she asked between gulps.

Celia modestly removed her own bag and sat at the kitchen table. "It makes me feel like I got a good grade, you know? Like A-plus."

Imogene finished the entire bag and dropped the empty in the kitchen sink.

Celia gasped. If she'd consumed that much blood that fast, she would have been on the ceiling, literally, clinging to it like a giant, redheaded bat. Instead of the ceiling, Imogene clung to the countertop with both hands and swung her boot-clad feet back and forth. Celia could tell she was riding out the high. Blood gave vampires a hell of a rush. Celia compared it to caffeine via IV. Imogene, meanwhile, breathed a little faster and shook her head a couple times. Then, she hopped off the counter and stretched her arms over her head.

"All right, let's go out." She clapped her hands and moonwalked.

"Go out? You want to go out right now?"

"Yeah." She wheeled her arms in the air at an invisible punching bag.

"But, I, um…" Celia looked down at herself. She'd put on her black yoga pants to appear more formal. Other than that, she wore an oversized Minnie Mouse tee and white socks.

"Clothes. Where are your clothes?" Imogene barked.

"In my bedroom."

"Okay." She grabbed Celia by the wrist and tumbled her out of her chair. Celia stutter-stepped to keep up with Imogene's way above normal human speed. Then, Imogene shoved Celia on the bed and told her to drink up. She reached into Celia's closet and threw things over her shoulders. "No, no, no," she muttered.

Then, Imogene found Celia's faded Freddie Mercury off-the-shoulder sweatshirt and flipped her glasses onto the top of her head.

"This is fucking fabulous!" she shouted. "How do you own something like this?" Imogene's irises were gone, pupils blown full black by the influx of human blood. "Put this on. Do you own anything other than sweatpants?"

"They're yoga pants," Celia said.

Imogene stared at her, eyebrows squeezed together above her nose.

"I own a pair of jeans."

"Good. Put them on. Let's go."

"Where are we going?" Celia was afraid to ask.

"Lazaret, bitch. We're going to Necto."

Celia decided to consider Dr. Savage's advice, make friends, and hit the town with a mad woman.

Imogene owned a fast car—something black and topless. She also paid little attention to speed limits or oncoming traffic. Celia kept her hands over her face most of the ride.

Imogene took Beach Drive past Happy Gas and all the way down Admiral Key to the bridge where they crossed the Gulf of Mexico inlet and saw the pathetic lights of downtown Lazaret. Lazaret liked to believe it was a city, but it wasn't. Celia would know; she grew up there.

It was a stack of office buildings with squat restaurants and rooftop bars. It was a coven of homeless people and shopping carts. It was a shithole, but the freckle on the ass of Lazaret was Necto. Celia had never been there because it was considered hip. Her whole life, she'd been to one bar in Lazaret—Tequila Sunrise, a place for high schoolers with fakes. It was where she met Danny.

Imogene parked behind Necto. Celia could already hear the music from inside, and panic struck. "I can't go in there," she said. She clutched to the door of her car like a sailor in a storm, afraid of going overboard.

"Here." Imogene reached into her back pocket and pulled out a small, round, yellow pill. "Take this. It'll calm you down."

Celia swallowed the pill, thinking for a moment that there was a reason they said not to take candy from strangers…and Celia had never met anyone as strange as Imogene. But if the yellow pill could calm her down, so be it.

Imogene seemed to know everyone at Necto. She high-fived humans and kissed this one guy with glasses right on the mouth. The bartender immediately poured them two shots.

"What is it?" Celia asked over the late nineties techno music.

"Who cares," Imogene shouted.

The shot was something sweet and burny. The next thing Celia knew, there was a rum punch in her hand, and Imogene dragged her to the dance floor. Celia didn't dance, not that Imogene asked. She started doing all these crazy breakdance moves. It was almost as if she was in her own music video, but people were into it. When Imogene wasn't dancing, dudes surrounded her—guys who looked like they'd fallen off the cover of *GQ*.

Since being turned, Celia had developed this embarrassing new habit; she stared at men's necks. It was one of those things her therapist told her she wasn't supposed to do as a vampire. Apparently humans considered it off-putting. Celia didn't see how this was fair, since men stared at women's breasts all the time—not hers, but other women's. At Necto, she stared at the ceiling and watched the lights move around, until she felt Imogene dragging her to the bar for another shot and rum punch. When Celia asked about Imogene's cocktail choice she replied, "What? It's beachy, bitch."

It was about an hour into their festivities when things got fuzzy. It was like the night at Tequila Sunrise with Danny when Celia got way too drunk and woke up immortal. This was a different feeling, though. This wasn't just drunk. This was—*I gotta dance!*

Celia felt like she danced for a very long time. And there were more rum punches and more shots and she felt really relaxed until she vomited—all over Imogene.

Outside, Imogene screamed at her. "What's the matter with you?"
Celia wavered on her feet in response.

At least Imogene was in a dark t-shirt, so the vomit wasn't that
obvious. Celia wanted to tell her that. Plus, it was only rum punch.
Celia could smell it—like peach juice and bananas. She realized it was
the way Imogene always smelled.

"You're so new, you're still puking? Real vampires aren't even
supposed to be able to throw up." Imogene tore off her sunglasses
and stuck her nose right in Celia's face. "You are a total fuck up. Find
a ride home."

And in the middle of downtown Lazaret, Imogene took off her t-
shirt and threw it in the gutter. She had on a red satin bra underneath
and only then did Celia realize Imogene was way too hot to be friends
with a loser like her. Imogene put her glasses back on and returned to
the club. Somehow, in Celia's pill-induced haze, she found a cab.

Celia didn't know what time it was when she got back to the
Sleeping Gull Apartments, but she walked right past all the quiet,
closed doors with their lights out. She didn't smell Woodsy BO Guy;
instead, she heard the call of the sea. Once she felt sand under her
toes, she peeled off clothes—the Freddie Mercury sweatshirt, gone,
and her bra landed in the bushes. She fell on her face trying to get her
jeans off, but she finally wrestled free. She even took off her cotton
underpants before diving headfirst into a moonlit wave.

Under the cold water, she was still buzzing hard, and the mystery
pill left a blissful echo as she rumbled and tumbled through the
waves. She caught a mouthful of salt water and spit the taste of vomit
into the sea.

Celia loved the ocean—had since she was a kid—but once she got
old enough to realize she was the "fat kid," she refused to put on a
bathing suit. Days at the beach stopped, but since she'd been a
vampire, the night had become not something scary but, rather, a
comfort—a way to hide her stretch marks and insecurities. So Celia
swam at night, often. Maybe that had been Danny's real gift; he gave

her the ocean back.

She didn't know how long she floated, but she was still wasted when she got out. She wandered naked up the empty beach, weaving, ankles unsteady in the ever-moving sand. She didn't notice him until she smelled smoke and pine and happiness, and by then, she was six inches from his chest.

The man was way taller than Celia, which wasn't saying much since she was short. Still, she had to tilt her head up to see his face, which made her head spin and made him grab onto her naked arm to keep her upright. A cloud of smoke surrounded the guy, blue in the night-light. She could only really see his outline—weird, curly hair; freckled nose in the moonlight; relaxed shoulders. It was Woodsy BO Guy. Even surrounded by weed, she smelled his skin.

"I thought you were a mermaid," he said.

Literally, the last thing Celia remembered was running naked up the beach screaming, "I'm not a mermaid! I'm not a mermaid!"

CHAPTER THREE

After The Mermaid Incident, she fell into a death-like slumber. She didn't wake until about 9 p.m., which was really late for Celia, who usually woke with the sunset. She wasn't hung-over. She wasn't even sure vampires could be hung-over. She sipped slowly on a bag of blood, her stomach still lacking confidence. She put on her soft Minnie Mouse t-shirt from the night before and felt bad for herself.

Then, halfway through her pint...*the smell*. Woodsy BO Guy was right outside her front door.

Knock. Knock.

She wanted to hide. Her canines descended on their own accord. They'd never done that before. Apparently, from what she'd heard, it happened whenever a vampire was hungry or turned on, but Celia drank enough to never be hungry and her sex drive was somewhere in the negatives. Yet, there they were; the damn pokey things had escaped their caves. She put her hand to her mouth.

Then, his voice: "Mermaid? Are you alive?"

Oh. My. God.

She sprang to her feet and dropped the bag of blood on her bedroom floor. Sudden panic made her canines retract, at least, but

20

still, she couldn't answer the door, not with him out there, smelling like that.

"Mermaid?" He continued to knock.

Celia lay down on the floor as if the man could see through walls.

"I'll call the police if you don't answer. Tell them I smell a dead body."

Just what Celia was scared of, the police showing up on suspicion of a dead body only to discover blood all over the carpet. She stood and found her robe. She draped herself in oversized plush and took a long sip from her spilled blood bag before slowly approaching the front door.

She leaned her nose against it. "I'm fine. Thanks," she said.

She could feel him out there, the heat of his ear against her door in the shape of a seashell. "I need visual evidence."

"No, really, I'm fine." She scratched at the door like a dog wanting to be let out. His smell—*oh, goodness, that smell*. Celia was warm and out of breath.

"Come on, Mermaid. I won't leave until you open the door."

She opened the door just a little so he could see the side of her face.

"Hey," he said. The scent of weed from the night before had covered most of his normal smell—that and Celia's panic. In that moment, his smell attacked her full bore.

Once, when she was going through a really fat phase, Celia gave up pizza for a week. Then, her stupid parents ordered delivery, and she almost tackled the pizza guy because that pizza smelled so good. That was how she felt, like tackling tall, dark Woodsy.

"So. I saw you naked last night."

She closed her eyes. "Yeah."

"I brought your clothes." He held up her discarded ensemble, neatly folded in his huge hands.

Celia reached through the three inches of open door and tried to pull her clothes inside. She had to open the door a little more to get her jeans.

"I'm Ian," he said. "I just moved in."

Don't stare at his neck. Don't stare at his neck.

It was a really nice neck—long and thin. His Adam's apple bounced when he swallowed. Shit, she was staring at his neck.

"Celia." She blinked. "I'm Celia."

"It's really dangerous to swim alone at night. You know that, right?"

"I was drunk."

"Yeah, well, don't do it again, okay?"

She chewed her bottom lip. "I like swimming at night."

Ian glanced toward the sea. He had nice cheekbones and a freckle on his throat. *Don't stare at his neck.* "How about next time you take a dive, you come get me so I can make sure you're safe."

She felt tipsy on his smell and his sympathy. She'd known the guy for five minutes—his scent a bit longer—and he already wanted to keep her safe. Celia had known her parents for twenty years before they died, and the only thing they worried about was her cholesterol.

The most mystifying thing: Ian was way out of Celia's league. He was surfer boy cute—tall, lean, spindly. His hair was wild, like a nest of black baby snakes, wiggling in the sea breeze. In the fake illumination of their nighttime apartments, she couldn't really see the color of his eyes, but they were big and crinkled on the edges, permanently amused.

And he was worried about her.

All this put together made Celia's canines descend again. She covered her mouth with her hand. "Okay, thanks." When her fangs came out, she spoke with a slight lisp, so "thanks" really just sounded like a hiss.

She closed the door in his face, locked it, and raced to her bedroom to finish her bag of A-positive.

What exactly did Celia know about Ian?

He really liked to ride his bike. He took the sleek, black beauty out on a two-hour ride the following day. He came back soaked in sweat and with more freckles than when he left.

He had a scar on his right leg in the shape of, strangely, a bite mark.

He had a mother who was alive. He talked to her on the phone on the front porch outside. He laughed a lot. He touched his mouth when he talked. Celia found this to be very distracting.

Finally, if she thought he looked good in the night-light, *well*. She had trouble swallowing when she saw him in the sun. And her stupid fangs wouldn't stay in her head.

How did she see Ian in the sun? Vampires obviously explode and die in sunlight, but Celia was sneaky. By destroying an old black t-shirt (*Fraggle Rock*; a gift from her mom who had no idea Celia didn't like *Fraggle Rock*), Celia made an ingenious facial covering with small holes for her eyes. She then donned a pair of huge, ugly eighties sunglasses she bought thinking they looked cool. The front windows of her apartment were covered in thick, plastic blinds. She cut a little rectangle in the middle of one of them, and she stood there all day when she should have been sleeping.

She assumed Ian must work from home. Or he was unemployed. Maybe he was on vacation? He didn't go anywhere, except for the bike ride. She wasn't sure if he owned a car.

He did glance at her door once, when he got back from his ride. By then, he was drenched in sweat. He had a blue bandana on his head to keep sweaty curls out of his eyes—and his eyes were blue. Not like Imogene's, though. Imogene's eyes were dark blue, kind of like her personality. Ian's matched Celia's beach cruiser—powder blue. He looked at her door that day like he was thinking about knocking, but he didn't. He just walked past and drool dripped down Celia's chin onto the floor.

Dr. Savage asked if Celia had met anyone, made any friends, since their last session. Celia didn't want to talk about the Imogene debacle. She hadn't heard from that crazy vamp since she'd hurled on her shirt. Celia decided to talk about Ian instead.

"His hair is kind of fluffy but not exactly like a clown wig. It's just…it looks…it's black but I think it has some red in it. I just want to squeeze it." She moved her hand in the cold air of Dr. Savage's office but stopped when she realized it looked like she was squeezing a breast.

"So you've been talking to this Ian fellow?"

"No, no. Just once." She pulled at her yoga pants. "He touches his lips a lot. I don't know why. Like when he's talking, he'll just reach up and touch his mouth."

"Do you want to touch his mouth?"

"What? No." *Yes.*

Dr. Savage leaned forward in her slick leather chair. "Are you stalking him, Celia?"

"No." She fumbled and almost knocked over her cold cup of tea. "I just like the way he smells."

"Maybe you should ask him on a date."

"I don't want to."

"Celia." Dr. Savage sighed. "Sexual relations are a good gateway to discussing your first bite."

The leather couch made its usual embarrassing fart sound when Celia moved. "I don't want to have sex with my neighbor."

"His name is Ian."

Celia crossed her arms and took the pose she used to take when her dad told her to stop eating so much ice cream. She squirmed. The couch farted.

Dr. Savage put down her pen and paper and put on her therapist smile. She had no wrinkles, none. "I understand this is a very difficult time for you. The first few months are hard on most vampires. It's important to get beyond Danny and make your first human connection. It's important to take your first bite. It's part of moving on."

Moving on from what, Celia wondered.

Before she left, Dr. Savage gave her an assignment. She was supposed to keep journaling and talk to Ian—like have an actual conversation that involved more than grunts and cowering behind her front door.

In response to this, for days, Celia successfully avoided leaving her house except to go to work—and even then, only when she was sure Ian was not outside.

A couple nights later, she did a careful Ian check before she left for Happy Gas. She leaned against her kitchen wall, and yes, good, he was in what she assumed was his bedroom, if his apartment layout was the same as hers. His scent was close enough for her to know he was home but far enough away to know he wasn't lingering by the front door, waiting for her to walk outside.

She exited her living space and tiptoed down the porch so as to not disturb Heidi and her sonar hearing. The last thing Celia needed was her landlady bellowing about the most recent episode of *True Crime* and how some husband somewhere killed his wife with something.

Ian's bike was parked next to hers, and she touched it, once, with the tip of her finger on the handlebar. Then, disaster struck. She noticed the back tire of her beach cruiser was flat and lifeless, much like her hair. She sighed and tiptoed back to her apartment.

Then, she heard Dr. Savage in her head: *Talk to Ian. Talk to Ian. Talk to Ian.*

Ian would have a bike pump, wouldn't he?

Celia paced back and forth outside his apartment. Unaware of impending doom, she paced…until his front door opened. She could hear the waves at the beach, but she felt like a wave of Ian washed over her. His scent wrapped her up like a too-warm and mildly suffocating blanket.

He wore a light blue button-down and khaki shorts. His feet were bare. Celia couldn't look at his face, because his face was near his neck and she was not supposed to stare at necks.

"Were you just creeping around outside my apartment?"

"Uh…do you have a bike pump?"

He chuckled. "Yeah. Got a flat?"

Celia giggled.

"Hang on." He turned around which gave Celia the chance to notice his sparsely decorated living space. There were unpacked cardboard boxes on the floor and one framed photo she could see of Ian and three other guys who looked a lot like him. Ian didn't have a TV, which Celia thought was weird. But then, she backed up suddenly.

His whole house…

Smelled. Like. Him.

She covered her mouth with her hand.

When Ian stepped outside, he had no respect for personal space, which made Celia take rapid, shuffling steps backwards until her butt ran into the balcony handrail. He gestured toward their bikes, and Celia walked fast.

He glanced at the orange Happy Gas apron she wore over jeans and a white tee. "So night shift, huh? I was beginning to think you were a vampire."

Celia laughed until she almost choked.

Ian knelt next to her bike and attached the pump to her back tire. "Where do you work?"

"A gas station by Dry Dock Café."

He stood up. He made her feel like an oompa-loompa. "I have no idea where that is. I'm still kind of lost here."

"Oh, so you're new. To Admiral Key?"

"Yeah, I just moved here from Panama City."

"You have nice hair," Celia said.

He smiled.

Beautiful. Brings out his freckles "Oh, God," she whispered.

"Have you lived here long?" He used his bare foot to pump air into her tire. She had the weirdest yearning to suck his toes.

"Who?"

"You. Have you lived here long?"

"Oh, well, you know."

He paused in pumping and looked at her with a half-smirk. "I like your style, Celia."

"Huh?" He couldn't be talking about her clothes.

"People are so concerned about what everyone else thinks. You're not afraid to be really awkward. I dig it."

Celia laughed for real—not the laugh she used for customers or pretty girls who annoyed her. Lit by the porch light behind them, she could make out every centimeter of Ian's face, from the powder blue eyeballs to tan skin to light salmon-colored lips that looked soft.

"Um…" he said.

She'd been gawking. She saw blood rush to his face in a pink haze.

"What do you do?" She sounded like she'd sucked a hot air balloon full of helium.

"I'm a gamer. Legitimately. Companies pay me to test new computer games. Find flaws, hidden clues. You know?"

Celia was a blank slate.

"Boring stuff if you're not a geek." He smiled again. She was beginning to notice Ian smiled a lot.

"I owned a computer once," she said.

He laughed. His laugh was like his voice, only deeper. He cleared his throat. He leaned over and squeezed her back tire before bending down to unhook the pump. "You're good to go." Ian looked up at her. "Is it safe for you to ride at night?"

"You seem really concerned with my safety."

"You seem like you do some kind of dumb things."

Celia thought of Danny. "Yeah." She leaned down to unlock her bike and fumbled over the combination twice before getting it right. Before she could dislodge her bike from the rack, Ian grabbed it and set it down on the sidewalk.

"Thanks," she muttered, climbing on.

"Do you work tomorrow night?"

"Yes," she said.

"What about the night after that?"

"No."

"Cool." He put his hands in his pockets and walked back toward their apartments. "See ya later, Mermaid."

Celia cringed at the memory.

When she got to work, Ralph looked up from his surf magazine. A picture of a guy with a big, turquoise wave wrapped around him was on the cover. "You're totally late, Celia. My mom is gonna be pissed." He slapped the magazine closed and walked right at her. Celia had to scoot to the side to avoid being run over by the pissed-off teen who waved his magazine in her face as he left. "Your hair looks like a rat's nest. Haven't you heard of a brush?" The bell *clonk-clonked* above his sun-bleached, pointed head.

She ended up behind the counter where she continued with her research—the angsty love path of Bella and Edward Cullen. She was a little turned off by the whole glittering in the sun thing. She thought it was totally unrealistic. Celia knew if she stepped into the sun, she would go up like a piece of hair to a match—probably smell the same, too. She hoped the author realized she'd given a completely fabricated account of vampire life. Talk about misinformation.

Celia didn't have any customers. It happened sometimes. Then, at 3 a.m., the door *clonk-clonked* and then (*clomp-clomp*), Imogene walked in wearing an INXS t-shirt and a leather jacket, with the white earbuds in her head, tape player on her hip. Celia put her book down immediately.

"I'm sorry I threw up on you."

Imogene sighed from behind her red sunglasses and walked back to the coolers. She again passed up the beer and this time went for strawberry-banana juice. She put the juice between the two of them and tilted her sunglasses up.

Celia continued, "I didn't even know vampires could throw up."

"Only the really new ones," Imogene said, then pulled out her earbuds and sniffed the air. She latched onto Celia with her hand in her hair and almost dragged her across the counter. She sniffed some more. "What is that?"

"Huh?" She teetered on the tops of her toes.

Imogene stuck her nose right against her head and snarfed a mouthful of air. "That smell. It's the same smell that was in your house the other night." She took a long, deep breath. "It's fucking fantastic."

Celia knew Imogene smelled Ian. When Celia thought of Ian, two words came to mind—*fucking fantastic*. He was beginning to feel like her secret. Sure, she'd told Dr. Savage about him, but that was in doctor-patient confidence. Celia didn't need to worry about her therapist sniffing around her place. But Imogene, well.

She sniffed at Celia's ear like she wanted to smell her brain. "It's not that A-positive shit you've been drinking. A-positive doesn't smell like this."

"Um, can you…" She twisted her head in Imogene's hand, and Imogene let go.

She tapped her chipped fingernails on the gas station counter. "I'm sorry I bitched you out the other night. It wasn't your fault you threw up."

"What was that pill you gave me?"

"Klonopin," Imogene said. "Anxiety pill, but you're not supposed to drink on it."

"Then, why'd you give it to me?"

Imogene shrugged her thin shoulders. "You looked like you were flipping out. Anyway, you wanna hang out again at your place?"

"Are you just using me for my blood dealer?" Celia asked.

"Maybe a little."

Celia shrugged. "Okay."

Imogene put her sunglasses back on her face, which Celia was beginning to notice was really, really pretty when she wasn't sneering. "Cool." She pushed her strawberry-banana juice closer. "Why don't you guys sell rum? You should really sell rum. It's so much easier than having to steal it from bars."

"You steal liquor from bars?" Celia rang her up.

"I steal things all the time." Imogene nodded. "I once stole a statue of the Virgin Mary from a Catholic church." She considered this for a moment. "I think it's still in my house somewhere."

"Oh." Talk about a one-way ticket to Hell.

"So when can I stop by your place again?"

"Well, Tuesday, I guess," Celia said.

Imogene turned to leave but stopped in the doorway. "Can you get something other than A-positive?"

Celia wanted to tell her no—she'd recently seen Steve and bought her weekly allowance—but she also wanted Imogene to like her, so she said, "Sure."

"You're all right, Merk." She waved her hand in the air. The door *clonked* in honor of her exit.

CHAPTER FOUR

Due to the need to impress Imogene, Celia called Steve The Blood Dealer. Celia really did not like seeing Steve. When she made blood pick-ups, she tried to stock up for a while so she didn't have to go back again until she was desperate.

Before the change, she never met any "dealers." Celia wasn't a drug kid, not like the cool kids at Lazaret High. Dealing with criminals wasn't her shtick, and even though Steve had a reputable looking job at Lazaret Memorial Hospital, his behavior was anything but.

Celia suspected he hated her guts. He was short, really short, and Hispanic. He had black eyes—really, black eyes. He looked like he had no soul, but as a fellow vampire, maybe he didn't? Celia hadn't given much thought to the whole God-body-soul thing. Just because she was immortal, she didn't plan on getting philosophical, although maybe that was why Dr. Savage wanted her writing a journal—like through self-inspection, she'd find some deeper meaning. Dr. Savage was all about *deeper meanings* and how everyone was connected and positive life forces, blah, blah, blah.

Celia took a cab to Lazaret, since she couldn't ride her powder blue beach cruiser all the way down Admiral Key, over the bridge, and into the city. She brought her red, plastic cooler and two hundred bucks—the going rate for a week's worth of blood for a vampire of Celia's size—plus a little extra for Imogene.

When she showed up at Steve's lab, as planned, he looked up and said, "What are you doing here?"

She hugged her red, plastic cooler. "I said I was coming tonight."

"Yeah, okay." He lifted his black eyes away from a microscope. Steve always wore scrubs, and his shoes were always covered in white paper bags. It sounded like skates on ice when he walked.

Celia followed him toward the cooler. The smell of blood was in the air, and Celia drooled just a bit. She moved behind her angry midget blood dealer until he stopped and turned to face her. "You got the cash?"

"Yu-yeah," she stuttered. She pulled the rolled bills from her purse.

Steve The Blood Dealer had the money out of her hand before she could stutter again. She put the cooler on the floor and opened it, waiting for him. He started pulling blood-filled bags from the icy shelving. She watched him closely. He liked to annoy her with B and O sometimes, when he knew dang well she liked A-positive. A-plus, like a star on her imaginary vampire report card.

She wondered what Dr. Savage would think of that.

That night, she allowed for all varieties, since that was what Imogene wanted. Once the cooler was full, Celia tripped getting out of the lab. She almost spilled bags of blood all over the floor, but Steve just shook his angry little head. "Damn newbie," he said.

When Celia got home, she put the blood in the fridge and *The Lost Boys* on TV as kind of a joke. She got the feeling Imogene was an eighties kid, based on her choice of music and dancing style—plus the weird plastic sunglasses. Very Molly Ringwald—if Molly Ringwald wore combat boots and scared the shit out of people. Celia even lit some candles to give the place more of a vampire feel.

She was considerably surprised when Imogene knocked on her door at ten. She said she was a late sleeper, so Celia wasn't expecting her until at least eleven, but she didn't mind early company. She opened the door, and it wasn't Imogene. It wasn't even Heidi, the annoying landlady. No, it was Ian with a six-pack of beer.

Being unprepared for his blood cologne, Celia's fangs came shooting out, and she covered her mouth.

"Hey." He smiled.

"Hewoh," she muttered behind the palm of her hand.

"Do you play Scrabble?" He held up a rag-tag box covered in duct tape.

"I'm acthally very good ath Scrabble." Her voice came out muddled, filtered through her fingers.

"That's excellent." He walked past her, a wave of woodsy clean but no BO. Actually, he smelled like he'd just showered. She thought he even had on aftershave.

Ian walked into her apartment like he owned the place and set the six-pack of Natural Light on her living room table. He wore jeans torn at the knee and a white button down, sleeves rolled up. His feet were bare; Celia wondered if he actually owned shoes.

"Beer?" He pulled a can from its plastic loop and looked like he was about to lob it at her.

She held up the hand that wasn't covering her mouth. "Yeth. Can you just give me a thecond?" She pointed to the bathroom and left before he could say another word.

His scent followed her in there, wrapped around her like bungee cords. Celia looked in the mirror. Yep, fangs at full attention. She was glad she'd put some effort into her appearance for Imogene. She had on a dark blue v-neck tee and the only pair of jeans she owned. She even had on little stud earrings, and her red hair was up in what she thought looked like a cool eighties side ponytail. All that was fine for Ian, but shit, she couldn't go back out there with her damn canines poking out. She wondered if this was what it was like for guys in high school when they got boners in gym class. Back then, the boys joked they'd think about baseball or grandmas to get the protrusion to shrink, so Celia thought about the one thing that truly disgusted her: Ralph.

Amazingly, her fangs retracted in record time, but her gums ached. She felt like this was all just *bad*. She had Ian in her apartment, and all she could think about was...

Neck. Neck. Don't stare at his neck.

She almost passed out when she left the bathroom, because Ian was on her couch with his head leaned back, neck gratuitously exposed. She wanted to nibble the freckle on the side. The fangs were coming back out, so she meditated: *Ralph, Ralph.* Her mantra worked.

"Did you know you have cracks in your ceiling?"

"No." She didn't know where to sit, so she stood.

Ian lifted his head. "Do you have a date tonight?" He took a sip of beer, then threw her a can, which she tried not to drop.

"N-no. Uh, a friend is stopping by later." She realized then she needed to get Ian safely back to his own abode before Imogene arrived.

His light eyes brightened. "Great. I really need to start meeting people. So far, I've only met you and crazy Heidi and one other girl. I don't even know where to go out around here. You should take me out sometime. Show me some good dives."

"Oh, I don't really..." She cracked open the beer and drank about half. Celia didn't even like beer. "I don't go out much."

"Too busy swimming in the ocean at night?"

She sat down on the edge of the couch farthest from Ian. "I like swimming in the ocean at night."

He nodded, watching her.

Oh, God. She forced a swallow. She was already crazy about so much of this man: eyes, neck, hair, mouth, and even toes. Now, she was growing pretty fond of his voice, too—baritone with just a touch of Southern accent from growing up in Northern Florida.

"So you said you're good at Scrabble." He put his beer down and reached for the ramshackle box that might have been produced before either of their birthdays.

"Yeah."

"I need a worthy adversary," he said.

Celia finished her first beer and realized she should slow down, which was hard to do since Ian had already placed another fresh beer in her hand. She watched him unpack the Scrabble board, which was in good condition compared to the box itself. He moved to sit on the floor, giving her full reign of the couch. She looked at the glowing red numbers on her VCR, which read 10:07. She had about forty-five minutes to get Ian out of her house. Even then, Imogene would know he'd been there. He was operating like some kind of human air freshener, filling her hallways and dusty corners with the smell of rainy forests, clean musk, and rare beef.

He held the silver bag up for Celia. "Pick a letter."

She chose a B.

"Damn it. What are the odds of that? There are two of those in the entire bag." He chose an E, which meant Celia got to go first.

She had a whopper, too: "exonic." With the double word score in the center square, that was thirty points on her first go.

"That's not a real word," Ian said.

"Yes, it is. It's a sequence in nucleic acid that forms messenger RNA."

"What the...?" He laughed. "What?"

"I was a biology major for two years." She drank more beer.

Ian gaped up at her from the floor. "You're a Scrabble hustler, aren't you? You're gonna trounce me."

"No, just lucky on the first one," she said.

He stared at the letters hidden on his letter tray. "Why were you only a biology major for two years?"

"My parents died. Their car got pushed off a bridge by a hurricane."

She could tell he didn't want to, but he snorted as the intro to a guffaw. He looked away from her, his eyes crinkled around the edges. "Jesus, that's not funny. I don't know why I'm laughing."

Then, Celia started laughing, too. Maybe it was the beer or maybe the ease of his amusement. "No, it is kind of funny. I mean, their car got pushed off a bridge during a hurricane with Kenny G in the CD player."

The sound of Ian's laughter dwindled into a quiet, shaking hiss. Although the sound lessened, she could tell by the way his shoulders shook that he was only further into hysterics.

"How embarrassing, right?" she said. "Of all the CDs." She shook her head. "I didn't really like them anyway."

He calmed down enough to speak. "So you just dropped out of school?"

"I didn't really like college that much."

Ian opened a second beer for himself. "Where did you go?"

"University of Miami. I wasn't pretty enough to go there, anyway."

"Bullshit," he whispered.

She didn't look at him, she couldn't. She just sipped her beer. "I assume you went to college."

"University of California, Santa Barbara."

"I've never even left Florida. I've only been to Lazaret and well, here. I mean, the islands." She nodded at the front door as if the Gulf Coast islands were standing in a line outside.

"We should go on a road trip," he said, moving letters around. He said it like they'd been friends for years.

About an hour later, Celia had kicked Ian's ass in Scrabble, and she was drunk. They finished off the six-pack, and he went back to his place for whiskey. Ian said he liked cheap beer and whiskey, preferably by a beach bonfire.

They were both sitting on the floor by then, backs against the table, staring at *The Lost Boys* on mute. Ian took a sip of whiskey from his red plastic Solo cup. "You have a boyfriend, don't you?" he said.

"No. But I bet you have a girlfriend."

He made a noncommittal noise.

Celia slurred, "My therapist says I need to get out there again."

"Bad breakup?"

She shuddered.

"Tell me about it," he said.

"You don't wanna hear about that."

"Yeah, I do. Tell me." In her drunken haze, Celia wanted to eat Ian's smile.

"Danny," she said. "His name was Danny. I met him at a club."

Ian leaned back against the table, which scooted into Celia's couch and almost knocked her sideways. "I think it's dangerous to meet people at bars."

"Yeah, well, I don't meet people anywhere."

"Why not?" he said. "You're so cool."

Celia snickered. "I am absolutely not cool."

"Yeah, you are. You play Scrabble."

"I don't think that usually defines cool."

Ian refilled her plastic cup. "So tell me about Danny."

Celia didn't think about that night much, because it turned out to be a lie. She did remember it, though—a packed club, sweaty bodies, her feeling out of place in a knee-length dress that covered her pouch stomach and flabby arms. Then, later, the venom high. Something most people don't know, and Celia certainly didn't until that night— vampire fangs expelled venom that incapacitated victims in high quantities. She remembered she felt euphoric with Danny—until he disappeared. Instead of saying all that, she just told Ian, "He was way too hot for me. I should have known."

"Known what?"

"That he was…bad. He lied to me. He told me he could change me, make me better."

Ian was quiet for a second. Celia noticed the TV screen picked up the blue in his eyes. "No one should try to change you."

"I wanted to change."

"Into what?" he said. "A unicorn?"

She laughed and shoved him. "No, just someone better. Have you seen *Pretty Woman?*"

He paused and touched his mouth. "I think."

"You think? How do you think? You'd remember."

"I'm not really into many movies."

"We'll have to change that," she said, feeling brave.

He poked her in the shoulder with his long fingers. "You're not supposed to try and change people."

"Shut up, Ian."

He glanced at her.

"In *Pretty Woman*, this street girl becomes this hot, classy lady, and I always wanted someone to do that to me. Give me, like, the best makeover ever. And Danny did that. Or he said he was going to. It hasn't really worked out."

Ian nodded. "So you left the stupid prick."

"He left me," she said. "It was just a game for him."

"His loss." Ian downed the rest of his cup.

She elbowed him. "How about you? How many girls are you seeing right now?"

"I don't know if I'm really *seeing her*. She's not really…" He sighed. "I met her at a bike shop when I was getting new tires. She's a competitive cyclist, too. I mean, she's beautiful, but…" Ian smiled at her. "She doesn't play Scrabble."

Celia tried to play it cool and not look at his neck. "Why are you with her, then?"

He rubbed his hand over his forehead and pushed his fingers through his hair. "You're gonna think I'm a dick."

"What?" she said. "Nuh-uh."

Ian took awhile and stared at Keifer Sutherland on the TV, which gave Celia the perfect opportunity to ogle his cheekbones. Then, he said, "She's really good in bed. Everyone needs a fix."

Celia was silent, because she knew he was right: everyone did need a fix. Shit, she was beginning to understand her therapist.

"See, you hate me now," he muttered.

"No!" She put her hand on his knee, and somewhere in her drunken haze, she realized she had her hand on his knee and pulled back. "I'm just not that sexual of a person."

Then, her undead head almost exploded, because he put his hand on the side of her neck and whispered, "Wonder if we can change that."

Shakily, Celia said, "You're not supposed to try and change people."

Ian chuckled and licked his bottom lip. If Celia's fangs could have made a noise, they would have said "boing!" Just as he leaned in, her front door banged open, and they both dropped their drinks.

Backlit by moonlight, Imogene looked like a fuzzy phantom. "Well, goddamn," she said and lifted her sunglasses off her face to the top of her head. "Hello," she said to Ian. She clomped over to where they sat on the floor and sat next to him. She then licked his cheekbone. "You smell delicious."

"Thank you." Ian was completely unfazed. Celia wondered how many women had licked his cheekbone before, like this was a daily occurrence or something.

"I'm Imogene." She held out her hand to him; he took it and gave it a shake.

"Ian."

"Ian. Yeah." Imogene nodded, never once taking her eyes off his throat.

"Hey, Imogene," Celia said as whiskey soaked a puddle into the carpet between she and Ian.

"What up, Merk?" Imogene still didn't look at Celia. She was just staring at Ian's neck, which reminded Celia: *I thought we weren't supposed to do that!*

"Imogene, would you come to the kitchen for a second?"

Ian moved to stand. "I can leave if you want girl time."

"No." Imogene latched onto his bare forearm. "No, stay. We'll be right back." Even though Celia had suggested the change in location, Imogene was the one who dragged her into the kitchen. "That—" she pointed toward the living room, "lives through there." She pointed at the kitchen wall.

"Yeah, he's my neighbor."

"My neighbors are stinky bums," Imogene said. She lowered her voice to a hiss. "Can you believe that guy? He smells like sunshine and rainbows."

"I consider it more woodsy," Celia said. "Like a magical fairy forest."

Imogene shook her head. "Whatever. I'm gonna destroy that neck."

Celia thought it was probably a mix of the alcohol and her sudden need to protect Ian that made her hold onto Imogene's skinny upper arm and shove her against the fridge.

Her eighties sunglasses flew down on her face and landed crookedly on the end of her nose. "Ow."

"You will not touch him."

The edge of Imogene's mouth turned up. "Merk. You got a hard-on for this guy?"

"No. He's just...my neighbor, and you will get nowhere near his neck."

Imogene lifted her chin and gestured to the living room. "Dude, he is epic first bite material. Girls don't get so lucky."

"No, I wasn't thinking about that." Celia realized her hand was still in a claw around Imogene's arm, so she let go. "He's just my neighbor and new friend."

"Shit, Celia, haven't you seen *When Harry Met Sally?*"

"Of course."

"Women are not friends with guys like that," Imogene said. She pointed a wicked finger in Ian's direction. "Hot guys. Guys that make you go 'mmm.' You can't sustain a friendship with that."

"Yes, I can." *Probably not.*

Imogene turned around, pulled a bag of O-negative from the fridge, and started to slurp. "You should bite him tonight."

"What? No."

"Why not?" She gulped. "You're both drunk."

"How do you know we're drunk?"

Imogene finished the bag and started talking really, really fast. "It smells like a middle-aged cowboy in here. Like whiskey. Plus, you're actually conversing with a human male, which based on your behavior at Necto, never happens. Like, ever. Plus, he's got the half-lidded thing going on over those..." She sighed. "Dreamy baby blues."

"He is dreamy, isn't he?"

Imogene grabbed another bag of blood. "Duh. Now, get out there. I'll be back in a second."

Celia took a deep breath and returned to the living room, where Ian was going through her rather eccentric collection of VHS tapes. He looked up at her from the floor. "You have all the original *Star Wars* movies."

She shrugged.

"You are so cool." He went back to picking through the drawers of her entertainment console. "I like Imogene," he said. "She's, uh, weird."

"You have no idea," Celia whispered, but he didn't seem to hear.

Then, there she was, shoving Celia forward so she almost fell down in Ian's lap. With her newfound vampire grace, she just stepped on his hand instead, which he didn't notice.

"You have no alcohol in your house," Imogene said.

"I'm not really much of a drinker."

"Says the drunk girl." Imogene did her Butthead laugh.

Ian stopped poking around in her things and leapt to his feet like a ninja. "Next door!"

The vampires both gaped at him.

"I have booze next door." He didn't wait for their response. He just turned and opened the front door. He left it open as he stepped out into the night.

At Celia's side, Imogene did the robot. She then followed, which meant Celia had to follow, because she wasn't leaving Ian alone with Imogene.

His door was open when they reached it. In the lamplight from inside, Celia saw Imogene's eyes were black with blood overload. Celia was surprised she wasn't twitching or spinning her head in circles like in *The Exorcist*. It was kind of a relief, though, to know Imogene was full and less likely to suddenly impale the guy Celia was really starting to like.

Ian's pad was pretty empty, just a lot of boxes. Still, there was that smell—the smell of Ian. Imogene must have noticed it, too, because for a second, she just stood there in his living room with her mouth open like she could taste him in the air. He clunked around in the kitchen, and Celia reached for the one and only framed picture in his house—the one she'd spotted momentarily nights before: Ian with three other guys, arms around each other on a beach, wearing huge smiles. Then, Celia looked closer and realized they had to be brothers. One of them had Ian's eyes; another one had his hair. All were tall and muscly and cute. Celia imagined his house was a very popular place to be in high school.

He returned from the kitchen with beer—more cheap Nattie Light, which was fine with Celia, since the whiskey was probably pushing her luck. Imogene had yet to bring out any of her little yellow happy pills, thank God. Ian stood in front of Celia, and then, Imogene scooted up to her side so their hips were touching.

"He has brothers," she said excitedly, as if he wasn't standing right in front of them. She finished half her beer in a loud gulp.

"Youngest of four," Ian said. He took the picture from Celia. His eyes glowed with alcohol and what she assumed was joy.

"You get beat up a lot when you were a kid, then?" Imogene asked.

He chuckled. "No. My brothers are pretty awesome, actually." He set the picture down and the beer, too. "I have something to show you." He pointed at Celia and moved toward a cardboard box on the floor.

Imogene went right for Ian's stereo.

"Not too loud," Celia told her, "or the fake person will come get you."

"She's scary," Imogene said in reference to The Wig, so she did indeed keep the volume down. It was a Dave Matthews Band CD, circa mid-90s. Celia had owned it once but had it stolen when a bunch of bullies took her backpack in high school.

She turned back to Ian. She watched his long fingers traipse through worn paperback books in the cardboard box on the floor.

Then, behind her, Imogene switched from DMB to the radio, where she scanned until she found Marvin Gaye singing "Let's Get It On."

"Look." Ian's voice at Celia's side made her jump. In his hands, he held two plastic boxes. When she looked closer, she realized what they were and plucked both boxes from his open palms.

"These are originals. Still in the box." She stared at the Luke Skywalker and Han Solo action figures in her hands. She looked up at Ian in awe. "How do you have these?"

"I went to Comic Con in San Diego when I was in college. They weren't cheap, but I always kind of wanted to be Han Solo."

Celia mooned up at him. "You'd be a really good Han Solo."

Ian chuckled. His sun-made freckles were like constellations on his face. She wanted to connect the dots and name one "Celia."

Marvin Gaye was soon replaced by David Bowie, "Let's Dance," which made Imogene spin like a crazy gypsy around an invisible fire pit. Ian watched her, smiling. Celia watched him, smiling, which was when Imogene knocked Celia upside the head and spilled her beer all over Ian's chest.

"Shit," Celia said, hand to her face, which was when she realized why Imogene had smacked her in the skull. Her fangs were hanging over her bottom lip. She covered her mouth as Ian took off his soaked shirt, which made Celia's fangs throb. Her knees went weak. All coherent thought went the way of waves at low tide. She watched him walk to his bedroom while random words flashed through her brain…

Abs.

Farmer's tan.

Muscle.

Mole, upper back.

Fangs.

Neck.

Need to bite neck.

Then, Imogene smacked her again. "What's the matter with you?"

Behind her hand, Celia muttered, "I have no conthrol over them."

"You need to fucking practice. This is embarrassing."

Ian came back in a tight white t-shirt, which didn't help, because it just showed off how cut he was—skinny cut, cyclist cut. Plus, the drunker he got, the bigger his hair seemed to grow, which made Celia want to squeeze it.

Things evolved—or devolved—from there. Beer turned to more whiskey, which seemed to be Ian's normal order of things. Celia realized Imogene loved to dance. She danced to anything, but her moves were always very much MTV music video. Ian seemed impressed. He liked to dance, too, but it wasn't good dancing. He danced like the stoners back at Celia's college: eyes shut, weaving to the music, like he should have been stoned at a Phish show instead of in a living room on Admiral Key.

Celia, meanwhile, sat on the couch and drank because neither Imogene nor even Ian could get her to dance. She enjoyed her hazy buzz. She thought she was beginning to like alcohol.

Celia wasn't sure how they all ended up in Ian's bed. She was sure he was exhausted. Human beings do tend to sleep at night, after all. Plus, they were all wasted, even Imogene, who wouldn't stop talking about how rum punches were her favorite drink and why didn't Ian keep rum punches at his house?

Ian and Imogene talked a lot, actually, while Celia weaved in and out of dreamland—or Alcohol Land, she supposed. She heard random words like "Hawaii" and "Patrick Bateman" and "prime bud." She remembered feeling really warm and Ian's bed was really soft and one time, she realized her fingertips were tangled in the edge of his t-shirt.

Next thing she knew, someone flicked her in the ear. "Wha...?" She opened her eyes, and Imogene stood above her, hands on her hips, sunglasses snug on her pointed face.

"We have to fucking go," she whispered.

Go where? Where am I?

Ian made a small sighing sound, which was when Celia remembered she was in Ian's bed. Not only was she in Ian's bed but her face was in his armpit and her hand was up his shirt. His head was thrown back over a pillow, and she stared at his neck freckle. Her fangs went "boing!"

Then, he cleared his throat. "What time is it?"

"Almost sunrise," Imogene said loudly.

"Sugar!" Celia shrieked and sat up. Fangs went the opposite of "boing!"

Ian sat up slowly. "I think I'm still drunk." He rubbed his eyes.

"We need to go." Celia stood and Imogene nodded in agreement.

She leaned forward and ruffled his hair. "Nice meeting you, Ian."

"Oh, yeah, I was gonna get your number."

Imogene latched onto Celia's wrist and said, "I'll get it to you tonight."

"Mm," he muttered and fell back against his pillows.

Imogene dragged Celia toward Ian's bedroom door.

"Bye, Ian," Celia said.

As he closed his eyes, he whispered, "Mermaid..." then fell back to sleep.

The edge of the sky was already purple when the girls stepped onto the front porch of the Sleeping Gull Apartments.

"Keys, keys, where are your fucking keys?" Imogene spat.

"I didn't lock it." Celia walked into her apartment.

Once the door was shut, Imogene leaned back against the front wall. "That was so stupid. I've never been this close to sunrise." She pointed at Celia. "You're a bad influence."

"Are you kidding? You are a *terrible* influence!"

She laughed and shook her head, then yawned. "God, I'm tired." She kicked off her huge combat boots as she made her way to Celia's bedroom. By the time Celia got there, Imogene had reserved the right side. Celia sprawled out on the left, thankful for her tinfoil-covered windows.

Imogene chuckled. "I still smell like him."

Sleepily, Celia said, "He kind of stays with you."

"He should be your first bite."

Celia snuggled into her pillow. "He has a girlfriend."

"Coulda fooled me," Imogene said. "Seemed like he only had eyes for you."

"He's out of my league."

Imogene snorted. "No, he's not. I mean, physically he is, but mentally, he's really just a huge dork." She yawned again. "You're both dorks."

Celia sighed out a deep breath.

Imogene patted her shoulder. "You're doin' good, Merk. Might even be a real vampire someday." Seconds later, she was snoring.

Celia sniffed her hand, the smart little hand that had earlier found its way onto Ian's bare skin. She fell asleep with her hand on her face, and through the kitchen wall, she heard him snore.

CHAPTER FIVE

Dr. Savage made Celia the usual chamomile tea, because it was supposed to be relaxing or something. Celia's therapist had the little fountain in the corner going. The sound of falling water was supposed to be relaxing. Or something.

"You seem tense, Celia."

Celia wanted to scream at her. *Wow! That degree is really working out for you!* Instead, she sipped her tea. It tasted like dirt with honey.

"Why are you tense, Celia?"

Dr. Savage was in a skin-tight turquoise business suit. She looked like a mix between futuristic heroine and eighties attorney. She had on wire rim glasses, which matched her silver pumps.

"Celia?"

She sighed. "Imogene keeps coming to my house, but you know I like my privacy."

"Imogene is good for you, Celia. She's another vampire who's been around. Have you asked how old she is?"

"No," Celia said. "I didn't think women liked that."

Dr. Savage smirked and crossed one long leg over the other. "Celia, it doesn't matter when you're immortal. I'm more than two hundred years old."

"Well, you look nice."

She pursed her lips. "Making a personal attachment to another vampire is good. It helps you make other vampire friends and build a support group."

Celia tried not to make the couch fart, but she was annoyed and she moved around until the couch, indeed, farted. "But she's not introducing me to other vampires. She just comes to my house and drinks my blood supply. And I hate going to see Steve because he's scary and he hates me. What if he cuts me off?"

"Your inheritance isn't running low, is it?"

"No. I'll never spend all that money." Celia sighed.

Dr. Savage reached her manicured hand out but didn't touch Celia. "Then, he won't cut you off. Calm down."

"Okay, the other night, Imogene was over when I left for work, and when I got home in the morning, she smelled like Ian. She said she'd been hanging out with him…without me."

"How does that make you feel?"

"Tense!" Celia pulled on the frizzy hairs around her head that had escaped the ponytail.

"Are you jealous of Imogene?"

Celia thought about the way her so-called friend looked, the clothes she wore. She thought about her curly hair—that kind of matched Ian's—her skinny person cheekbones, too, and the way she could just talk to guys and make them like her without even glamouring them. Celia thought about the way Ian seemed to like Imogene and worried a little that maybe Imogene was glamouring him. Celia knew vampires could glamour people; Dr. Savage warned her about it. They could make people forget things or even like them. Celia had never tried it before.

All those thoughts must have showed up on her face, because Dr. Savage wrote a bunch of notes on her stylish leather-bound notepad.

"Do you think Ian wants to date Imogene?"

"Why wouldn't he?" Celia shouted. "She's pretty and weird and they talk about things like Europe—because of course, they've both been to Europe. Not that it matters, because he said he's already dating someone."

Dr. Savage tapped her silver pen against her bottom lip. "Have you met this other woman yet?"

"No." The tone of Celia's voice sounded a little psycho, even to her own ears.

"Okay, let's stop talking about Ian for a second. What about your first bite? You said Imogene took you to Necto, right?"

"Yeah."

"I think you and Imogene should go out again and make a connection for the night. Once you get your first bite out of the way, you'll feel empowered, maybe even enough to approach Ian."

"And tell him what?" she asked. "Break up with your slutty girlfriend and date chubby, asexual me?"

Dr. Savage paused. "Is his girlfriend slutty?"

"I don't know. I like to tell myself she is." *Slutty and trashy and dumb.* "But I don't want my first bite to be with some stranger at a bar. I want my first bite to be..." She looked at the ceiling.

"I know. Special." She heard amusement in the doctor's tone.

Celia looked at her therapist and wondered, aloud, "What was your first time like?"

Dr. Savage smiled. "We're not here to talk about me."

Celia nervously plucked at her t-shirt. "Imogene doesn't even remember hers. She said it was just some guy she picked up in Lazaret. She says I'm blowing things out of proportion."

Dr. Savage leaned back and recrossed her legs. "You need to do what's best for you. We're all different, Celia. Take your time. Meditate. I always feel that meditation brings me back to my center."

Yeah, Celia thought, *try that when Ian and Imogene are arguing over better beaches: France or Spain.*

After her session, Celia dreaded going home because she knew what she would find—Imogene and Ian on her couch, watching one of her favorite eighties movies because Imogene was trying to show Ian all he'd missed. Apparently, to her horror, the only movies he really knew were *Star Wars*. Sometimes, Celia caught Imogene with one hand absently in his hair. Celia was beginning to think it was like the cheekbone thing: women licked Ian's cheekbones; women played with Ian's hair.

But when she got home from her appointment, Ian was on the front porch on the phone and Celia's apartment was dark. He smiled when he saw her. "Hey, bro, I gotta go." He paused. "Yeah, my woman just showed up." He winked at her, which actually made her feel worse. "Okay, yeah, love you." He hung up. "I was wondering where you were."

"I…had an appointment."

"At ten o'clock?"

She made her way to her front door.

Ian's front door was open, and she could hear quiet tracks of reggae dancing out with the lamplight. "Are you okay?" he asked.

"Yeah, I'm…yeah." She didn't look at him. She just unlocked her door and thought about swimming in the ocean. She needed to swim in the ocean.

"Celia." He stopped in her doorframe but didn't come inside, like he was a vamp in an old movie that needed to be invited in. "What's up?"

"Nothing." She could practically feel the waves against her skin. She needed water—now.

"You're going to go swimming, aren't you?"

She looked up at him, shocked. "What?" *How did he know that?*

"I'm going with you, and I'm taking a flashlight." He disappeared, barefoot, in the direction of his place.

Hurriedly, Celia drank some blood and changed into her bathing suit. There was no need for mermaid sighting, number two. She wrapped a towel around herself. Even though Ian had already seen her naked, she didn't want to remind him that she wasn't as skinny or pretty as Imogene.

When she stepped outside, Ian was waiting on the front porch with an *X-Files*-sized flashlight that could have possibly lit the opposite side of the gulf. He had on shorts, even though it wasn't really that warm that time of night. She could see the weird scar on his lower leg again, the one that looked like a big bite mark. She kind of wanted to ask, but she also kind of didn't. He had a tightly rolled joint behind his right ear.

"After you." He gestured with his light the size of the sun. For a second, Celia almost worried it might send her up in flames.

They walked down the patio past Heidi's place. Once Celia's toes were in the sand, she glanced up at Ian. "Where's Imogene?"

"I think she had a date."

Celia pulled her towel tight. "You're okay with that?"

"Why wouldn't I be okay with that?"

Celia kicked a little shell, which disappeared from the line of Ian's flashlight into salty sea air. "I thought you guys were, you know, hitting it off."

"Me and Imogene?" He laughed. "No, we're not like that."

"But she touches your hair."

He shrugged. "I like when women touch my hair."

Celia did something freakish. She reached up and tucked a piece of his dark hair behind his ear, and it happened again—the pink haze surrounded his whole head, and the smell of his blood smacked her, center forehead.

He paused walking and looked at her. Celia heard him swallow.

"Does your girlfriend touch your hair?"

Ian looked toward the black sea and scratched his scalp. "She's not my girlfriend. I think that's kind of over."

"You broke up with her?"

"No, I'm just..." He started walking again, the flashlight beam an extension of his movements. "I'm twenty-five years old, and I think

I've been shopping in the wrong aisle."

"Which aisle would that be?"

"The same one as Imogene, where everyone is shallow and just looking for a good time. Not saying Imogene is a bad person."

Celia sort of wondered.

"I'm just sick of the party scene and meaningless sex, you know? I'd like to find someone with a brain. Someone real." He paused. "Plus, I'd like kids someday. The women I've dated are not exactly maternal." Celia saw the glint of his teeth in the semi-darkness.

"No, girls like Imogene certainly aren't maternal." Celia smiled a little—just a little.

"Anyway, I haven't broken up with that girl, no. I'm just thinking it might be a good idea."

"Oh." Celia nodded just as Ian stopped moving. She turned to look at him, frozen on the beach, and was surprised by the look in his eyes. "Ian? Ian, are you okay?"

They were about three feet from the edge of breaking waves, and he had his flashlight pointed at the sandbar like it was one of those creatures from *Alien*. Ian always seemed relaxed, yet there he stood, shoulders tense around his ears, a look of abject horror on his face— and Celia wasn't even naked.

She grabbed his arm and shook. "Ian!"

"What? Yeah." He looked down at her. "Do you really need to swim at night?"

"It makes me feel better."

"I could think of other things that would make you feel better."

"But..." She looked toward the waves. The dark shimmer beckoned, as did all the slurping, sliding sea creatures below.

"Just be careful, okay? I'll stand right here," he said.

Then, Celia did another crazy thing. She actually asked him to swim with her.

His response was unexpected. He turned the color of printer paper and shook his head. "No. No, no, no. Not gonna happen." The flashlight in his hand trembled.

"I'm sorry, I—"

"It's not you. Celia." He shook his head. "It's uh…Let's just get this over with. Ten minutes. I'll time you."

"But, I—"

"Celia. Please." God, she thought he looked so scared. For a guy who lived by the ocean, he seemed really uncomfortable with it. The look of horror on his face almost made her turn back to the apartments, but Celia needed her ocean.

She turned away from him, dropped her towel, and ran to give Ian as little time as possible to be reminded of her soft center. But he wasn't kidding about keeping her safe. Every move she made, the flashlight found her, which the fish really didn't like. Celia didn't complain, because at least Ian wasn't shaking anymore. Even underwater, she could feel his heartbeat and smell his skin.

When she came up for air, he yelled at her, "Time's up, Mermaid!"

She did one more underwater roll and then made her way up to the uneven beach, past broken seashells that poked at her feet bottoms. Ian put the flashlight down so he could wrap the towel around her body. Really, he wrapped her like a babe in swaddling clothes. Then, he rubbed his big hands up and down the outsides of her arms.

"Aren't you cold?"

"No," she said.

"All right, inside."

She giggled when he took her hand.

Ian took Celia to his apartment. He hung her towel over the outside deck and wrapped her in a well-worn cotton robe. "Second hand store," he said. "But it's comfy."

She agreed it was. Then again, she felt kind of liquid after her night swim, the heat of Ian's palm still lingering across her skin. She was in his house, on his couch, surrounded by his smell and his books. It looked like books—and comics—were the only thing he owned, plus a few photos. Most of the cardboard boxes were gone, but there were stacks of comic books on his floor, and he'd hung a couple big photos: some more with his brothers and other ones with friends. There was just one of him alone, on a beach at sunset with a surfboard.

He came back from the kitchen with a mason jar half-full of what Celia knew was cheap whiskey. "Just a little nip," he said. "To keep the cold away." He pulled the joint from behind his ear and sat next to her. He didn't light it—just put it on the table in the center of his living room. Celia got the feeling he carried joints out of habit, like a security blanket or good luck charm.

Ian kind of melted into the couch so he was shorter than her. His long legs extended halfway across the room. She watched him smile. "Oh, go ahead. I know you want to."

Celia wasn't even nervous. With the mason jar wedged between her knees, she dug her fingers right into his hair.

Yes. This. This is good.

Ian's hair was so soft, and she ran her fingers through it like he wasn't there—like it was just her in a room with a mop of fluffy black curls. There were no judgments, just curls. But then Ian made a noise. It was a really good noise. That was when Celia remembered Ian was actually attached to his hair, and she was wrist-deep in it.

She moved his hair a little so she could see his face. His eyes were closed. He looked sleepy. She didn't have to lick her teeth to know her fangs were out. She leaned over him, and all she could hear was the *thump-thump-thump* of blood through his veins. She leaned closer. Was this the moment she'd been waiting for?

Then, she drooled on his face.

Ian's eyes popped open, and he touched the wet spot above his eyebrow. "Do you have a runny nose?"

Celia dragged her hand out of his hair and covered her face from nose to chin. "What? Maybe." She stood up. "I need to go."

"Huh?" She realized he probably couldn't understand her very well, what with her fangs and her lisp and her whole hand muffling the sound.

"I have thom things to do," she said. She started walking toward his front door, but he stopped her with a hand on her arm.

"Celia. Why do you keep running away from me?"

"I'm not. I just—thom things."

He kept one hand on her arm. The other one went to the side of her face, and he did the thing she liked, where he licked his lips. She felt like his *X-Files* flashlight from earlier had magically reappeared and was shining directly on his mouth.

Then, Celia realized what he planned to do, and she totally flipped out. "Oh my God!" She stumbled backwards, hand still on her mouth. "I have to—" She ran right into his front door. As she tried to swat at the little Tweety birds around her head, she heard Heidi outside. Celia practically tore Ian's door from its hinges and stepped out into the night.

Heidi was shouting something about *True Crime*, and how could Celia be noisy when Mr. Walters just murdered his mistress? The distraction made Celia's fangs suck back into her skull, at least, which was when she decided, why not? Go mad.

In that moment, she hated her own guts. She was an idiot. She was a wuss and a failure. She was a damn vampire, and she couldn't deal with her first bite. She had a shit job. Her only friend was a crazy fellow vampire who used Celia for her blood connection, and there was Ian, standing in the doorframe, looking like Celia had just called his mom a See-You-Next-Tuesday. She did the only thing that could possibly make the situation worse—she kissed him.

CHAPTER SIX

Following the kiss, Celia ditched Ian on the front porch, refused to answer the door, and called Imogene.

"I need your help."

"Merk, you need all sorts of help."

"Yeah," Celia said, "but this is about one thing in particular."

She explained the situation. Imogene said she was happy Celia had kissed Ian. Her exact words: "Someone needs to suck that mouth." Celia told her she hadn't actually "sucked his mouth." The kiss was more like a peck—still, just a peck, and Celia had realized her problem.

She told Imogene, "I can't control my fangs."

"Hang on," she said. Through the phone, Celia heard some weird eighties punk jam in the background. Then, all was quiet. "What do you mean?" Imogene asked.

"I mean," she paced around her place, "they just come out. At bad times. A lot when I'm around Ian, they just pop out, and I can't control it."

"I know. I've seen."

"What am I supposed to do?"

She heard Imogene sigh across the line. "I guess you have to practice."

"Practice? What do you mean?"

To Celia, it sounded like Imogene was sitting down on leather furniture—*squish, squish*, but not *fart, fart,* like at Dr. Savage's office. "I mean, I don't know, like, develop your self control. I know, come out tonight. I'm at a party."

"How does that help?"

Celia heard the music again, weakly this time, and she recognized The Cure. "Come to this party. We'll get you around a bunch of dudes. Get close to their necks, okay, and then, when your teeth go boing, practice suckin' 'em back in."

Celia looked down at her damp bathing suit. "You're serious?"

"Yeah, there are tons of guys here. You can practice all night long. Shit, you could have your first bite tonight!"

"But I want my first bite to be special," Celia whined. Somewhere deep inside, she knew she really wanted her first bite to be with Ian.

Imogene mocked her. "Special, schmecial."

Celia couldn't believe Imogene talked her into it. She had to take a stupid cab because Imogene was all the way out on Barkentine Beach, this touristy island where the bars all played Jimmy Buffet and there was no such thing as a "local." The party was at a ritzy, yellow, three-story beach rental. Celia smelled sunscreen, lots of sunscreen.

Strangely, Imogene answered the front door like she owned the place, but then, she leaned in and whispered in explanation, "I could smell Ian on you."

The house was packed. It reminded Celia of party scenes in movies like *Say Anything* or *Can't Hardly Wait*—a bunch of people trying to look cool, drinking from red Solo cups, and playing odd drinking games that involved quarters and shot glasses. Imogene was right; there were men everywhere, but none of them was Ian.

"Okay." She put her boney arm around Celia and led her to the kitchen. "Let's get you a drink."

"I don't want a drink."

"You need a drink."

Celia knew Imogene was right; she was hella nervous. She'd done her best to go from just-swam-in-the-ocean to don't-you-wanna-hit-on-me? Not that Celia knew what option two really looked like, so she just put on a flowery peasant blouse over her jeans. If she was physically comfortable, she thought maybe she could feign emotional comfort as well. Plus, alcohol helped, even if it was beer. Imogene poured her a foamless yellow brew from a keg surrounded by ice in the kitchen sink.

Imogene moved through the crowd like a ghost, and Celia followed until they reached the balcony, which overlooked the entire party area. These were vacationers. They were all half-sunburned with weird tan lines. They wore things that looked too beachy like t-shirts with "Admiral Key" on the front or brand new flip-flops on their sunburned toes. The girls were all in short, summery dresses that looked practically bridal.

"What am I doing here, Imogene?"

"You see all these guys." She waved her hand over the room like she was conjuring a spell. "They're fang practice."

"Fang practice?"

"You're gonna find guys who look kind of like Ian," Imogene said.

"Nobody looks like Ian," Celia whispered.

Imogene groaned. "God, you're disgusting." She pushed her red sunglasses off her nose and looked anywhere but at Celia. Then, she pointed. "See that guy right there in the blue shirt? He kind of has Ian's cheekbones. Over there, that guy has blue eyes."

"So what's the point of this?" Celia asked.

"You can't control your fangs around Ian. I've seen it. It's embarrassing. So if you ever want to bang him—"

"I don't want to bang him!" she shrieked, loud enough for people to turn and look.

"Yes, you do. Every girl wants to bang Ian. So if you're ever going to do it, you need to stop..." Imogene popped her fangs out and hissed with one hand in the air like a claw.

Celia was in awe. "See, how do you do that? You can just pop 'em out whenever you want."

Imogene put her hand on Celia's shoulder and winked over her glasses. "Merk, I'm a bit older than you." She looked back to the people playing Beer Pong below. "Now, you're going to hit on guys, get close to guys, dance with guys, and when your fangs go boing, you practice sucking them back in."

Celia wrung her fingers. "Won't guys notice when my fangs come out?"

"No." Imogene laughed, Butthead-style. "We're all on X." She cackled again. "Me, I got one of my favorites here, so I might be busy. Find me later." She walked away.

"What?"

Imogene didn't look back.

Celia was completely alone at a beach party, which had never happened in her entire life. She decided standing on the balcony was not a way to blend in, so she went downstairs and refilled her beer. Considering she'd never used a keg before, it was all foam, but she sucked on the foam and tried to look cool.

She wandered around and caught some nice smells. Some of the guys reminded her of Ian, but they just didn't smell right. This one guy smelled like German cheese. Plus, there was the mix of all the women's perfumes, reminiscent of too-sweet vanilla and dead funeral flowers.

She went out to the back porch that overlooked Barkentine Beach. She could see the dark waves crashing on the beach, but she couldn't hear them over the sound of Depeche Mode's "Enjoy the Silence." She'd always kind of liked that song, so she did her best to join in the ever-moving crowd of humanity even though she didn't dance. She caught glimpses of Imogene inside, doing her thing and looking like she should be in a rap video.

Imogene said she was older—it made Celia wonder how old.

She felt someone's hand in her hair, which made her glance over her shoulder. A short guy stood there with a backwards baseball cap and a piercing in his bottom lip. "Whoa," he said. "You have the most beautiful hair, like, ever." He ran his fingers through it and weaved a bit on his feet.

"Thanks?"

"Totally, can I, like, just stand here and touch your hair?"

"Yeah, um…" He didn't look anything like Ian, but he was cute in that little druggy guy way. He was obviously high out of his mind, so Celia thought, *Hmm. If I get this over with, I can go home.* She said, "You wanna walk on the beach and touch my hair?"

"Yeah." He nodded as if she'd solved world hunger.

With his hands still on her head, they wandered down the back porch steps and into the sand. The waves were only about ten feet from the prime vacation house.

"What's your name, beautiful fire goddess?"

She almost choked on her own spit. "Uh, Celia."

"Celia." He nodded. "Yeah."

"Um, what's your name?"

"Everyone calls me Stoner."

"Uh-huh."

They walked down the beach toward Admiral Key when he stopped Celia with his hands still moving through her hair like warm, sausage-sized brushes. "You wanna make out?"

This is going well. "Yeah. Okay."

He had to use her hips to support his small stature, but his lips did eventually find Celia's, kind of. He sort of hit the outside of her mouth and then navigated right until their lips were just…well, he was sucking on her lips. Celia focused. She knew her fangs would come out any second, and he did smell nice. He smelled like shaving cream. So Celia was waiting, waiting for the boing. Stoner kept kissing her, and she even got close to his neck at one point. She could hear his pulse, so she didn't get it: where was the boing?

This went on for fifteen minutes or so, and that was when she realized there would be no boing—a fang no-show. No one had ever mentioned performance anxiety!

Celia left Stoner on the beach, because he seemed perfectly content making angels in the sand. She threw her red Solo cup under the porch and approached the house to find Imogene. She now had a whole different set of problems to figure out.

When Celia found her, Imogene was wrapped around a blond guy like vines around a tree. She was giving him hickies, and he didn't seem to mind. He had his hands on her ass, rubbing his palms in circles like he was shaping pottery.

Celia tapped Imogene's shoulder, and she responded with, "How's practice, wench?"

"Not good. I need to talk to you."

"Yeah, let's go upstairs." She dragged blond guy behind her, and Celia did her best to follow, despite the ever-increasing crowd who smelled worse and worse. Celia wanted the sea air again. She wanted Ian's apartment.

Instead, they ended up in a bedroom that smelled of pool water and sunshine sweat. Imogene closed the door behind them and shoved the guy on the bed.

"Okay, watch this," she said. She straddled him, and Celia wanted to tell her she didn't show up to watch porn. But Imogene didn't take off his clothes; she just leaned over him and took off her sunglasses. She looked down and whispered, "You are crazy about me, and this is going to feel so good."

"Yeah." The dude put his hands on her thighs.

"Come here." She beckoned Celia forward. She kept her dark eyes focused on the blond guy, whose light eyes looked hazy, tired. "You've never glamoured someone, right?"

"No," Celia said.

"It's super easy." She took a deep breath. "Just make eye contact and think, 'Relax.' Then, say what you want your victim to feel. For instance, Paul is crazy about me and likes when I drink his blood."

Celia took steps back. "You…what?"

"Come here," Imogene insisted. She shifted her eyes long enough to stare Celia down, and even Celia felt almost glamoured. She now understood why Imogene wore sunglasses all the time; she was a glamour tsunami. She continued, "I'll just take a nibble so you see what it looks like and what to do. Got it?"

"Uh…"

Imogene didn't give Celia a chance to leave. She just dipped down and bit into blond guy's neck. He didn't even jump. He just laid there and let her take what she wanted, and it wasn't *just a nibble*. By the time Imogene was finished, Celia could have walked home and back.

Finally, she sat up and wiped her mouth. She sighed. "Now I'm really fucking high." She laughed. "Okay, here's the important part," Imogene slurred. She took a razor blade from her back pocket, which made Celia think her mentor was going to murder someone. She reached out her hand to stop Imogene, and Imogene glanced up. Her lips were tinted red from blood, and her fangs were still out. She looked scary as shit, honestly, which made Celia fall over. She landed on her ass, which made Imogene laugh some more. "It's just me. God, Merk. Come here and watch. Stop being a spaz."

"What are you going to do, Imogene?"

"Watch."

Celia crawled over and watched. There were two bloody spots on the blond guy's neck. With a flip of her wrist, Imogene connected them like dots with her razor blade. Instead of bite marks, it looked like he just had a cut. Then, in front of his face, she snapped her fingers.

"Whoa," he said, coming to. "What happened?"

Imogene patted at his neck with the bed sheets. "Dude, you cut yourself on a beer bottle. Again." She rolled her eyes.

"Shit, I hate when I do that." He sat up slowly. "At least it doesn't hurt."

Imogene rolled off him. "Better get back downstairs. Get a napkin or something, huh?"

"Yeah." He looked Imogene from toes to tits. "God, you're hot."

She blew him a kiss as he left the room.

"You've fed on him before," Celia said.

Imogene lay back on her folded arms. "I thought I told you he's one of my favorites."

Celia stood. "And then he just forgets."

"That's the point of glamouring. You should try it sometime." She put her glasses back on and sat up. "It's fun."

"Wait, I need to..." Celia took hold of Imogene's upper arm. "I had performance anxiety."

"Heh?"

"I had this guy on the beach, and we were kissing, and I was even near his neck, but my fangs wouldn't come out."

Imogene pursed her lips in a duck mouth. "I don't think they make vampire Viagra, dude." She turned to leave the room.

"But, Imogene..."

"Try again," she said. "It's a party, duh."

Celia just wanted to go home.

CHAPTER SEVEN

Celia knew she needed to see Dr. Savage; instead, she avoided her therapist. She avoided Ian, too, which was really hard since he was her neighbor. If anyone knocked on her door, she wouldn't answer, and she went *Mission: Impossible*-style to get to her bike for work.

She got to Happy Gas safely. As usual, her boss, Omar, was just leaving, but had enough time to tell Celia how she looked nice in her orange Happy Gas apron she'd taken to wearing when she rode her bike. Then, Omar left to do whatever huge bald men do on Tuesday nights on Admiral Key.

Ralph was closing up shop, but he took the time to give her a look of disdain. "Don't you own any other pants?"

Celia ignored him. She waited for him to leave so she could read more of *Twilight*. The book was taking her forever to finish, because she wasn't learning anything. There were no vampire-affirming life lessons, but anything to avoid Ralph.

The empty bell on the front door *clonk-clonked*, and Celia almost dropped her stupid book when she looked up to see Ian standing there in one of his nice, tight t-shirts and army green shorts. His hair was windblown, and under the ugly fluorescent lights, he looked really tan. She'd missed his smell. At her apartment, she kept candles lit to make it look like a true vampire lair. In reality, though, she was just trying to cover up the way Ian's scent crept through her kitchen wall.

"Hey, I tried to catch you before you left, but I must have missed you." He glanced outside. "I biked here."

"Oh, hi, Ian." She hugged the book to her chest.

Suddenly, Ralph got animated. He slammed the register drawer shut and started stuttering and grabbing his forehead. Celia thought he might be having a seizure, but then he said, "You're Ian Hasselback."

"Yeah. Hey, man." Ian reached across the counter and shook Ralph's hand.

"I have worshipped you since I was a fetus."

Ian laughed. "Thank you."

"Celia!" Ralph grabbed her upper arm, and it kind of hurt. "Why didn't you tell me you knew Ian Hasselback?"

"I didn't know his last name."

She was immediately ignored.

"Bro, I'm Ralph. The time you rode that gnarly cruncher in Biarritz, that was bitchin.' Do you still hold the record for that?"

"I think so." Ian nodded, even though Celia understood nothing that was being said.

Ralph stood on the tips of his toes like he might take off like the Challenger and explode. "Do you have the...Can I see the...You know, Banzai Pipeline?"

"Sure." Ian smiled, and Ralph rounded the counter. He looked down at Ian's calf, and so did Celia—the one with the bite mark the size of a human head.

"Whoa, bro, that is vicious." Ralph's voice broke. "How big was that Great White anyway?"

"I don't really remember," Ian said. "I just remember punching him in the face."

Ralph let out a loud sigh of air. "Wicked. Is it true you haven't been in the water since?"

"Yeah."

"But, man, you're Ian Hasselback. You're the best!"

Ian looked sheepish. "Thanks, Ralph. So you surf?"

"Yeah, but I'm not that good. Not like you."

Celia had never heard Ralph say anything humble. It made it hard for her to swallow, especially considering she had about a million questions to ask Ian. For starters, what the hell were they talking about?

"Can we hang out some time? Just talk surfing?" Ralph's brown eyes were wild and bright.

Ian smiled politely. "Sure."

"Holy shit, I can't wait to tell everyone I know." He pushed the receipt machine button next to the register and tore off some paper. "You live on Admiral Key now?"

"Yeah, just moved here."

Celia watched Ralph write down his phone number. He had the handwriting of a five-year-old. "And you're friends with Celia?" Ralph snickered.

"Hey, man, Celia's cool." Ian's blue eyes watched her watching him.

"Oh. Okay." Ralph handed the paper to Ian. "Call me anytime, but I gotta go. Some of my buddies got some dank weed down on Ship's Bell. You wanna come?"

"Maybe next time." Ian nodded.

"Yeah, totally." Celia had never seen Ralph smile so hard. As he pushed the door open to the outside world, he shouted, "Ian Hasselback, yes!"

Ian turned to Celia, his smile wrinkles in full bloom.

"What just happened?" she asked.

"Hmm?"

"Ralph doesn't know about anything, but he just geeked out over another man. Who are you?"

"Ian. We've met."

Celia hid her vampire book behind the counter.

"I used to surf," he said.

"Oh."

"I was really good at it."

"But you don't even go near the ocean," Celia said.

He leaned back on his heels and looked away from her. "Three years ago, I was surfing off the coast of Oahu, and a Great White tried to take me out." He winced. "I almost lost my leg."

The feeling came over Celia sort of like a shark attack. One second she was fine, talking to Ian. Next thing she knew, she couldn't breathe. She felt like someone had tied a rubber band around her esophagus.

"Oh my God, oh my God," she wheezed. She had the fleeting thought: *Apparently, Ian smells good to animals, too.*

"Celia." Ian circled the counter and put his hands on her shoulders.

It wasn't enough. She shoved her face against his chest and latched onto his back. Next thing she knew, she was choking on sobs. She wondered what the hell was wrong with her.

Ian seemed to understand, because he rubbed her back and whispered, "I'm okay."

Then she recognized what was happening. She was freaking out at the thought of Ian being dead—freaking out over the thought of some sea monster taking a bite out of his leg and leaving him, bleeding, to fight for his life.

She felt his mouth right by her ear. "I'm okay, Celia."

She didn't feel embarrassed, her nose crushed against his breastbone. She should have been embarrassed, having a meltdown about the near-death experience of a guy she barely knew. But Ian had a way of making her feel not embarrassed about anything. Even The Mermaid Incident didn't bother her anymore.

Ian didn't stop holding her until she stopped crying. She didn't even know vampires could cry. She kind of wished they couldn't.

The next time Celia visited Dr. Savage, there was a man there—a human man. The doctor and the human stood in the little lobby outside her office together, where she played quiet sitar music on the stereo and burned incense to help relax clients.

The human was attractive in that soap opera star kind of way—spikey but stylish blond hair, big brown eyes, and carefully planned five o'clock shadow. He had a cute butt, which Celia only noticed because Dr. Savage had her hands on it.

"Celia!" Dr. Savage looked up, surprised. "You're early."

"I can go." Celia gestured to the door.

"No, it's all right." She smiled. Her business suit was green that night, with a slight sheen like lizard skin. She had on her red-bottomed Louboutin heels, which made her a couple inches taller than the traditionally pretty human with his hands on her hips.

"See you in the morning?" he whispered.

"Mm-hmm." She kissed him once, quickly, but Celia noticed, as he walked away, Dr. Savage looked like she wanted to eat him.

He sort of smiled at Celia as he left.

"Come into my office, Celia." She gestured toward the open door, and Celia could already hear the fountain inside. "Can I get you anything?"

"No." She shuffled past her therapist and sat on her favorite farting couch. "Who was that?"

Dr. Savage picked up her leather bound pad of paper and sat cross-legged in her swivel chair. "We're not here to talk about me."

"Are you dating a human?"

She put on turtle shell glasses. "Yes."

"And it's working out?"

"Dean and I have been together for a year."

"And he knows…" She flashed her top teeth at the good doc—no fangs. Celia still couldn't get 'em to boing unless Ian was around.

"Of course."

"He's okay with it?"

Dr. Savage smiled, tight-lipped. "Do you have on a new perfume?"

"No." Celia was embarrassed to tell her she'd been wearing the same shirt for the past two days. After hugging Ian at Happy Gas, Celia had been pleasantly surprised to realize his scent had stuck to her clothes. She refused to wash her shirt and was still debating whether she would ever wash it again.

Dr. Savage sniffed the way Imogene sometimes did—which made Celia nervous. Then, she stated the obvious: "Is that Ian?"

Celia cleared her throat and tugged at her shirt.

"Well." Dr. Savage chuckled. "No wonder you've got a crush on him. You've been close to him lately?"

"Yeah," Celia said. "A little."

"By the smell of you, very close."

"I had a meltdown on him."

Celia thought Dr. Savage was trying to wrinkle her brow, but her wrinkle-free skin wouldn't let her. "A meltdown, Celia?"

She shook her head. "That's not why I'm here. I need to talk to you about something in particular. I have a problem."

Dr. Savage shifted gracefully in her seat, but she still leaned forward, Celia assumed in an effort to catch shadows of Ian's scent in the air. "Okay. We're here to solve problems."

"Right. Okay. It's about my fangs. They don't work right."

"Could you elaborate?"

"Yes." Celia picked at her fingernails. "Imogene says I either have premature ejaculation or limp dick."

"Um." Dr. Savage pursed her lips together. "I don't think I understand."

Celia got up and walked to the window of the office that

overlooked St. Arthur's Circle where all the posh clothing stores stayed open late for drunken tourists with too much money.

"The other night, I went to this party with Imogene, and...but that's not really the problem." She shook her head. "I can't control my fangs when Ian's around. They just..." She gestured to her mouth. "Boing."

"Boing?"

"That's the sound I pretend my fangs make," she said. "So when he's around, sometimes, they just pop out, and I have no control over them, and it's embarrassing. The other night, Imogene thought I could go to this party and practice." Celia paced. "Boinging them out and then pulling them back in. But they wouldn't boing. I had performance anxiety. Have you ever heard of that?"

"Celia, why don't you sit down?"

She sat down and folded her hands in her lap.

"This is an easy thing to fix," Dr. Savage said. "Just takes some practice."

Celia barked out a petulant sigh.

"It's obvious why your fangs come out when you're with Ian. You're attracted to Ian. As you know, our fangs distend when we are sexually excited or hungry. You've done well controlling your hunger, but you've never met anyone like Ian since your turn. You need to learn to control yourself. It takes practice."

"But why won't they come out when I want them to?"

"Nerves." Dr. Savage nodded. "We're going to work on some exercises, but then we really need to talk about Danny."

"Why?" Celia howled.

"Because I feel that most of your repression and anxiety stem from your experience with him."

Celia crossed her arms, reverting to her five-year-old self. "I don't want to talk about Danny anymore."

"That's the problem. You need to work through your feelings about what happened."

"There aren't any feelings," Celia said. "He just left me."

"He rejected you, Celia, which is why you're afraid that all other men will do the same. Even Ian. That's why you fear your fangs. You fear judgment, rejection. Your fear manifests itself in your fangs misbehaving."

"Look." She poked out her bottom lip. "I promise we'll talk about Danny next time if you just help me with this fang thing. Can't we just do that tonight?"

Dr. Savage leaned back in her chair and looked at Celia over the top of her glasses, probing.

When Celia got home later, all was quiet at the Sleeping Gull Apartments. It was 3 a.m., so when she walked into her kitchen for a snack, she heard Ian snoring through the thin wall. The sound was way more soothing than Dr. Savage's fountain and stupid sitar music. Celia took a couple sips of A-positive and headed to the bathroom.

Contrary to popular lore, vampires did have reflections. They showed up on cameras and video. It was a good thing, too. Celia couldn't imagine going through a whole day with a booger on her face and not knowing it.

It was time to practice. The exercises she and Dr. Savage had put together were simple. She had to think of two different dudes. One dude: Ian. The other dude: Ralph. She couldn't use Danny, because Dr. Savage said they still weren't sure how Celia felt about Danny. The exercise needed to be clean-cut, obvious—a guy she liked and a guy who annoyed the shit out of her.

What she was supposed to do was, first, think about Ian—not just his name or his face but all of him: his crinkly blue eyes, the freckle on his neck, and the length of his toes. She avoided the shark bite scar because she was still pretty freaked about that whole thing. So back to Ian and his good stuff: his curly hair, the way he sounded when he laughed, the way he smelled.

That did it. *Boing*! The fangs were out. Celia admired them in the mirror. She had to admit, they were pretty freaking cool.

The second part of her exercise was to think about Ralph. Ralph with his stupid gelled hair with highlighted tips and his stupid hemp necklaces—the way he said, "Ceeeelia," like he had a speech impediment. Ralph: stupid, annoying Ralph.

Holy shit, her fangs went back in. She leaned forward and pulled at her upper lip. Nothing. Nada. Gone.

Celia called Imogene immediately, and she said, "Go bite Ian," the mere suggestion of which made Celia's teeth go boing without her consent. Apparently, more practice was necessary.

CHAPTER EIGHT

Celia was working on her fang trick—and getting pretty good at it—
when someone knocked on her front door: Ian, obviously, based on
the woodsy BO scent wafting around her living room. She looked at
herself in the mirror. Still awkward with a round face and too-big
nose?

Check.

She opened the door to a sweaty Ian wearing one of his spandex
biker outfits. He held a helmet in his hand, and he was still out of
breath. "Do you work tonight?"

"No."

"I broke up with that girl," he huffed between gasps of air.

"Oh."

He smiled at Celia like she'd said something funny. His black hair
was plastered to his forehead. There was a drop of sweat on his nose,
which made Celia want to suck on his nose. Luckily, just at that
moment, she thought about Ralph.

"Do you want to hang out tonight?"

"Why'd you break up with that girl?" she asked.

He sniffed, and the bead of sweat went flying. "Uh." He chuckled and touched his bottom lip. "She wasn't what I was looking for."

"Oh. Okay."

He squinted at her like he was waiting for her to solve a math equation. When she didn't say anything like "x equals 34," he ran his hand across his sweaty head. "So can we hang out tonight?"

"I was going to watch *Pretty Woman*."

"I'll watch it with you." He pointed at his house. "I just gotta shower. Give me fifteen."

"Wh…" She watched his cute butt walk away and thought *Ralph, Ralph, Ralph.*

Celia closed her front door and called Imogene, because that was what she'd been doing lately whenever she had a thought about anything.

"God, what now?" Imogene barked on the fifth ring.

"Ian broke up with that girl," Celia whispered.

"How do you know that?"

"He just told me."

Imogene paused. "He's not sitting right next to you, is he?"

"No, he's taking a shower. Then, we're watching a movie."

Celia heard the sound of Imogene's huge boots, dancing. "You're totally gonna fuck."

"Imogene! No, we are not!"

"Then, bite him! Bite him! Bite him!" Celia had never pictured Imogene as a cheerleader.

"No. Stop it. We're watching a movie."

"He broke up with that skanky girl for you, dumbass!"

"How do you know that?" Celia curled into a ball on her couch and started rocking back and forth.

"Because you kissed him the other night, and he obviously likes you. And he just told you he broke up with the other girl. He just announced he's available. To you. Now, stop being a dumbass and tear his clothes off!"

"I don't tear clothes off," Celia said.

"How's your boing practice?"

She glanced at her cracked ceiling. "Good. Unfortunately, I have to think about Ralph all the time, but it works."

"Well, keep thinking, Merk, because you're about to be curled up on a couch with the guy of your dreams."

She stood up. "Oh my God, you're right. Oh my God."

"Merk, Merk, deep breaths."

Celia tried to breathe deeply, but she felt like her uvula was choking her.

"Merk, you got this. Ian is the nicest, dorkiest hot guy I've ever met. He's not intimidating, right?"

"No."

"And we trust him?"

"Yeah."

"So everything's gonna be great."

"Right." Celia nodded. "Yeah."

"Are you wearing yoga pants right now?"

"Shit. I have to change." She hurried to her bedroom, but before she hung up on Imogene, she heard her voice…

"You should be paying me by the minute, bitch!"

Celia's closet was a disaster. She had nothing to wear—nothing. Ian had seen her in the same jeans practically every day, so she went for her one dress, the one she'd worn the night she met Danny. The color was good. The navy blue went well with her red head. It tended to cover all her sensitive areas: the soft places on her stomach and upper thighs—not that it mattered since Ian still occasionally called her "Mermaid." It wasn't like he didn't know what he was getting himself into.

She pulled her hair into an orderly ponytail and put on a hint of blush, plus mascara. She almost poked her eye out with the mascara brush, she was so out of practice.

In the mirror, she said, "Ralph." Quickly: "Ralph, Ralph."

She went to her VHS collection to prepare *Pretty Woman*, which was right on top since she watched it once a week. She put it in the VCR. Then, she thought about putting a padlock on her fridge, because what if Ian brought beer over and wanted to keep it cool and opened the fridge to find bags upon bags of human blood?

Celia did the deep breathing Dr. Savage taught her once and that Imogene apparently approved of as well. There was just no time to calm down, though, because right then, Ian knocked on Celia's front door.

She turned on the TV for some background noise. *Jeopardy!* was on. Then, she opened the door. He didn't have beer, as she'd feared. He did have a bag of popcorn in one hand, though.

He wore the holey jeans she liked, bare feet, and a black button-down that matched his hair. The top three buttons were undone. She wondered if he'd done that on purpose or if he'd just not noticed, because Celia noticed. She noticed the edges of his collarbone, the shadow at the base of his neck, the neck freckle—dear God, the neck freckle!—and every inch of skin that ran from chest to chin.

She giggled in greeting.

Ralph, Ralph, Ralph.

"Wow, you look really pretty." He leaned across the threshold and kissed her cheek.

She giggled in reply. *Ralph.*

He walked past her, and she closed the door behind him. He stood in front of her TV and said, "Caduceus."

"What?"

He gestured to *Jeopardy!*. "Symbol for medicine."

"Oh. Are you good at *Jeopardy!*?"

"Yeah."

"Were you the really smart kid in school? Because you don't seem like it."

He looked over his shoulder at her and smiled.

Then, Celia realized she'd insulted him. "I didn't mean it that way," she said. "I just meant no pocket protectors or Steve Urkel pants. You seem like you would have been one of the cool kids in high school."

"I was too busy surfing to get good grades," he said.

She took a step closer. "You surfed a lot, huh?"

"Since I was eight."

"And now you won't go near the water."

He turned away from the TV and toward her. "I go near it." He smiled again.

"You seem like the happiest person I've ever met."

He shrugged. "What's there to be sad about?"

"Nothing. Right now." She clasped her hands behind her back so he couldn't see her picking her fingernails.

"I brought popcorn. We're watching a movie?"

"Yeah!" She grinned. "Yeah, it's my favorite." She handed Ian the box with Julia Roberts and Richard Gere on the cover. "I know you said you might have seen it, but that means you haven't seen it because it's so great you'd remember." With him standing in front of her, she switched the input on her TV, and the screen glowed blue.

Ian carried the empty VHS box with him to the couch and sat right in the middle. Celia had no choice but to squeeze in next to him, and he made no sign of scooting over. He opened the bag of popcorn. The cloying scent of butter was almost enough to make her feel sick. He held the bag out to her.

"No, no, thanks," she said.

"More for me." He crunched a kernel and put one of his arms over the back of the couch—not around Celia but over her.

She felt kind of tingly as she fast-forwarded through all the copyright warnings and old rom-com trailers. Then, it began: *Pretty Woman*.

Ian's commentary was quiet and mostly to himself between chews. For instance, "Hey, that's George Costanzsa," or "Did Richard Gere ever not have gray hair?"

At one point, he grabbed the controls from Celia and hit Pause.

"So Julia Roberts is a hooker?"

"Yes."

"And she's the protagonist."

"You use words like 'protagonist'?"

He scratched his hair, which sent off a wave of men's shampoo smell. *Ralph.* "Oh, is this where the phrase 'hooker with a heart of gold' comes from?"

"Yes, exactly!" Celia said.

"Okay, keep it rolling."

Ian got surprisingly angry at the bitchy women on Rodeo Drive who wouldn't let Julia Roberts shop. He didn't understand the whole no-kissing-on-the-mouth thing, so Celia tried to explain that kissing was too intimate, to which he replied, "What part of sex isn't intimate?"

Celia made him shut up when Vivian (Julia) finally got to go on her shopping spree. Celia loved that part—all those people running around, giving her outfits to try on, and everything fitting perfectly, of course, and looking great.

Ian cheered when Vivian got to go back to the bitchy lady's store and tell her off. Celia found his exultation to be adorable. Plus, although he'd been silent about all the classic eighties music in the film so far, he finally did say, "I know this one!" when Roy Orbison started singing.

Celia hadn't noticed it, but at some point, her hand had traveled to Ian's knee. His hand was on her shoulder, and his fingers would sometimes sneak up the side of her neck.

"People always fall in love during montages," he said to the screen as Vivian and Edward returned to their hotel for another night of hooker passion. "Wouldn't it be nice to know what they were talking about?"

Celia shook her head. "No, I like montages better. Then, you can fill in the blanks."

"Shit, she's going to kiss him," Ian said.

"Shh…"

He was right, of course. Vivian broke her rule and kissed Edward and of course ended up falling in love, because that's how movies worked: people kissed, fell in love, and lived happily ever after—following totally awesome shopping sprees.

Celia was so focused on the kiss on TV that she didn't notice Ian next to her, leaning forward. Then, his hand was on her face, turning her head to him. He kissed her. Not like the quick peck she'd given him days before. Theirs was movie kissing—open mouth, little bit of tongue. He tasted like butter and…Ian.

Celia's gums burned, so she said, "Ralph."

He paused. "Did you just call me Ralph?"

"It's a long story."

"Okay." He leaned in again, but she smiled against his mouth.

"The movie's not over." She half-heartedly pushed him away.

He made a humming sound. He was leaned over her, his hand on the outside of her thigh, and she had no idea how it got there so fast. He did eventually back off because he said he had to see how it turned out. Celia was relieved since she loved the scene where Vivian talked about being locked in the attic as a kid. She always dreamed her white knight would come and save her from the high tower, but he never did.

Ian made it to the part where "It Must Have Been Love" by Roxette started playing. That was when his warm lips found the side of Celia's neck.

"Is it almost over?" he whispered.

Was what almost over? Celia's head was filled with cumulonimbus clouds, and each lightning strike made the sound, "Ian…Ian…Ian."

"Wait," she squeaked when his hand moved even higher on her thigh. "It's the big ending." She pointed to the screen. "See, Edward gets over his fear of heights to get to Vivian." She looked up at Ian. "He's her white knight."

Celia didn't know if Ian was smiling at the utter cuteness of the movie or at her. When he ran his thumb over her bottom lip, she concluded her, which was so weird. She'd never had a guy look at her like that before, except maybe Danny just before he bit her.

"Can I kiss you some more?" he asked.

"Yeah." She nodded and didn't even have to think "Ralph." What was happening to her wasn't about blood anymore. This was…something else. For some reason, she wanted Ian's entire body on top of her, and she'd never felt that way before. Usually, Celia didn't even like stuffed animals on her lap, but she was super pumped when Ian somehow maneuvered her whole body onto the couch and laid down next to her. His hands were in her hair, and he kissed her neck. She felt flushed and kind of like she had to pee.

Then, his mouth was on her mouth again, and she did her best to keep up.

"You've kissed a lot of girls before, haven't you?" she asked.

"No." He smiled with his nose pressed against hers. "Yes."

Celia returned his goofy grin and dug both her hands into his thick, black hair.

"Bedroom?" he whispered.

The clouds in her head scattered. The heat left her loins. She sat up suddenly, and, due to her unnatural amount of strength, knocked him completely off the furniture and flat on his back between the coffee table and couch.

Ian stayed there and stared at the ceiling. "Too fast?"

Celia put her hands over her face. "I am so sorry. Are you okay?"

He sat up and leaned his elbow on the couch. "Yes. That was a completely reasonable response to my question. Way too fast."

She curled her legs up under her. "It's just, I'm different." She wasn't even talking about the vampire thing either. "I've only had sex twice, and I don't really remember either time." *Why the hell did you just tell him that?*

She expected some kind of…reaction. There were a few options:

1. Ian would ravage her and make sure she remembered.

2. Ian would freak at her inexperience and never touch her again.

3. Ian would say they should just be friends.

In classic, unflappable Ian fashion, though, he just said, "Huh." He climbed back on the couch next to her. "You're a really good kisser."

"I am?" she asked.

"Yeah." He slouched down in the couch, and she had the same feeling she'd had the other night: the need to touch his hair. Then he went even further and laid his head across her lap—which actually made it even easier to play with his hair. He curled his long legs up so he could fit on her couch and said, "So what other favorite movies you got?"

Let the eighties education begin.

CHAPTER NINE

There were so many things to talk about with Dr. Savage except Danny, like how Ian had by then seen *The Dark Crystal, Say Anything,* and *The Neverending Story*—which just wrecked him when Artax died in the swamp. Celia thought he was going to cry. He held her so tight, if she'd been human, his fingers would have left little blue circles on her skin.

Of further interest, she was doing much better with her fangs. She didn't have to say "Ralph" half as much anymore, even when Ian and she were cuddling on the couch and he moved her hair so he could kiss her upper back—and *oh, God!* Celia wondered why people didn't talk more about upper back kissing?

Despite all this, Dr. Savage wanted to talk about Danny because Celia promised she would.

To talk about Danny, she had to first talk about Terrance. Terrance was a chubby frat boy at the University of Miami. Celia lost her virginity to him freshman year. It was her first time being drunk, and he seemed to like her all right, so when he invited her to his room, she said, "Sure." She hadn't really thought things through.

She remembered there was nothing special about her first time. It was over in three thrusts, and she left Terrance passed out, face-first, with his pants around his ankles. When Celia got back to her dorm, she looked at herself in the mirror and expected to look different—womanlier. Instead, she was just Celia with bloodshot eyes.

She partially blamed that botched sexual experiment on her obsessive behavior in regards to her first bite. It was the last "first" she had left as a woman/vampire, and damn it, it was going to be special.

Which brought her mind back to Ian, who fell asleep wrapped around her on the couch the night before. Only when he was still, sleeping, did she notice the *thump-thump* of his pulse and remember he was full of blood. Sometimes, she just sat there with her fangs out, staring at his neck. She didn't think there were rules about staring at men's necks when they were asleep.

She got through all these meanderings before Dr. Savage stopped her. "Celia! Danny!"

"My friend Layla." Celia paused. "When I say 'friend,' I just mean she didn't ignore me in high school. She invited me out to celebrate her college graduation, probably because she felt bad for me, and we went to Tequila Sunrise, this sort of trashy bar in Lazaret." She shrugged. "I got drunk."

Dr. Savage made a note and looked up over her glasses. "Then what?"

"I was dancing. Well, I was standing in a crowd, moving my hips. I had my hair down, which was probably what caught his attention. Danny likes red hair."

She remembered he started dancing around her, and he could not have looked more out of place. He was in a full three-piece suit. His dark hair was combed back over his head like Redford in *The Sting*.

Due to Ian, Celia had come to realize there were different levels of hot. Ian was cute-hot. He was boy-next-door, the hot you wanted to marry. Danny was bad boy hot—hot as a blowtorch, hot as in you-will-never-meet-my-mother. And that night at Tequila Sunrise, he was all over Celia.

She told Dr. Savage he whispered weird things to her over the music:

"You're a hell of a dame."

"Wanna blow this juice joint?"

"Let me make you beautiful, baby."

It was like Terrance all over again.

Danny invited Celia back to his hotel, and she went. They were both completely hammered—or, as Danny said, "ossified." They had sex, but there was nothing really sexy about it. Afterward, he kept kissing her neck.

More weird things were whispered:

"Do you want to be perfect?"

"Let me make you perfect, baby."

Yes, yes, okay.

"Then, he bit me," she said, "and the booze mixed with his vampire venom until I thought we were floating on the ceiling. Maybe we were floating on the ceiling. Can vampires float on the ceiling? I've thought about it before, like bats, but—"

"No, Celia."

She sighed. "So Danny bit me and then made me drink some blood from a cut on his wrist. I threw up. I threw up some more." She tugged on the hem of her shirt. "When I came back from the bathroom, he woke up long enough to say, 'Hey, you're a vampire. Stay out of the sun.'"

"What happened in the morning, Celia?"

She hated the next part, but for the sake of therapy, she continued. "At 4 a.m., the hotel room alarm went off, but Danny was gone. The only evidence he'd even been there was a note with phone numbers for Steve and you—and a used condom in the trash, because I'm all for safety. Danny laughed about that." She threw her hands in the air. "So poof! Vampire! But when I looked in the mirror, I wasn't Kate Beckinsale. I was just me, again, stuck as me forever."

"Why do you want to be someone else, Celia?" Dr. Savage asked.

"I don't want to be someone else. I want to be me, just better."

"Why?"

"I'm worried Ian is going to look at me some night and realize he's out of my league and wonder what the hell he was thinking."

"Ian seems to care about you, Celia."

She shrugged. "So did Danny."

When Celia got home that night, Ian was on the porch with Heidi. The landlady was in her usual cat puke-colored robe with her big, white-yellow wig. Celia heard her wild, crazy voice over the sound of waves—big waves. A storm was coming.

"After she used the hammer, she chopped his body up into pieces and left him for the gators," Heidi said. "Can you believe that? Probably made the gators sick!"

Ian sipped a drink that actually sort of matched Heidi's robe.

"You need to watch *True Crime*," she continued. "You just never know what kind of monster lives next door." She waved at Celia, which brought Ian's attention to her arrival.

"Hey." He smiled. "See you later, Heidi."

She held up her saggy-skinned arm, covered in gold bangle bracelets. "Good luck tomorrow!"

He walked up to Celia and kissed her on the cheek. He held up his glass. "Kale smoothie?"

"Gross," she muttered.

"I have a bike race tomorrow. Will you come?"

"Hmm?" Celia stood on the porch with her keys in hand. She smelled rain somewhere down the beach.

"It goes all the way down the key, but it ends in St. Arthur's Circle. Thought you could come cheer me on in my spandex." His eyes crinkled in mirth.

Celia wanted to say yes, but then she thought about bursting into flames. "I can't."

"All right." He sipped at his health sludge.

She put her hand on his cheek. He was the first man she'd ever been so comfortable touching in her whole life. She'd never even hugged her dad. "Does anything bother you?"

He thought hard about her question, chewing the side of his bottom lip. "You swimming in the ocean at night."

She sighed and unlocked her front door...to find Imogene on her couch with a bag of blood in her hand.

"Jesus!" Celia slammed the door, which made Ian go tumbling backwards against the porch railing.

"I almost dropped my smoothie," he said.

Then, a raindrop hit Celia, square on the forehead. Ian kissed it away.

"Can you give me a second?" she asked.

"Sure." He shrugged and stood there as the raindrops picked up speed.

Celia squeezed through her front door. Imogene was still on her couch, but the blood bag was gone. "Sorry?" she said.

"How'd you get in?"

"Merk, I'm a thief. And a vampire. The only thing cooler would be if I could turn into mist."

Celia nodded. "Yeah, I've thought about that, too."

Imogene stood, and she was way more glammed up than usual. She wore the same red plastic sunglasses, but she had on a black glitter top that was totally see-through with a black bra underneath. She had on black skinny jeans, and holy shit, no combat boots! Imogene was in black spike heels!

"It's Saturday," she said. "Let's go out."

"Um, Ian—"

"He can come. We're not going to some bloodsucker cult. There's this dive bar on Barkentine that I like. There's a killer band playing tonight. A female guitarist. For real." She stepped past Celia and opened the front door, where Ian stood being pelted by rain. "Come here, you stud," she purred.

He smiled at her and gave her a one-armed hug that lifted her feet off the floor.

"Where have you been?" he said into Imogene's purple hair.

"Pining after you." She licked his cheekbone, as usual. Celia noticed Imogene was different around Ian. She brushed wet pieces of hair from his forehead, which kind of made Celia's stomach twist when she realized she should be the one doing that. "We're going out tonight. You in?"

He frowned and looked at the now empty smoothie glass in his hand. "I have a race tomorrow morning."

"You don't have to drink." Imogene turned toward Celia and shoved her toward her bedroom—a silent command to stop wearing fucking yoga pants. Celia was hearing Imogene's voice in her head by then. "Just come hang out," she continued. "There's this band playing at Drift Inn you just gotta see."

"Drift Inn?"

"Yeah, it's this really skungy bar. They even let you smoke inside."

Celia heard the sound of his laugh from her bedroom and also the sound of his refusal.

"I'd really love to, but I can't. I wanna kick some pavement ass tomorrow."

"Wah, wah, then get the fuck out of here."

Celia was staring at her closet when he stepped into the room. "I've been kicked out of your apartment," he said.

"I don't really want to go out," she whispered.

"You should. You have to work the next three nights."

Celia stuck out her bottom lip.

Ian pushed her out of the way of her open closet door and started going through her things. It was mostly t-shirts, but she kept her favorite shirts on hangers, which was how he found one Celia hadn't worn in a year that said, "Bite Me" on the front with a pair of fangs underneath.

"Perfect," he said, though he didn't seem to understand why she laughed so hard.

She stopped laughing when he reached for the bottom edge of the well-worn white shirt she had on. He didn't ask her permission before pulling the shirt over her head and tossing it on the floor. He kissed her collarbone once, twice.

Ralph.

Ralph, Ralph, Ralph.

Then, he pulled the "Bite Me" tee over her head and down her torso. When the shirt was in place, he kept his thumbs against her hips and rubbed softly. "Now, you're ready to go out." Then, he kissed her with that magic mouth of his—that mouth that made her think of things like Atomic Fireballs and the Fourth of July.

Imogene catcalled from the doorway, but when Celia tried to pull away, Ian just held her chin and kissed harder. Despite Imogene's presence, he said, "Come over when you get home tonight?"

She nodded. *Ralph.*

Ian high-fived Imogene on his way out, and Celia stood there, legs in metaphorical cement.

"That was fucking hot," Imogene said.

"Ralph."

"What?"

"It's how I calm myself."

Imogene crossed her arms and leaned on the doorframe. "By ralphing?"

"I think about someone I hate. It keeps the fangs in when Ian's around."

"Ah, getting the premature ejaculation under control, huh?"

"Yeah, but he makes it really difficult."

Imogene nodded. "No shit. Nice shirt." She flashed her fangs. "Let's get the hell out of here."

It rained in earnest as they made their way down Admiral Key. Luckily, Imogene's convertible had a top, but the top didn't make her drive with any more caution. Neither did the rain. She actually seemed amused by the puddles she threw up whenever she lost control of the vehicle. She was a menace.

The streets of Barkentine Beach were dead, but the bars were full. Many establishments had their doors wide open, and Celia could see crowds inside, hiding from the storm. Stages were brightly lit, filled with longhaired old hippies and wrinkled backup singers.

The Drift Inn was at the end of the main drag, and Imogene parked crooked in two spots like she owned the whole block. "Good thing we're not witches," she said.

"Huh?"

She flipped her glasses up at Celia. "We'd melt!" With that, she went running across the street. Celia took off after her, glad she'd changed out of her white t-shirt from earlier—not that anyone was going to give her half a look next to Imogene and all her wicked glory.

The Drift Inn had a reputation for being dirty, stinky, filled with biker dudes…and totally rad. Imogene was right about the smoking thing. When they stepped inside, Celia was baptized in blue haze. The jukebox played Elvis, and there wasn't an open seat at the half-circle bar.

"Let's go make some guys move," Imogene said.

The place was smaller than one might expect for having a multi-island-wide rep. It was just a half-circle bar with a stage the size of Celia's closet and a unisex bathroom—oh, and a mannequin, dressed in a silver glitter gown and purple wig. Oddly, she resembled Imogene.

Imogene walked up to two huge guys in leather vests with long, white beards. She lifted her red sunglasses and said something, which made them immediately get up and try to buy her a drink—which was harder than one might think. There was only one bartender at The Drift Inn, and he was this old guy who looked like a grumpy Santa. He had on a huge Mexican sombrero; glasses; and a shirt that read, "Fuck you, I have enough friends." He even ignored the huge biker dudes until Imogene put her glasses on top of her head, wiggled her hips, and boom, there he was, grumbling about rum punches and peach juice. She ordered one for Celia, too, and they sat down, elbow-to-elbow with the new, old, and barely coherent.

"What do ya think?" She gestured to the crowded area as if it was a vast mountain range.

"Cool," Celia said.

"Yeah, the band should start in, like, an hour. You and Ian a thing now?"

"I guess so." She stirred her tall, pink drink but didn't take a sip.

"God, you look miserable. You were just orally attacked by the most adorable human on the Key." Imogene stuck her bony elbow in Celia's rib. "What's the matter with you?"

"I keep thinking he's going to break up with me."

"Break up with you?" She drank half her rum punch in one gulp, kind of like the way she drank blood. "Are you even official? Like girlfriend-boyfriend? Because you can't break up with someone if you're not even official."

"Well, he could stop wanting to see me because I'm chubby and awkward and he's...not."

"God, enough with the fucking pity-party." Another rum punch materialized in her purple-painted fingers.

"It's just, nothing in my life has ever been easy. Even when I was a kid, I stressed over the organization of my toy box. Now, this thing with Ian is moving along, and it's just too easy. Something has got to go wrong."

"Like him finding out you suck blood to live?"

Celia shrugged. "Yeah. That would be bad."

Imogene shoved Celia's rum punch close to the edge of the bar so she had to catch it before it fell in her lap. "Drink that. All of it." She sighed. "Look, there's this music guy in South Carolina. Not the kind of shit I usually listen to, right? Kind of sappy, sweet. Written after 1989. But there's this one song he wrote and played for me once. I don't know what it was called, but it was about love and how this guy didn't…" She tipped her head and took a slurp from her straw. "It was about this guy who was looking for love and then he met this girl—this one girl. And the chorus was something about 'I never knew it could be this easy.'" She shrugged. "I think that's what happens when people are supposed to be together."

"Oh," Celia said.

"Yeah." Imogene nodded. "Let's do a shot."

Celia laughed.

Imogene was right, the band was cool. The female guitarist was killer, even though she kind of resembled the Crypt Keeper. The girls even made friends with some fishermen who smelled like shrimp. Guys smiled at Celia, even though they mostly just danced around Imogene, considering she could actually dance. But Celia wasn't as invisible as usual, which was nice.

They drove home drunk, the rain still coming down. When Celia suggested they go swimming, Imogene was all for it. She was naked before they reached the sand, but Celia kept on her bra and underwear. With all the booze in her system, she didn't feel so bad about herself.

Celia loved swimming in the ocean when it rained. It was hard to tell when she was above water, and the ocean felt warmer than the storm—unusual for early April. She liked being surrounded by water, and the air smelled a strange mix of wet flowers and salt. Of course, Imogene was obnoxious, rolling and shouting and spitting salt water from her mouth, washing it away with fresh rain. Celia did her normal duet with the fishies and floated until she could no longer tell the difference in sound between breaking waves and falling rain.

They ran up the beach together. Imogene didn't even put her clothes back on—just went right for Celia's front door. When Celia moved to follow, Imogene shook her head.

"He told you to go to him when you got home."

"Oh." Celia glanced at Ian's front door.

"So go to him. Duh." Imogene walked into Celia's apartment and slammed the front door in her face.

"Right. Okay."

Ian's front door was unlocked, and his apartment was warm. The scent of sleeping Ian felt better than the waves against her skin. She was soaking wet in nothing but panties and a bra. She crept to his bathroom and dried off with a towel from the rack. Then, she crept toward his bedroom, and she did kind of feel like Bela Lugosi, creeping around Ian's place with him unconscious and snoring ten feet away.

She didn't know if she was supposed to wake him or what, but she stretched out on his bed, above the covers. He was sprawled on his stomach, arms curled under a pillow. She'd never seen so much of his skin before, so she had to touch it.

He had freckles on his back, and when she touched them, he took a loud breath of air and squinted up at her in the dark. "Mm," he said and pulled her body closer with a hand around her waist. "You went swimming in the ocean."

"Imogene was with me."

"But I wasn't."

Celia wasn't sure he was really awake. His voice was slurred, deeper than usual. His hair was a huge halo of black tentacles. His eyes remained closed.

"Why aren't you under the covers?" he asked.

"I didn't want to bother you."

"It bothers me that you're not under the covers."

She smiled and slipped beneath his sheets. He pulled her even closer so their stomachs touched. Celia felt super nervous when she realized he was in nothing but boxers—and she was in sea-soaked underwear. His breath came out in warm, stale puffs against her forehead. Who would have thought sleep-breath could be so cute? His arms were around her, one leg tangled between hers. He let out a little sigh and was asleep again.

Celia leaned her head back some so Ian became less a fuzzy mess of features and more Ian. She moved one of her hands to the back of his neck and played with the shaggy hair there, in need of a trim. She guessed even in his sleep, he liked having his hair touched, because he moved his body even closer. They were glued together from the chest down.

It was shocking. Lying there, drunk, sticky with the sea, covered in clammy, half-asleep Ian, Celia finally got it. She finally understood what it was like to want sex.

She was sure other people figured this out climbing the rope in gym class in sixth grade, but the whole thing with Terrance had been just a rite of passage. With Danny, it was just because. So outside of the blood lust thing, she'd never looked at a man and thought, "Yeah, I totally want to be naked with him."

Imogene said this was because Celia had never had an orgasm. How can you miss pizza if you've never had pizza? Right?

It was then decided: Celia wanted to have sex with Ian.

It wasn't just about orgasms. She wanted to be closer to him. Literally, lying in his bed, there was no way they could have physically been closer, except for one very obvious thing that...well...

Dr. Savage said sex was a gateway to discussing the first bite. Maybe if Celia and Ian had sex, it wouldn't be so weird when she told him she drank blood to stay alive?

She went to bed happy. Ian snored, she knew this, but she slept anyway—for a while. Then, she had a nightmare.

In her dream, Danny met her on the beach. He wore the same three-piece suit as the night they met. "What's up, Mermaid?" he said. Then, Celia realized she was naked and ran back to her apartment screaming. She wasn't sure that really counted as a nightmare, but she sure didn't like it.

CHAPTER TEN

Ian got second place in his race. When Celia was leaving for work, he stood on the porch on the phone with his mom, but he still had time to wrap his arm around her shoulders and kiss the side of her head. He said he was going to start training super hard for a big race coming up, and Celia was reminded, again, Ian had a really cute butt.

Celia thought if they were in a romance movie, those days would be the perfect time for a montage, despite the fact that the female lead kept bags of blood in the fridge—and some in the freezer, the vampire version of popsicles.

On nights when she didn't work, she and Ian watched *Jeopardy!* together. Ian would come over after testing video games all day. Then, they would make out, which Celia had gotten better at, she thought. Ian hadn't asked about the "bedroom" since she threw him off her couch that one time, but her hands had been wandering. Ian's body felt nice.

She found it was getting a bit annoying, turning down his offers to make her dinner all the time. She figured it had to be annoying for *him*. He had to wonder why she never ate.

Sometimes, they went biking together after sunset. Ian had to practically pedal backwards for her to keep up with him. Her beach cruiser wasn't exactly built for speed—and neither was Celia. But Ian was good about it. Sometimes, he even rode around her in swift circles.

Sadly, being supernaturally strong didn't translate to having super endurance. A normal person would think they'd go hand-in-hand, but no. It was yet another one of those things no one bothered to explain to Celia before she became a vampire.

He visited her at work. He would show up at Happy Gas and buy Smartfood White Cheddar Cheese Popcorn, because he said it was the only edible item they kept in stock—this coming from a man who drank kale smoothies every day.

Celia finished reading *Twilight*, so she would have to wait to get the other books to find out if Edward ever turned Bella. She had hoped the book would give her some insight into Ian and their relationship, but it didn't and she'd mastered how to be an angsty teenager years ago.

Then, the romantic montage halted when, one night, Ian came walking out of her kitchen with a bag of blood in his hand. "Why do you have blood in your fridge and freezer?"

He must have found her popsicles, too.

She needed to glamour him—immediately. But she felt kind of guilty about glamouring Ian. Plus, she had to face facts, Celia had no idea how to glamour someone. She'd seen Imogene do it, but she had only a vague understanding of how it was done. She needed Imogene, but she thought Ian might get even more suspicious if, instead of answering his question, she made a phone call.

"Celia?" he said.

Think, stupid, think. "I'm anemic."

"Probably because you never eat." He glanced at the bag: B-negative, Celia's least favorite.

"I have an eating disorder?"

He looked back at her as she sunk deeper and deeper between two cushions in her couch. "You do?"

"Yes."

"So, what, you put blood in your cereal?"

"I have an IV."

"Where?"

"It's being washed." *Did IVs need to be washed?*

"Hmm." He shrugged. "Okay." He turned and walked back to the kitchen.

Hmm, okay? That was it? She was off the hook that easily?

Ian came back and laid his head in her lap with his long legs folded over the arm of the couch. She stuck her fingers in his hair. She knew from experience that playing with it momentarily erased his brain. Instead of humming happily, though, his eyes popped open. "I knew you were a vampire."

Holy fuck, he figured it out!

Then, he laughed. He had just found a fridge filled with bags of blood (and peach juice for Imogene's rum punches), and he was joking around. Celia suspected she was falling for a maniac.

Celia needed to talk to Imogene, but she wanted some privacy. Imogene didn't mind talking, so long as she could hunt at the same time. She whined until Celia agreed to go to St. Arthur's Circle and meet her at a bar called Daiquiri Deck, where they served…daiquiris.

They sat out on the second story porch. The nights were getting warmer and warmer in southern Florida. Summer was raring to go, ready to drench the air in never-ending humidity and the sweet scent of flowers—with just a hint of rotting fish. Tourist season was in full swing, so Imogene had her pick of the litter.

She was playing "Marry-Fuck-Kill" when Celia started poking at some blue and green frozen mixture called Kryptonite. Imogene's game really could have been called just "Fuck-Kill," because Celia had yet to hear her friend mention marriage—ever.

Celia said what needed saying: "I think I should bite Ian."

"Duh." Imogene watched a chubby tourist walk by on the sidewalk below. She said, "Kill!"

"I mean, nothing I do upsets him. Nothing surprises him. If I walked around naked all the time—"

"He would bend you over a table and ravage you."

Celia scoffed.

"What?" Imogene looked over her sunglasses at her. "You get his blood pumping, Merk."

"So should I bite him?"

"Fuck!" she said to a group of tan guys in boat shoes. "Of course you should bite him."

"Right." She took a chilly sip of her overly-sweet beverage. "So are we supposed to talk about it first?"

Imogene looked at her, shrugged. "I don't know. What would you say?"

"I'm a vampire, and I would like to suck your blood."

Imogene giggled; so did Celia.

"What do you say when you bite guys?"

"I don't say anything. Kill!" she said to a pale, skinny guy in jean overalls. "I just glamour them and drink my fill."

"You've never had a crush on someone?"

"Hell yeah, I have." Imogene finished her blood-red concoction called Planet Mars. "I have a crush on Ian."

"You do?"

Imogene waved to the waitress, who nodded when she lifted her empty plastic cup. "Look, I'm attracted to men all the time. Doesn't mean I want to keep them around."

"I want to keep Ian around."

"Duh. Fuck!" she yelled at a guy on a motorcycle.

Celia rested her head in her hands. "Maybe I should talk to my therapist."

"Screw your therapist. I'm your therapist."

"A terrible thought," Celia said.

"Look, just bite him. I'm not sure if you remember, but being bitten feels really good. Plus, once the venom gets into his system, he'll be all high and shit. He'll be more open to discussion when he's high."

She thought of the occasional cloud of pine that floated around Ian. "He's been high around me before."

"Venom is a different kind of high. How do you not remember this?"

"I was really wasted when…" She shrugged as a waitress brought another Planet Mars and Kryptonite, not that Celia needed it.

"Just do it. Just get it over with. Then, you can stop thinking about it. Plus, it'll explain the creepy bags of blood in your fridge."

Celia shook her head. "He's gonna break up with me."

"Merk. The man's had blue balls for weeks. And he just came upon your Dracula stash. If he's willing to put up with both of those things, a little bite isn't gonna scare him away. Kill!" she shouted to a couple of tourists with cameras around their necks.

"How do you know he's had blue balls?"

Imogene pushed her glasses up her nose and slurped at her red drink. "Let's just say, when he's around you, the blood travels south."

"How can you tell?"

"You can see it." Imogene paused. "You can't see it?"

Celia sighed. "How old are you?"

She made a disgusted noise and looked down into the street.

"Imogene, you're so much better at this than me. How long have you been a vampire?"

She folded her hands on the table. "Since 1985."

Celia quickly did the math in her head but didn't say the number out loud, just in case Imogene wasn't as cool about throwing her age around as Dr. Savage.

"How did you…I mean, who did…"

"God, stop doing that fucking Rain Man thing."

"Sorry." Celia sipped her drink and turned the second one, untouched, in a slow circle on the white tabletop.

"I was a club kid in Miami. Met this vamp named Wharf."

"His name was Wharf?"

Imogene laughed. "Yeah. I was living on the streets of Miami, so I followed him to Lazaret, and," she shrugged, "the sex was spectacular. Neither of us were very good at monogamy, though, so we went our separate ways."

"You're not homeless now, are you?"

"Nope." She lowered her glasses and winked. "I'm a good thief, Merk."

Biking home, slightly buzzed, Celia wasn't sure meeting Imogene had helped her at all. Her mind still wasn't made up about biting Ian or talking to Ian about being a vampire or…anything. Her mind was really kind of fuzzy from the Kryptonite, although she'd held herself to a limit of two.

She rode up the little rock driveway to the Sleeping Gull, but that was when…

Blood. Lots of it. Ian's blood.

She fell off her bike and landed with an "oof" in a hibiscus bush. She didn't even bother locking her cruiser up for the night. She just kept walking in a sort of haze until she spotted Ian on the steps of their apartments.

He was in one of his spandex bike outfits.

"Ian?"

He looked up at her. "Hey. Slight wipeout."

Slight? All the flesh from his left shin was gone, replaced by torn, dripping red.

"Could you get me some hydrogen peroxide?"

He said something else, but by then, his voice sounded like the Charlie Brown parents: *wah-wah-wah*. Celia crept closer. The scent of his blood was thick, heady. There was no chance of a "Ralph" moment. No, it was too late. Celia's fangs went boing, but Ian was too busy looking at his own mangled leg to notice.

That was when she attacked him.

She called Imogene. Together, they dragged Ian into her apartment. That was when Imogene finally got a look at him. "What the fuck did you do to his neck?"

"I don't know." Celia was hyperventilating.

"There are, like, three different bite marks," she said, but she could barely speak, she was laughing so hard. "What, do you stutter bite?"

"Imogene, this is not funny. I attacked him without his consent, and I destroyed his neck."

Imogene was still laughing. In fact, she had to sit down on Celia's couch to avoid falling over.

"Oh my God." She paced. "Oh my God." Celia thought it was like the Great White all over again! Too bad Ian hadn't punched her, too. His blood was all over the inside of her mouth. The flavor was totally unlike the bagged stuff she bought from Steve every week. Ian tasted like summer barbeques and lazy days by the sea. His blood coursed through her, and she felt like she could have leveled a building or flown to the moon.

"How do you feel?" Imogene must have noticed the wild look on her face.

"He's gonna break up with me!"

Imogene shook her head. "How do you feel, Merk?"

She took a couple deep breaths. "I feel great," she said. The lights in the room were brighter, the colors more vivid. Imogene's body seemed to glow—all purple, of course. Celia's brain floated, and

Ian—despite the whitewashed pallor of his skin—looked like a golden god on her living room floor.

"Better than the bagged stuff, right?"

Celia couldn't seem to catch her breath.

Imogene pulled a yellow pill from her pocket. "Want a Klonopin?"

"No. No. I need to be ready for when he wakes up."

Imogene put the pill away, stood, and put her arm over Celia's shoulders. "Congratulations, Merk. You just popped your cherry."

Ian groaned, and they both jumped. The only movement Celia could see came from his fingers, which clasped and unclasped the strings of her apartment carpet. Surprisingly, Imogene went all Florence Nightingale. She let go of Celia and knelt at his side. "Ian?"

"Mmmm," he said.

"Hey, dude. You all right?"

"I don't...what the heh..." He blinked his eyes open. "Did I get roofied?"

Imogene chuckled. "Not that I know of."

"Celia..."

"She's here." Imogene glanced over her shoulder.

Ian didn't look at Celia. Actually, his eyes slipped shut again. Then, he said, "Did you bite me?"

Imogene took the opportunity to pull her white earbuds from their hidden place in her cleavage. She poked one into her ear, then the other, and said, "I'm gonna step outside."

Celia gave her a look that said traitor.

Then, Ian threw up. Celia suddenly knew she couldn't live without him because if she still thought he was cute, chucking all over her living room floor, she would think he was cute doing anything—and there just wasn't enough *cuteness* in the world. She didn't know exactly how to voice this revelation, so instead, she spilled her biggest secret. "I'm a vampire."

Ian leaned up on one elbow and wiped his mouth with the back of his arm. He seemed to notice the puddle of blood surrounding his lower leg, soaking her carpet. "Do you have any hydrogen peroxide?"

"Yeah," she said.

"And maybe a mint?"

"I have chewing gum."

He gave her a bleary-eyed thumbs-up.

She heard his voice as she rifled around in her bathroom: "Celia, a towel, too. Something you can toss after."

"Okay." She rushed back to him, piece of foil-wrapped chewing gum extended. Then, she set the peroxide and towel by his leg and stood up again. She felt almost scared to be near him and his blood and the smell of him and...blood. She could have gone for round four on that neck.

Ian leaned up and poured peroxide on his leg. Compared to the nonexistent skin on his shin, the shark bite scar on his other leg looked almost appealing. He wrapped his new wound with the towel and laid back down on the floor, chewing gum.

"Ian?"

"What did you say a minute ago?"

"Oh. I'm a vampire."

"Right. That." He took a deep breath and opened his eyes again. "So you really did bite me?" The wounds on his neck would still be numb from the venom; she knew that much, so Ian still had no idea that she'd stutter-bit all over his perfect skin.

"I didn't mean to bite you. I was gonna talk to you about it first, but then, I came home, and you were all..." She gestured to his leg. "Open wound. I couldn't help it."

Then, he did it: he reached for his neck. His long fingers found one bite mark, then another, another. "Oh my God," he muttered and looked like he might puke again.

"I know," she said, "you're a mess, but it was my first time, and everyone's first time is kind of awkward. I like your neck a lot, and I want to be your girlfriend. One bite probably would have sufficed, but once I got started, I just…you taste really good."

He held up his hand in a silent, "Please don't talk anymore." He wrestled into a seated position and leaned against her entertainment center. "You want to be my girlfriend?"

She nodded, then shrugged.

He took a loud breath in through his nose.

"You're going to break up with me, aren't you?" she shrieked.

"Celia, just…" He put his hand on his forehead.

She sat on the edge of her coffee table.

"Night shift," he said.

"Yeah."

"Bags of blood instead of food in your fridge."

"Right."

"You'd think I would have seen this coming." He scratched his chin. "Do you have any juice?"

She shook her head no.

"There's some in my fridge," he said. "Could you get it for me, please?"

"Yeah." She stepped out onto the porch, but Imogene wasn't there. Celia thought she saw her friend dancing near the beach as she walked into Ian's apartment and brought back an entire jug of organic apple juice. Celia watched him dazedly put his chewed piece of mint gum on her table and chug three-quarters of the bottle.

He was starting to look a little better, not so green. His blue eyes weren't quite as glazed. He looked drunk instead of like someone tripping balls. "Imogene…"

Celia nodded.

"A vampire," he said.

"Yes."

"How many vampires are there?"

"I don't know," she said. "We're not really into social networking."

He nodded as though this should be obvious. "Are you going to kill me?"

"No!" Celia slid down to kneel in front of him. "No, no. That's not what this is about. See, humans and vampires develop relationships, and well, yeah, there's feeding." She paused. "But there's devotion and friendship and *Jeopardy!*. Vampires and humans…they date."

"Is this usually how the conversation goes?"

"I don't know. Like I said, you're my first time."

"Oh." He got this look on his face like he understood the gravity of the situation—like he'd just taken a teenager's virginity. "How long have you been…?"

"About four months now."

"And Imogene?"

"Since 1985."

"So then, you're new," he said.

"Yeah.

"And I'm your…" He paused. "First."

"I always wanted my first time to be special."

What a relief when he smiled at her. All his tan wrinkle lines popped out like a moonrise. "I guess I don't have to worry about you swimming in the ocean at night, huh?"

She smiled back at him. "No."

"So no sunshine."

"No."

"No food."

She shook her head.

"But you can drink alcohol."

"One of the perks."

"Do you have super strength and stuff?"

"I can rip a phone book in half."

He chuckled. "What else?"

"Um, I have a really strong sense of smell. And there's this thing Imogene does called glamouring where she makes people like her or makes them forget things. I don't do that, though, I swear."

"Good to know."

"Yeah, I mean, I would never do that to you." Celia looked down at her hands, folded in her lap. "I'm really sorry I bit you, Ian."

"Well, you should always have honesty in a relationship."

Her head shot up. "You're not going to break up with me?"

"You want to be my girlfriend. Would be dumb to break up with you before we even get started."

"Even though I look like Nosferatu when I wake up?"

"You don't look like Nosferatu when you wake up," he said.

"Even though I destroyed your neck?"

He shrugged. "It's kind of funny really. I finally meet a girl I see a future with, and she drinks blood to stay alive."

Celia tried to laugh, but it came out like her usual nervous half-choke donkey bray. Then, she realized he really looked a mess. "Do you want to wash up?"

"Yeah. Can you help me?"

"Sure! Let me just get Imogene."

"You have super strength," he said. "Why do you need Imogene?"

She paused in her open front door. "You're surprisingly hard to move. Your long appendages are like huge limp noodles."

He laughed and leaned his head back against her TV.

Celia found Imogene, dancing by herself on the beach. Celia had to pull an earbud out to get her attention. "Can you help me move Ian?"

"Shit, Merk, you didn't bite him again, did you?"

"No, he wants to take a shower, but you remember how his arms and legs—"

"Huge limp noodles." Imogene nodded. "Okay."

The girls went back, and Ian looked half-dead with his eyes shut. He glanced up when they arrived. "Hey, vampire," he said.

Imogene closed the front door. "Oh, good, he already knows. Hey, walking blood bag."

"Gross," he said.

They got on either side of him and helped him stand. Together, they walked him to Celia's bathroom. Once there, they sat him on the toilet seat. The scent of blood wafted off him like steam from a pot roast. Celia sort of jumped when she saw Imogene's fangs were out.

"What?" she lisped. "I'm not gonna bite him. Really ith more the thought of him getting naked that did thith." She gestured to her teeth.

"Ian, how are you going to shower if you can't stand up?"

"Bath," he muttered.

"Great," Imogene said. "You get the bath water ready. I'll take hith clothes off."

"Out." Celia pointed to the door.

"No fair!"

"Imogene, there is blood in the fridge. Go. And put your damn fangs away."

"You're no fun." She closed the door behind her, and Celia ran the bath water.

Slowly, Ian kicked off his shoes and socks. His spandex suit unzipped from chest to hips, but then, he just sat there, slouched against the back of Celia's toilet. Admittedly, it would have been easier with Imogene's help, but Celia was feeling very defensive about her human. Yes, she was already thinking of him as "her human."

As she peeled him out of his sweaty, blood-soaked spandex suit, she did her best to avert her gaze. Celia felt guilty for a lot of reasons. One, she'd attacked him and possibly almost killed him. Two, she felt kind of date-rapey with him unconscious and nude in her bathtub. He sort of woke up once he was in the water, although Celia washed his hair for him. It wasn't long before the bath water turned red from all his open wounds, but by then, Celia had gotten him pretty much cleaned up.

She did need Imogene's help getting him out of the tub and to the bedroom. Her friend refrained from most commentary. Just one sentence—"You lucky bitch"—before Celia told Imogene to hush. She wrapped Ian's leg in an ace bandage and put neon-colored Band-Aids on his neck. Then, she wrapped him in her sheets, and he was asleep, dead to the world.

Imogene and Celia stood there, watching him sleep. She put her arm around Celia's shoulders. "Well, Merk, so it begins. Navigating a human-vampire relationship. You should probably see your therapist tomorrow."

"You *think?*"

Celia wasn't sure what time it was when she woke up, but it wasn't time to get up. Her alarm had yet to wheeze-shout as it did every night at 8:30 p.m., but she did wake up. She opened her eyes, and Ian's face was right in front of her with his hand on her cheek.

"I didn't mean to wake you," he said.

"Are you okay?" she muttered in half-sleep. The neon Band-Aids on his neck glowed.

"I was thinking about my parents," he whispered.

Imogene huffed from where she slept at the bottom of the bed, curled in a little ball like a house pet, but she didn't wake up.

"You're gonna have to meet them."

"I am?"

"They meet all my girlfriends," he said.

Celia grinned. "I've never been a girlfriend before."

He said, "I've never dated a vampire before."

She leaned forward and kissed him. She was a little off target, and their noses mushed together until Ian had the presence of mind to turn his head. Then, he opened his mouth and kissed her harder—until he hissed and pulled way. He put his hand on his mouth.

"What?"

Hand still on his lip, he squinted at her in the dark. Then, she realized: her fangs had gone boing. She covered her mouth.

"You're not still hungry, are you?" he whispered.

Celia shook her head.

"Wh…" He pulled her hand away from her mouth and pushed at her upper lip until he could see her fangs. "Whoa, those are sharp. If you're not about to bite me, then why are they out?"

Celia was mortified to explain.

"Celia?"

"They come out when I'm…excited."

He got a huge grin on his face. "When you're turned on?"

She nodded, hand back on her mouth. She closed her eyes. "Ralph, Ralph, Ralph."

"What are you doing?"

"It's part of my fang control. I have to think about someone I despise."

"That surfer kid from Happy Gas?"

She nodded, eyes still shut.

"Hey, Celia," Ian said.

She opened her eyes a little.

"Fuck fang control."

He put his hand on the back of her neck and crushed their mouths together. Celia stuck her hands in his hair and pulled. She had the weirdest yearning to wrap her legs around his waist. She wanted…she wanted…what did she want? What was this all-encompassing heat? Why couldn't she breathe?

Maybe this is what it feels like to want to bang the hell out of someone, she thought, and the closer she got to Ian, the more she noticed he was naked under her covers and he obviously reciprocated her feelings. Celia made a sound like a growl.

That was when Imogene groaned. "God, I'm right here!"

Ian laughed and pulled his mouth away. Then, slowly, he moved his leg under the covers and shoved Imogene off the end of the bed.

She landed with a "hunh" on a pile of dirty laundry. "Dick," she said but didn't climb back on the bed. She stayed on the floor and was snoring in about thirty seconds.

Ian sighed and whispered, "To be continued. Until then, spoon."

"You need cutlery right now?"

He made a cough-chuckle sound in the back of his throat and guided her onto her side, facing away from him. Then, he wrapped his long body around her.

Oh. Spoon.

CHAPTER ELEVEN

When Celia went to see Dr. Savage, she was very excited to tell her about her first bite and how she was now somebody's "girlfriend." She was disappointed to find her therapist's office locked up and dark. Dr. Savage once told Celia her door was always open.

Liar.

The following evening, Ian rode Celia to work, despite his mangled shin. Plus, he told Ralph they'd hang out and talk surfing. The boys rode off together into the night—Ian on his rental (he was waiting to get his back from the shop after his wipeout); Ralph on his skateboard—but not before Ian made sure to kiss Celia, which made Ralph cackle and point like the annoying little brat he was. At least the twat didn't call her "Red" anymore.

Having finished *Twilight*, Celia had moved on to more adult vampire content: Bram Stoker's *Dracula*. She was pleased to find that so far there had been no glittery vampire sightings. In fact, Dracula was more monster than man. For some reason, this seemed to take some of the pressure off Celia to be a super seductress. Maybe it was the book or maybe it was Ian. She had a boyfriend who was super hot and sweet and seemed very interested in doing wonderful things to her body and she didn't even have to look like Kate Beckinsale!

Imogene came in to Happy Gas around midnight, and she looked funny. Her sunglasses were missing, and her curly hair was a huge mess on top of her head. Celia didn't think her friend even had on makeup. "Did you hear?"

Celia dropped her book. "Hear what? Is Ian okay?"

Imogene rolled her eyes. "Jesus, is everything going to be about Ian now?"

"Sorry. Hear what?"

"Apparently some human got deaded outside Tequila Sunrise the other night."

Celia didn't mean to be callous, but she figured people died all the time so she just shrugged.

Imogene did her hissy vampire thing where she flashed her fangs and put her hand up in the shape of a claw.

"Oh!" Celia squeaked. "One of us did it?"

Imogene nodded.

"But Dr. Savage said we're not supposed to kill humans."

"Duh. That's why things are kinda funny right now." Imogene glanced out into the night.

Celia followed her look. "Funny how?"

"Well, nobody knows who did it. It's gotta be an out of towner. Vamps are on the fucking hunt."

"We hunt each other?"

"Yeah," Imogene said, "when something like this happens, vamp's gotta go—doesn't matter who does the killing."

"Humans kill vampires, too?"

"Haven't you seen *Buffy*?"

Celia cocked her head to the side and nodded.

"We can't have one of our own running amok, killing humans, leaving fang marks. Whoever did this has got to be a newbie."

Celia took steps back, hand to her chest. "I didn't do it!"

Imogene snickered. "Merk, you don't have the balls to do

something like this, but newbies can be kind of bloodthirsty. I mean, look what you did to Ian's neck."

"I like his neck."

"I know." Again, Imogene glanced out into the empty gas station parking lot. "It just feels kind of spooky out there."

Celia held tight to the counter. "Hey, Imogene, would you go hang at my house tonight?"

She glanced up, smiling. "You got some B-neg waiting for me?"

"Ian's at home," Celia said.

She didn't know if she needed to say it or what she would say exactly. Imogene stared at her for a second, and then, it was like she got it. She nodded and said, "Yeah, Merk. I'll make sure he's okay."

Imogene leaned across the counter, grabbed Celia by the back of her head, and smacked a big kiss on her forehead. Then, she was gone, and Celia thought some more about Dracula: monster and man.

There was still no word on the mysterious vampire murderer, not that Celia gave it much thought, what with the "holiday" and all.

As it turned out, April twentieth was a day when people got high—really high. As soon as Celia woke at her usual time of eight-thirty, Ian was at her front door with a joint. He had to explain the whole thing to her, due to her ignorance, which he thought was surprising considering she went to college in Miami.

Legend had it that in the seventies, some group of high school kids used to meet every day by the bleachers to smoke up at 4:20 p.m. It became code. Four-twenty meant time to toke. Therefore, April twentieth had been embraced as a whole day of cannabis worship.

"I've never smoked before," Celia told Ian.

He put the joint behind his ear and counted on his fingers. "First bite. First joint. I like being your first. This is like Christmas."

Celia giggled.

"Come on." He dragged her to his apartment, where she was

surprised to find a cloud of smoke and Imogene.

"How'd you get here already?" Celia asked.

"It's 4-20. We only have, like, three and a half hours to get totally baked before the holiday's over. I drove here as soon as the sun set." In front of her was a bag of what looked like grass clippings and a box of rolling papers. Celia watched for a second. Imogene made joint rolling into an exhibit worthy of the Met.

Out his front door, Ian called, "Heidi!"

Celia grabbed his arm. "What are you doing? She'll evict us."

"Aww." He kissed her forehead. "You're so cute."

Then, there she was: their landlady, who'd obviously just come back from the beach. She was in her bikini with a see-through cover-up. Her wig was crooked. Her eyes were red.

Oh my God, my landlady is high!

"Light it up, Olive Oyl!" she shouted.

With the joint in her mouth, Imogene said, "I'm not sure I like that she calls me that."

"You do kind of look like Olive Oyl," Celia replied.

"Great." She lit the end of her joint, and the room was filled with the fresh scent of pine.

Ian sat Celia down on the couch next to Imogene. "Have you ever smoked anything before?"

"I think I tried a cigarette once."

Imogene handed the joint to Celia, and Ian knelt between her legs. "Just think about sucking air through a straw."

"Okay." She did what he said…and started choking. She coughed a cloud of smoke right into his face, which he happily inhaled.

Ian laughed, and Celia was momentarily distracted by the way his blue eyes wrinkled, the way his lips pulled back to reveal straight, white teeth. "One more try," he said.

Celia thought it went better the second time. By the fourth time, she was like an old pro. In school, she had always been a fast learner. Heidi, bless her, brought over a pitcher of margaritas. Imogene headed to the stereo and, after bitching about Ian's horrible hippie music, found one album on which they could agree: The Talking Heads.

Celia watched Imogene dance. Ian was crushed against Celia on the couch with his arm around her and his mouth on her neck. When "Once in a Lifetime" started playing, Heidi joined Imogene in the wild thrashing dance of the drunk. Celia kind of felt like David Byrne, asking, "How did I get here?"

When she ended up in Ian's bedroom, she really asked herself that question, because Celia was no longer herself at all. First off, Ian didn't drag her to his bedroom; Celia practically lifted him off the couch to get him there. New best friends, Heidi and Imogene hooted when Celia slammed the bedroom door and literally threw her boyfriend on his bed. She jumped on him like a spider monkey and ripped the buttons of his nice linen shirt.

He was breathing really hard, and she could hear his heart—*thud, thud, thud*—beating super fast. She leaned over him, which was when he said, quietly, "Celia?"

It was only then that she realized her fangs were out and she held his arms trapped above his head. She let go of him and leaned up, her hands flying to her face. "I don't know what I want right now."

"Oh-kay…"

"I just feel really hungry."

Ian chuckled, despite having been her prisoner five seconds before. "Side effect of the weed, Mermaid."

"I have blood at my house."

"You have blood right here." He pulled her down in a kiss.

She pulled back. "No, no, I can't."

"Imogene said it can be a lot of fun." He brushed the hair from her face.

"You believe everything Imogene tells you?"

He smiled. "Yeah."

"But won't it bring back shark flashbacks?"

"Only one way to find out."

Celia was so hungry. She had never been that hungry before, even back in her teenage fat days. Ian's blood thumped through his body, and he smelled so good—always smelled so good. She remembered the days when she used to lean against her kitchen wall to get a whiff. Now, she had him in front of her.

Mine, mine, mine.

She licked her lips, which were kind of throbbing, and went to dive, but he stopped her. She knew it; he was backing out.

"Not neck," he said. "Too obvious."

"Right." *Duh*, she thought. He still wore Band-Aids from their first debacle.

"Shoulder?"

She ran her fingers over his pecs. "I like your chest."

"Okay."

She was too high to hesitate, so she just dug in. His skin tasted sort of salty, but his blood was the way she remembered: heady, rich, like hot chocolate with cinnamon. He made this distracting noise when her teeth went in: somewhere between a groan and her name. His fingers closed tightly on her shoulders, and she felt his chest rise and fall at the speed of a dog panting in the summer heat. She stopped drinking when she felt his hand in her hair. She didn't want to leave him completely unconscious.

Well. He wasn't.

He flipped her over like an acrobat and started covering her whole body with his mouth. He pushed at pieces of her clothes to get to her stomach, her ribcage, her stomach...even lower.

Then, his fingers toyed with the button on her jeans.

Celia felt like she had to pee but also like her loins were on fire.

Ian's fingers made their way down the front of her jeans, and his mouth sucked her hipbone. Then, he moved his fingers a little lower, and she felt something akin to electric shock.

Celia panicked. "I'm not ready!"

He pulled back immediately and fell on the floor at the base of his bed. Celia rearranged herself and crawled to look over the edge.

"Are you okay?" she whispered.

There was a bite mark by his right nipple that dripped a little blood down the side of his chest. His shirt was gone; Celia had no idea where. The top button on his shorts was undone. She sort of wondered if she'd done that. His eyes were shut, his mouth wet, but his brow was furrowed. He looked…frustrated.

"Ian?"

"Mmhmm?"

"Are you gonna break up with me?"

"I just need a second."

Celia leaned her chin out further, pouted. "Can I get you a margarita?"

He finally opened his eyes. "Yeah, that would be great."

"Okay." She stepped over him and made sure her pants were on straight. She made sure to close the bedroom door behind her, too.

When she stepped back into Ian's living room, the girls were dancing to Prince. Heidi was hip-thrusting, which…talk about nightmare material. When Imogene saw Celia, she hooted and hollered, then ran at her and kissed her on the mouth.

She pulled back enough to wipe at the corner of Celia's lips and give her a glare. Celia was going to have to practice clean eating.

"Where's Ian?" she said.

"He'll be out in a second." Celia's voice must have sounded unnaturally high.

"Is everything okay?"

Celia nodded. There was no time to think about her apparent fear of orgasm. God, she wondered, was that what it was? Was she afraid of her own orgasm? She was a creature of the night. She could rip a phone book in half! Why was she afraid of sex?

Ian came back five minutes later wearing a black shirt and looking a little peaky—but everything was fine. He didn't seem weird or irritated with Celia. He just came out, kissed her head, and lit another joint. Four-twenty continued with but a small pause. Imogene occasionally snuck next door for some blood. Heidi went on and on about the most recent episode of *True Crime* about a horse jockey who got buried in a tub of toxic waste. She was full of useful information.

Heidi disappeared around two, after they'd all gone swimming in the ocean—except Ian, of course, who watched the stars from the beach.

At five, Imogene curled up on Celia's couch, singing lines of Pink Floyd. Ian and Celia curled up in her bed.

"You've got sand in your sheets," he said.

"We live at the beach. There's sand everywhere."

He hummed against the top of her head, then said, "Mermaid."

He was snoring when she started playing with his hair. She knew he liked it when she played with his hair.

CHAPTER TWELVE

Dr. Savage's office called to confirm Celia's appointment, which comforted her, since last time she showed up, her therapist was a no-show. On the bike ride there, Celia considered lodging a complaint. Then, she thought about Ian's bike and how Ian was so cute and how Ian liked to put his hands on tingly parts of her body, and by the time she got to the office, Celia didn't even remember her name anymore.

Dr. Savage looked tired. Celia had never seen her doctor look anything but photo-shoot ready, so the blue pallor of her skin and lack of makeup was just...shocking.

"Are you all right?" Celia asked.

"Wonderful, thank you." She smiled. Her eyeballs looked kind of nuts. "Come in, Celia. You smell different."

She plopped down on the couch in her jeans. She wasn't wearing yoga pants every day anymore—a huge step she hoped Dr. Savage would notice. "I had my first bite."

"I can tell." Dr. Savage smiled again, but her skin looked tight. Celia thought maybe she had Botox during her short time away. "Ian?"

"Yeah. He's my boyfriend now. Like, he calls himself 'boyfriend.'"

"Oh, Celia!" She laughed an unfamiliar and kind of creepy sound like Maleficent from *Sleeping Beauty*. "So Ian was completely open and willing to be your first?"

Oh, dear. Celia just knew Dr. Savage was not going to like this part, being all vampire/human peace and love. How could Celia put things delicately? "The first bite was kind of an accident." She cleared her throat. Not even the scent of lavender could make her explanation smooth sailing.

"What do you mean?"

"See, Ian rides bikes. I think I told you that. He's a competitive cyclist."

Dr. Savage nodded. "Ever since the shark attack."

"Yeah, so he wiped out the other night, and um, well, I came home, and..." Celia cleared her throat again because, frankly, her fangs were out at just the memory of having his neck skin between her jaws. She covered her mouth.

"Did you attack him?"

"It wuf a complete accfident."

Dr. Savage leaned closer in her sleek leather seat. Her brown hair was in a severe bun. She didn't have glasses on, so she couldn't even look over the brim of her glasses like usual. "You're not glamouring Ian, are you?"

Celia's fangs popped back in. "What? No! I don't even know how to glamour anyone."

"You promise? Because we are not allowed to do that."

Celia would never, ever, tell her therapist about Imogene's behavior, then. She shook her head. "No, it's for real. We really have a thing. I swear."

Dr. Savage took a deep breath and seemed to calm down. "Too many vampires out there use their abilities to the disadvantage of humans. They treat humans like their personal blood slaves. I could never see you being like that, Celia."

"No." She shook her head. "If anyone's being glamoured, it's me. Ian makes me feel…different."

The pen and paper were suddenly at the ready. "Okay. How?"

Celia looked to the ceiling and pictured Ian's smiling face floating near the light fixture. "I get all tingly when he touches me. I feel warm in my stomach but also kind of like I need to pee."

Dr. Savage looked like she was trying not to smile.

"What?"

"So you haven't been intimate with him yet?"

Celia sighed. "Well, he was doing something the other night, but I got all dizzy and felt like I was gonna wet the bed—and that's *not* sexy—so I made him stop."

"Do you like touching Ian?"

"Oh my God!" She was loud enough to make Dr. Savage sit back and recross her legs, as if Celia's voice was like a breeze about to knock her over. "Sorry, I didn't mean to yell. I just really like to touch Ian, yeah."

"Good." She nodded. "That's great."

"So why does he make me have to pee?"

Again, Dr. Savage looked like she fought a giggle. She assumed the pose Celia imagined mothers used when they told their daughters about the birds and bees—although Celia wasn't sure, because her mother had never talked to her about either. Her mother apparently didn't think Celia had anything to worry about. Instead, though, Celia now had a super hot two-hundred-year-old vampire goddess about to explain human sexuality.

"Celia, have you ever had an orgasm?"

"I don't think so."

"You would know."

"That's what Imogene says."

"Well, although I don't always agree with what she tells you, in this case, she's right." She paused and put down the paper and pen. "What you're feeling with Ian is the beginning of sexual pleasure."

"Orgasms feel like peeing?"

Dr. Savage shook her head. "No, but sometimes, when things are just getting started, women mistake the feeling."

Celia nodded. "So if he does that thing with his mouth again, I won't wet the bed?"

"No, Celia, you will not wet the bed."

"How do you know?"

"Because vampires rarely use the facilities, especially now that you've had your first bite. Your transformation is nearly complete."

"Oh, right."

"Now, you don't have to rush into anything with Ian—not until you're comfortable."

"That's the thing!" Celia smacked her own thigh, which caused a skin tidal wave across the farty couch. "When I look at Ian…" She closed her eyes and pictured him, all six-foot-something of him, long, lanky, standing there in Dr. Savage's office in one of his button down linen shirts, khaki shorts, barefoot, hair all a mess, and freckles, always freckles. He was smiling at her, because Ian was always smiling or laughing.

"Celia?"

"I want to have sex with Ian."

"Okay."

"But every time he starts to…" She moved her hands in the air like she was clawing an invisible net. "I start to panic. I literally throw him off furniture."

"Celia, are you afraid of intimacy?"

She shook her head. "I don't think so. I mean, I love when he spoons me and when we have sleep-overs—"

"But the idea of sex makes you uncomfortable." It wasn't a question.

"Not with Ian." She buried her head in her hands. "I don't know what's wrong with me. I was a pussy human. Now, I'm a pussy vampire."

"That sounds like Imogene talking."

"What if she's right?"

"Have you considered that you're afraid of sex because every time you've had sex in the past you've ended up rejected?"

Oh. Terrance. Danny. "Huh," she said.

"You're afraid that if you are intimate with Ian, he'll leave you, too."

Was Dr. Savage right? In college, Terrance had been a wham-bam-thank-you-ma'am, and they'd never seen each other again. She never even went to frat parties again. Danny, that was obviously rejection with a capital R. He was supposed to be Celia's prince, her Richard Gere. Instead, he disappeared and left her a note. Rejected, rejected; Celia always got rejected.

But Ian wasn't like that. Celia suddenly felt like a panda bear had been lifted from her chest.

"You're kind of good at your job, you know that?" she said.

Dr. Savage pressed her lips together. "Thank you, Celia."

She toyed with her hands in her lap. "Um, this might be a dumb question, but…what about birth control?"

"As members of the undead, we're no longer able to bear children," the doctor said.

Celia thought about Ian and how he wanted children and felt kind of sad, really.

When she got home that night, Imogene was on her couch, per usual. She was almost as much of a standard at Celia's apartment as her eighties film collection. Put her on a shelf, and she would have been a decorative item.

"See your shrinky-dink?" She had a bag of B-negative in one hand, her cassette player in the other.

"How'd you know?" Celia shut the front door.

"You always smell like a fuckin' massage parlor after you see her."

"Dr. Savage says lavender is soothing."

Imogene put an earbud in her head. "So is Phish."

Celia stood there, brow wrinkled. "Since when do you listen to Phish?"

"Ian told me to. Now, shut up, I'm meditating." She leaned her curly, purple hair on the back of Celia's couch.

"Are you ever going to pay me for any of the blood you drink?"

From over the rims of her sunglasses, Imogene opened her dark blue eyes, wide, and smiled. "Wow. Shrinky-dink gave you balls."

Celia sighed and headed for the kitchen. Then, she stopped, because Ian was outside her front door. Celia smelled him; Imogene smelled him, too, based on the way her brows were knit together in the center and she had duck lips.

Celia walked to the front door before Imogene could move.

When she opened it, Ian stood there in another of his super spandex bike outfits, covered in sweat. Celia had noticed he'd taken to riding at night. As usual, she had the yearning to lick the sweat from his nose, but she didn't, because if she couldn't have sex with him yet, she didn't think she should lick his face—it might send mixed messages.

"Hi." She smiled.

"I wanna take you on a date," he huffed, out of breath. He always seemed to come up with the craziest ideas post-ride.

"I've never been on a date," Celia said.

"Tomorrow?"

"I have to work."

Imogene was at her side in seconds. Celia thought maybe she really could turn into mist. "Take the night off." She poked Celia in the ribs.

"Can you take off work tomorrow night?" Ian asked.

"I've never taken off work before."

His light blue eyes looked up into the palm trees that surrounded the Sleeping Gull. Then, he licked his top lip. "You've never been on a date, and you've never taken a night off. I think you should do both."

"Me, too," Imogene agreed.

"Imogene, go away," Celia said.

As Imogene plugged earbuds back in her head and laid down on the couch, Ian's hand found Celia's chin and pulled her lips up to his. He tasted salty and Ian-ish. She'd kissed a couple guys in her life, and they always wanted to shove their tongues in her mouth like they were bobbing for tonsils. Ian's tongue just always kind of touched and tickled and made her want to open her mouth wide.

His kiss had the desired effect. Celia weaved on her feet when he pulled way and tried not to look as cross-eyed as she felt.

"So can I take you out tomorrow?"

"Where?"

"I'm not telling, but you have to wear a dress. It's a proper date. Wear a dress."

"Okay."

He glanced down at the hand she had clenched in the front of his bike outfit. She wondered when that happened. "I actually have to work tonight," he whispered. "But tomorrow, I'll be by at ten."

"Ten. Yeah. Okay."

He kissed her again, on the cheek this time, probably because he noticed her fangs were out.

As soon as Celia shut the front door, she turned to find Imogene staring at her. "What?"

Deadpan: "You don't have a dress."

"Yeah, I do."

"That fucking blue muumuu doesn't count. You need a dress."

Celia ran her hands over her full hips and looked down at her feet. "What kind of dress?"

Imogene put one combat boot on the living room table and stepped over. "You know that hot guy next door?" She pointed to Celia's kitchen. "His name is Ian, and he wants you to wear a dress tomorrow night. My guess, he's gonna be in a suit. Now, together," she took Celia's hand in hers, "let's think about Ian in a suit."

Imogene closed her eyes, so Celia did the same and was overwhelmed by a barrage of imagery, running the gamut from James Bond to Mr. Darcy, all with Ian's face. By the time she opened her eyes, Celia felt flush.

Imogene watched her. "How'd that work for you?"

"Uh…"

"Because I got Niagara Falls between my legs."

Celia opened her mouth to make a disgusted noise, but Imogene continued.

"All I'm saying is Ian's gonna look super hot tomorrow night. Like Billy Idol in 'White Wedding.' You need to look even hotter."

"But I don't—"

"I know, dude." She shoved her cassette player in the back of her tight jeans and took hold of Celia's wrist. "We're going to my place."

They got in the car, and Celia found herself wondering: where would someone like Imogene live? She pressed a couple buttons on the dash of her black convertible, and Prince sang about money and astrological signs. They drove down Beach Drive, off Admiral Key. They drove through Barkentine Beach. Thanks to Imogene's raucous tunes, Celia didn't have to hear another chubby beach bum sing yet another Jimmy Buffet cover in one of the many open-air bars. They passed the Drift Inn, which Imogene saluted with a friendly middle finger. As they crossed the bridge, the ocean shimmered black beneath the stars and far-off city lights of Lazaret.

To Celia's utter shock and bewilderment, Imogene lived in a beachfront shack on Mizzenmast—the poorest, most worn-down segment of the keys. Mizzenmast was a fishing community. It smelled of fish. Celia thought about asking Imogene how she had such a fancy car when she lived in such a super shitty house. She decided against it, because she was pretty sure she didn't want to know the answer.

Imogene flipped her keys in a circle on the edge of her finger and unlocked the front door. Celia was relieved when lights came on; she wasn't sure there would be electricity. In fact, due to the state of the place, she kind of wondered if Imogene was squatting.

"Landlord gives me a good deal," she said.

Okay, so not squatting but hopefully not paying more than fifty cents a month. Then again, it was beachfront property, even if the entire little house felt crooked and smelled damp. There was a single couch in the living room, no TV. The windows were covered in black velvet curtains. There was a stereo, of course, with huge speakers. Records and cassette tapes littered the floor, some in states of disrepair, all artists from the late seventies through the early nineties. The walls were blank; the kitchen was empty. A statue of the Virgin Mary sat in the corner, scary as a Chucky Doll. Celia vaguely remembered Imogene saying she'd stolen it.

Imogene wandered into a darkened back room, and Celia assumed she was to follow.

She ended up in Imogene's bedroom, and there, on racks surrounding an unmade bed, was a cornucopia of multi-colored fabric and high-heeled shoes.

"Whoa," Celia said.

"This is what a woman's closet it supposed to look like." She gestured to a dress the size of Celia's thumb.

"Where'd you get all these clothes?"

"I wanted to be a dancer in music videos." She shrugged. "Had 'em just in case."

Celia watched Imogene's hands move at immortal speed through one of the silver racks until she pulled out a lime green dress that might have fit Kermit the Frog.

"I wore this when I crashed my high school prom. I ended up fucking my history teacher." She shrugged. "My style wasn't very popular in the Midwest." She put the dress back. "Now, we need to find something for you."

"I can't wear any of your clothes, Imogene. They won't fit." Celia gestured to her friend, to herself, and to her friend again and then tugged hopelessly on a strapless purple satin number that could easily be confused with an expensive sock.

"Merk, I have tons of corset dresses. We'll just tie you in."

Well, that sounds painful.

They moved from one rack to another while Celia stood by and watched, wondering how long it would be before a heavy wave knocked Imogene's house over.

"With your hair color and sickly complexion, we should go blue."

"I have a blue dress."

"Bitch, you have a blue muumuu."

Sometimes Celia wondered if Imogene was a flaming gay guy in a past life—the angry kind that would snap his fingers a lot before he stole your boyfriend.

"Here. This one." She pulled a flash of blue from her collection. "Corset top. Flared skirt to cover your hips. And I have these fucking fabulous silver heels."

Celia took the dress when Imogene shoved it against her chest. "I don't wear heels."

"You're wearing heels tomorrow. You can't wear flip flops with that dress."

Celia muttered a random selection of letters.

"Ian said ten tomorrow night, so I'll be over at eight-thirty, the second your annoying alarm goes off."

"You never get up that early..."

"I'll do your hair, makeup, and strap you into that dress." Imogene reached under the bed and pulled out shoes that glittered in the buzzing overhead light. "Practice walking in these."

Celia held all her gifts against her chest. Then she began to cry. Imogene looked like she was trapped in the middle of the desert at sunrise.

"What the hell's the matter with you?"

"I don't know. I just..." She sniveled. "I just...I've never had a friend who wanted to help me before." She sniveled some more before she dropped Imogene's dress and shoes and wrapped her in a huge hug.

Imogene felt like a tree in her arms—a boney, pale, pissed off tree. But she didn't shove Celia away. She just said, "Emotions are gross."

Celia nodded and leaned over to pick up the blue dress and silver shoes.

"Don't fall apart on me, Merk."

Celia nodded again, and then followed Imogene to the car. She dropped her off outside the Sleeping Gull Apartments.

"Are you going out tonight?" Celia asked.

"Yeah, I'm gonna go bite somebody." She took off her sunglasses and gave her a wink. "Here's hoping you get laid tomorrow night."

Celia shuffled her feet. "Imogene…"

She laughed like Butthead and shouted, "I'm out!" before throwing gravel up on her way to Beach Drive.

CHAPTER THIRTEEN

At Happy Gas, Omar wasn't even annoyed Celia took the night off. He said she'd been looking kind of pale lately, anyway; maybe she needed the extra rest. Imogene would say she needed to get laid. On her word, she really did show up at Celia's place at eight-thirty, on the dot. Celia woke early and had already showered, as had Ian. Through the thin walls, she sometimes heard him singing in the shower. Ian was completely tone deaf, but he had an affinity for Queen.

When Imogene arrived, Celia pretended she hadn't been leaning against her kitchen wall. Ian smelled different that night. The woodsy BO was covered by something clean but spicy—cologne. It wasn't too much, not like women's perfume that made Celia sick to her stomach. His smell was nice, and Imogene commented on it as soon as she stepped into Celia's apartment.

"Just when you think he can't smell any better," she said, with a huge makeup bag under one arm and a curling iron in the other.

Celia sat on the couch, obsessively chomping on a stick of chewing gum.

Imogene eyed her over the red rims of her sunglasses. "Have you fed yet?"

"No."

"Feed, Merk. It'll calm you down. You're so nervous right now, you look radioactive."

Celia pulled an Imogene. She stood in the kitchen and chugged an entire bag of A-positive, which made Imogene slow clap behind her. The overabundance of blood in her system made Imogene's applause sound like thunder claps. Celia's sense of smell was on high alert, too. She moved beyond the fruity smell of Imogene, the salty smell of the sea, and even past the cologne to smell Ian's skin, his blood. She heard the sound of his heart. Her fangs went boing.

For the next hour, Imogene did horrible things that involved yanking on Celia's head until her scalp burned, poking her nose with concealer, and accidentally gluing her eye shut in a mission to replace Celia's red fringe with actual eyelashes. Then, the worst part was getting into the Dress of Death.

With Imogene behind Celia, she told her to smoosh her breasts against her ribcage with the palms of her hands. Imogene then struggled to clasp the multiple corset teeth that fought to hide Celia's pudgy belly while making her A-cups look somewhat respectable. Behind Celia, Imogene made sounds like someone being punched repeatedly. When she finally finished, Celia couldn't breathe, but her posture was incredible. And hey! She felt like she actually had a waist!

"Where are the shoes?"

Celia grumbled.

"Merk."

She gestured to where she'd hidden them under her bed. "I can't walk in them."

"Did you practice?"

Oh, she practiced—and broke two coffee mugs and the bottom half of her bathroom mirror.

"Put. Them. On." Imogene held the silver torture devices in her hands like gremlins that wanted to eat Celia's soul.

She squeezed her flat feet into the stupid shoes, and Imogene gave a low whistle. "You're comin' into focus, Merk." She dragged her to the bathroom and made her look in the half-broken mirror.

Oh. *Well.*

Celia looked…different. Imogene had styled her hair into a weird sort of sideways beehive on her head, but the red color really did go well with the blue dress. Her boobs even looked okay. All of Celia looked okay, really. Imogene had used some green eyeliner that made her green eyes pop. All her blemishes were covered in concealer. Plus, the shoes made her cankles into ankles. She thought she could have passed for attractive, even!

"Are the boobs too much?" Celia panted since she couldn't breathe.

"No way."

"I feel like I might fall out." She tried to push her boobs farther into the dress, but Imogene batted her hand away and pulled them to the top again. "Imogene!"

"What? They're just boobs. We all have them." She pulled at Celia's until they were, she said, "Just right."

That was just in time, too, because the scent of Ian arrived on Celia's porch.

"He's here!" they both hiss-whispered, then giggled. Imogene giggling was just weird to Celia. She was way more comfortable when her friend would sneer and call her "Rain Man." Imogene beat her to the door.

Imogene's original assessment of Ian's date attire had been correct. He was in a suit—a navy blue number with thin silver pinstripes and a light blue shirt underneath, no tie. He didn't seem like a tie kind of guy, Celia thought, considering he spent most days/nights barefoot. His black hair was wild and untamed, as usual. He smiled when he saw Celia and walked right past Imogene to give her a kiss on the cheek.

"I'm afraid I'll muss you," he said, still smiling. "You're like a twenty-first century *Pretty Woman*."

Squee!

Imogene arrived between them. "All right, I want her home by two o'clock, or I'm calling the cops." Celia quickly realized she wasn't talking about her. Imogene handed her car keys to Ian.

"Thank you, Imogene."

"And no sex in my car unless I'm invited."

"Okay," he said and took Celia's hand out into the night. The humidity from the day clung to the sidewalks, and she had to cling to Ian to keep up in her silver pumps. When they reached Imogene's car, Ian opened the passenger door for her.

"Where are we going?"

"I'll tell you when we get there."

Ian held her hand on the center console as he drove. While she tried to breathe in Imogene's corset dress, she watched the air toss his hair around, and he thankfully drove like a responsible adult.

Celia was so glad Imogene had forced a bag of blood down her throat earlier. She felt in full control of her boing, even though Ian looked good enough to bite. They drove toward Lazaret, but he parked Imogene's car by one of the nude statues in the center of St. Arthur's Circle.

Celia looked around as he circled the car to open her door. Shops and restaurants were everywhere, packed to the gills. Everyone wore Polo or Abercrombie in varied shades of pastel blue, pastel pink, pastel puke. She could see the doorway to Dr. Savage's office down the block. Then, Ian pulled her to her feet by their connected hands.

"Where are we going?" she asked again, pulling at the top of her dress to make sure her breasts didn't pop out and yell, "Surprise!"

Ian put his arm around her bare shoulders, and they walked together down the sidewalk. Instead of answering, he whistled the chorus of Queen's "Somebody to Love." Then, he kissed her forehead. "You look beautiful. Did I tell you that you look beautiful?"

"No."

"Must have just been thinking it." He pulled her tighter against his body, and...*Ralph.*

They crossed through the circle, past Daiquiri Deck, where Imogene had dragged her the other night.

"You know, I've only worn this suit twice."

"I'm surprised you even own a suit," Celia said.

"Weddings and funerals. A man should always be prepared." He kissed her forehead again. She wanted to lick his Adam's apple.

"This is Imogene's dress."

"I figured," he said with a smirk.

"Too much?"

"I'll protect your honor if I have to."

They walked down the sidewalk, inlaid with red brick, and then Ian dragged her to a stop. They stood in front of an overcrowded patio that led into a restaurant the color of dark wood. Celia could smell tomato sauce and wine.

Ian leaned his mouth down to her ear. "Best martinis in town."

"You don't drink martinis."

"I do when I'm being fancy." He opened the door for her, and the place reminded Celia of restaurants in movies where rich men took their mistresses—all dark corners and service staff who talked to you while making eye contact with your shoes. A jazz quintet played quietly in the back near the kitchen.

There was a reservation for Hasselback, and they were escorted to a shadowed booth that overlooked the patio and the streets of St. Arthur's Circle outside. When the waiter asked if they wanted an appetizer, Ian playfully bit her neck and then ordered them each something called "The Green Fairy."

"What food do you miss the most?" he asked. He was leaned toward her in their little booth, his hand on her leg and his nose in her hair. When he spoke, his breath blew out in a warm cloud over her collarbone.

"Pizza," she whispered, eyes half-closed with the nearness of him—and the slight feeling of dizziness from the corset cutting off her oxygen supply. "What would you miss most? And don't say kale smoothies."

He chuckled. "My mom's ravioli."

"What are your parents like?"

"Nosey. Overbearing. The most loving and supportive people you'll ever meet." He leaned back in the booth. "My mom was a flight attendant, so we got all these cheap fares when I was a kid. That's how I got to surf all over the world. Dad's an accountant who occasionally forgets to put on his pants."

"The absent-minded genius?"

"Maybe. Or maybe he just did a lot of drugs in the seventies."

The waiter returned with two chilled martini glasses filled with something green and ominous. When he left, Celia turned to Ian. "Tell me this isn't kale."

"Taste it. You'll love it."

She took a sip, and she felt like there were fireworks in her mouth. The drink didn't burn; it just woke her up. The flavors were multi-layered. One moment, she walked through a rainy forest. The next, she was surrounded by Easter candy. That was when she realized why the flavor was familiar: it did remind her of Easter! Jellybeans. Black jellybeans—but black jellybeans soaked in a fresh rainstorm.

"What is it?"

"Absinthe. Mostly. Not sure what else."

"Don't people, like, hallucinate on absinthe?"

"Only in Amsterdam."

She glanced at him.

"Don't ask." He grinned and finally, finally (*yes!*) kissed her on the mouth. "What about your parents? What were they like?"

Celia shrugged. "I feel like they were people who only had a kid because all their friends were doing it—not because they actually wanted a kid. So when I was born, I was just another piece of furniture or a new seascape painting, not an actual person."

"That's shitty."

"Yeah, but it's not like I was abused or locked in closets or fed dog meat, you know? I just had a lot of time to myself and read a lot."

"What did you read?"

She took another sip of spicy fresh forest. "I loved Nancy Drew. I used to pretend I was a detective. I would steal some of my mom's jewelry, and once she realized it was gone, I would pretend to follow the clues and find the missing piece."

Ian laughed.

"I guess it was the only way to get her attention."

He ran his fingers over the skin on the back of her neck.

"You're lucky," she said. "You had siblings."

"Ha. Well. Yeah, I guess. Years of wrestling matches and weird advice."

"Like what?"

"You should never marry the woman who gives you the best blow job of your life."

"Huh." She bit her lip and gave that some serious thought. "Seems counter-intuitive."

"My oldest brother Doug told me that. See what I mean? Weird advice."

They were silent for a second as the band played "Beyond the Sea." Then, she asked, "Doesn't it weird you out that I drink blood to live?"

He pouted his bottom lip and seemed to consider it. "It's just as weird as vegans."

"I think it's a little bit weirder," she said.

"Nothing's weirder than giving up cheese," he said between sips of green.

He said it with such dedication, she couldn't question him.

"Let's dance." He slid out from the booth and held his hand toward her.

"I don't dance."

He glanced over his shoulder. "Please don't make me ask the drunk guy."

She looked behind him, and indeed, there was a lonely drunk guy who danced to his own beat in the middle of other couples doing their best to slow dance without distraction.

"Ian, I really don't dance."

"You can stand on my shoes. I'll carry you." He half-smiled; she loved his smile wrinkles.

She allowed herself to be pulled from the booth. Once standing, she realized the corset was dangerously close to falling off. She gave it a hefty tug upward and prepared to hold her breath to keep her costume intact. Then, her tall, incredibly gorgeous, oddball boyfriend led her to the floor.

"Put one hand here..."

She shook her head, grinning like a fool. "I know where to put my hands."

"So you do know how to dance."

She huffed at him.

Ian was about as good a dancer as he was singer. Beat and tempo were sort of like suggestions, but with his chin against the side of her forehead, stylistic points didn't matter.

"I'm going to spin you," he whispered.

"Oh, shit."

She giggled as he did his best to look totally smooth. Of course, the illusion was ruined when the corset top flipped down, and her breasts were openly exposed to the entire dance floor—including the drunk guy who pointed and shouted, "Boobies!"

Ian wrapped her in a hug, and she felt the scratchy material of his suit against her nipples.

"Did that just happen?" she asked.

"Definite mermaid sighting."

"What do we do?"

He laughed against her beehive.

"Ian!"

"We waltz to the bathroom."

"I don't know how to—"

He didn't literally mean waltzing. He just held tight to her until her feet barely touched the floor and carried her away from gawkers. The bathroom was right near the entrance, down a dark hallway, which was ideal considering Ian didn't just let her take care of things on her own. No, he followed her into the single stall bathroom and locked the door behind them.

He glanced away long enough for her to pull the corset back up and shove her boobs down deep into the fabric in the hopes of avoiding another mermaid appearance. When she turned around, though, he put his hands on her hips and lifted her onto the bathroom counter. Luckily, it was a nice bathroom—not the kind you'd see in gas stations in horror movies, right before people get disemboweled. No, this bathroom had granite countertops, real fabric hand towels, and smelled like rose petals.

As usual, Celia was overwhelmed by Ian's mouth. *How on earth does he know to kiss my collarbone like that? How does he know about my sensitive earlobes? And who knew it felt so good to have your hair tugged?*

Imogene was going to be pissed about the beehive, but soon, ringlets of red fell down around them both. Ian tangled his fingers in Celia's hair. His other hand was on her lower back, bringing her closer. He stood between her legs, but he wasn't close enough. She needed him closer. She wrapped her legs around his waist, tightly, and he made a sound she'd never heard him make before: a low, guttural "nuh" that made her fangs go *boing!*

She wanted to bite him, right there, in a public restroom at an expensive restaurant. She reached for the collar of his shirt, and he pressed himself against her.

Oh...

Something felt different about Ian's body pressed against hers. Then, she realized.

Fire down below!

He made the "nuh" sound again, right against her throat, and he licked and sucked at her skin until she saw stars circling her head like in old school *Looney Tunes*.

"Ian." She clawed at his back. "I need…"

He pulled back, huffing and puffing, smiling. "*You* need?" He crushed their mouths together, and Celia mimicked his "nuh" sound, because she was no longer capable of navigating the English language.

There was a knock on the door, which made Ian pull away. Celia covered her mouth, considering her fangs were along for their date now, too.

"Just a second," he said. His voice sounded deeper than usual, which sent shivers through the base of her stomach. "We should probably get out of here."

She nodded and thought, *Ralph, Ralph, Ralph,* until her fangs went away, which was shocking, considering the way Ian looked—all ruffled and red-faced. She noticed his pants looked really tight all of a sudden. He lifted her off the bathroom counter and smiled.

"You are so hot," he said.

She pushed her newly freed red hair from her face. "Nobody's ever told me that."

He took her hand and led her back to their table. First, they had to pass a scandalized-looking older woman at the bathroom door. Of course, Ian winked at her, which made her go the shade of a plum. He paid their tab and, hands still connected, guided her back to the sidewalks of St. Arthur's.

"What next?"

She watched his bright eyes take in the still crowded streets. "Honestly, I'd love to take you home and get you in my bed, but as this is your first date ever, I'd better make it good."

She almost wanted to tell him, "Yes, please, yes, your bed—now and forever." But she wasn't Imogene. She didn't have the balls to say something like that, and she wasn't even sure what would happen once they got to his bed. Whatever had just happened in the bathroom had been good—real good—but was she ready for whatever came next?

He walked her past rows of shops filled with clothes she would never be able to pull off. A bunch of chubby tourists ate ice cream outside the local creamery. There was a shoe store with a pair of stilettos covered in crystals. Ian paused outside the Tube Dude shop. Tube Dudes were big, metal statues of stick figures, all smiling, doing any number of things: holding a mailbox, waving, fishing—but always smiling. Ian posed by one, and Celia laughed when she realized he kind of looked like a Tube Dude: lanky, tall, with an unshakable grin.

"You're my Tube Dude," she said, and he gave her a hug.

They ended up walking away from all the shops and tourists until they made it to a waterfront park overlooking the harbor that separated St. Arthur's from Lazaret. The city lights reflected off the harbor water, and she smelled the comforting scent of sea creatures and seafood.

Ian leaned his elbows on the edge of the boardwalk that poked like a pinkie finger into the water. "Do you know anything about astronomy?"

She stood next to him and leaned against his shoulder. "Nope."

"Me neither."

"You know every answer on *Jeopardy!*, but you don't know about constellations?"

"Must have skipped that class at school."

"How many nights have you spent on beaches under the stars?"

"Several," he said. "But I wasn't usually looking at the stars."

Celia wasn't dense. She knew what he was saying, which made her think: *God, how many women has he been with? How experienced is he?* Based on what she knew of him from Ralph, Ian Hasselback had been a world-class champion surfer until the shark attack. Women liked champions and surfers and men who looked like Ian.

All of a sudden, Celia felt really nervous and twitchy, which was probably why she blurted out, "I've never had an orgasm."

His brow furrowed. "What?"

"I've never had an orgasm."

He turned to face her, one arm still resting on the boardwalk bannister. He looked like he might cry. "That's the saddest thing I've ever heard."

"Well. It's not like genocide or jokes about disabled people," she said.

He drummed his fingertips. "Do you want an orgasm?"

She shrugged. "I think so."

He stood tall and posed like Superman. "Do you want me to give you one?"

She thought about all the times he'd made her feel like she was about to pee—or the times when she felt like there was something on fire between her legs. No one but Ian had ever done that to her before, so she said, "Sure." She thought Dr. Savage would be proud.

Ian took her hand and started walking.

"Where are we going?"

"Home."

"Wait, you're going to give me an orgasm right now?"

"Well, not *right* now. We're in a park."

"Oh," she said. Luckily, she had super human speed. Otherwise, she never would have been able to keep up with the pace of Ian's long legs. She considered kicking off her heels, but Imogene would have killed her.

By the time they got to the car, Ian was practically carrying her. She giggled. "Ian!" He didn't even open the passenger side door. He just lifted her into the convertible and slid into the driver's seat like a runner into home base.

If she thought Ian was a conscientious driver, she was wrong. He drove like a maniac back to the Sleeping Gull Apartments, which made her laugh. She kept her hand on his knee for the ride.

They made it back in record time. Even Imogene would have been impressed. Ian carried Celia like his new bride from the car to her front door, which he kicked open. Imogene had her sunglasses poised on the end of her nose. She chewed absentmindedly on the top of an empty blood bag and watched *The Lost Boys* on TV.

"What are you doing home already?" she asked.

"I'm going to give Celia her first orgasm."

Imogene pushed her sunglasses up on her head and actually looked interested. "Can I watch?"

"No."

"Typical." She flipped her sunglasses back down. "I'm gonna hang out with Heidi." She *clomp-clomped* in her big old boots onto Celia's front porch, and Ian used his foot to slam the door behind her.

With her hair hanging loose over her shoulders and her dress, again, about to fall off, Ian carried Celia to the bedroom and plopped her down on the edge of her bed. She giggled as he took off his suit jacket and threw it on the floor, then knelt between her legs and put his huge hands on the outside of her thighs. The way he carried her, touched her, he made her feel small. No one ever made her feel small, but with Ian, Celia felt like a forest sprite.

He looked up at her and smiled. "Hell-oh."

She realized what he was looking at and covered her fangs. She chuckled behind the palm of her hand.

"I think she's excited."

She nodded.

"Lie down," he said.

She started lying back, but he stood up.

"Wait, wait." He pulled a pillow from the top of her bed and put it behind her head. He used his fingers to brush hair off her forehead and kissed her nose, which made her giggle some more.

He was right, Celia was excited. She felt like a little kid on

Christmas morning, about to open her last present only to find a pony inside.

Ian resumed his position on the floor between her legs. That's when it started.

Celia had her eyes closed, so she couldn't be sure what exactly Ian did down there. She experienced the occasional sensation of having to pee, but then she remembered she couldn't pee, so she didn't have to worry about that. In fact, after the initial couple seconds, Celia didn't worry about a damn thing.

Her mind was empty. If there was such a thing as negative thought process (and there might have been; she did know Ralph), she experienced it. There were vague images, like the time she glanced down and put her hand in Ian's hair. There was the flash of his bright blue eyes. Other than that, it was all a lot like her first bite: black out, blotto, gone.

Things went from "it started" to "it happened" pretty damn fast. By then, she had one of her hands woven between Ian's fingers. His other hand was...busy. She was reminded of the way the ocean felt at night: the power of it, the way it threw her around, the way it made her feel free. Orgasms were kind of like that for Celia—only better.

She closed her eyes tight. She felt her whole body stiffen, and Ian's mouth...his mouth...

She was disappointed when he pulled away. She wondered if she'd done something wrong, so she sat up to find him on his back on her bedroom floor. He held the hand she'd been holding in front of his face. His adorable smile wrinkles were turned down in a grimace.

Then, she noticed his pinkie was at a ninety-degree angle.

"I think I need to go to the hospital." He groaned.

An hour later, Celia was still in her annoying corset-top dress, sitting next to Imogene (in sunglasses) and Heidi (in her robe) in the waiting room at the Admiral Key Urgent Care. The place smelled like gauze and stale, sickly blood. Celia stared straight ahead, silent.

Then, all of a sudden, Imogene let out a massive guffaw she must have been holding in since they'd hopped in her car back at the Sleeping Gull. "You broke his finger coming?"

"He's gonna break up with me." She felt her bottom lip quiver.

Imogene kept laughing, couldn't seem to stop. "If he hasn't broken up with you already because of…" She slapped her knee. "He's not going to break up with you over a broken pinkie."

"I've done much worse to my ex-husbands." Heidi nodded. Her wig was crooked.

"And we're not even sleeping together yet," Celia whispered.

"You're not?" Heidi shrieked. "If I were thirty years younger, I woulda hit that as soon as he moved in!"

Celia sighed. "Heidi, can you give me and Imogene a second?"

She stood up and retied her cat puke robe before stepping toward the rack of out-of-date magazines.

"How am I ever going to have sex with him?" Celia hissed. "I'm going to kill him. Squeeze him to death with my thighs or something."

"Turn him into one of us." Imogene shrugged.

"What? No. We've never even discussed that. No." She smoothed the skirt of her dress. "Dr. Savage says humans and vampires can have healthy, fulfilling relationships."

"Your therapist sounds so annoying."

Celia sighed.

"How was it?"

Celia made an indecent noise, which made Heidi glance back at them with her over-plucked eyebrows lowered. "Amazing. I wasted twenty-three years of my life not doing that."

"Yeah. I found mine in ninth grade in the back of a station wagon. Haven't really stopped since."

"I want to have sex with him."

"Duh," Imogene muttered. "Just don't have your hands on anything important when you…" She started laughing again.

The door from the sick people area opened, and there was Ian. He was still in his dress shirt (untucked) and slacks (slightly wrinkled). His black hair was wild, as usual, but perhaps more so from Celia's earlier tugs. In his left hand, he held an orange prescription bottle. He had an amused look on his face as he held up his right hand to showcase his metal-encased pinkie finger.

"Oh my God." Celia stood up. "Are you gonna break up with me?"

He smiled. "No, but I'm probably going to tie you to the bed next time."

Imogene sucked air in loudly through her nose, and Heidi put her hand on her chest and went, "Oh!"

Ian popped the top off the orange bottle, tossed a pill into his mouth, and chewed. "Vicodin," he explained. "Used to get it all the time for surf injuries. Home?"

Imogene drove them all back to Sleeping Gull, she and Heidi in the front seat. Ian kept his arm around Celia in the back, and he looked awfully pleased for a guy with a broken bone. Maybe it was the painkillers. They got dropped off. Imogene said she was hungry, but when Heidi asked if she was headed to Denny's in Lazaret, Imogene just laughed and sped off in her nifty convertible.

Back at Celia's place, alone, Ian fell down on her couch and stretched his long legs across the coffee table. He rested his eyes. She thought he was asleep until he said, "Don't you need to feed, sweetie?"

The pet name almost made Celia pass out cold.

She headed to her bedroom where she happily put on her beat up yoga pants and a turquoise t-shirt. She went to the kitchen and poured Ian a glass of water before grabbing herself a bag of A-positive. She settled next to him, and he leaned his head against her shoulder.

"So that was a first date," he muttered.

She glanced at his hand and remembered what he did for a living. "Can you play video games like that?"

He waved his right hand, played an invisible piano. "My ring finger will work overtime."

Celia opened her bag of blood and took a little sip. "Thanks for…" She chuckled. "Everything."

"You're welcome." He sniffed and nuzzled closer to her. "Movie?" he asked.

She didn't want to get up, so she picked up the remote and scanned the channels. She left it on a *Mythbusters* marathon and wanted to tell the whole world she'd busted a myth of her own: perfect boyfriends did exist.

CHAPTER FOURTEEN

Imogene had raised an interesting point in the Urgent Care lobby, so Celia decided to enlist the help of her therapist who knew more than Imogene—or at least used fewer cuss words to communicate, which made her sound more intelligent.

Dr. Savage had her perfect brown hair loose around her shoulders that night. It fell in perfect ringlets around her perfect cheekbones. She had turtle shell glasses on, green slacks, and a cream-colored silk shirt. Despite all Celia had with Ian, the way Dr. Savage looked still made her feel bad about herself.

"How are things with Ian?" She sipped what smelled like chamomile tea with a blood chaser.

"I need to talk to you about that."

"Yes." Her lips were tinted slightly red. She was alert, awake, glowing—not like their last meeting when she looked unsteady and tired.

"I broke his finger," Celia said.

"How?"

"In bed."

"Okay." Dr. Savage nodded and wrote something down, probably, "What an idiot."

"You have a human boyfriend, right?"

Dr. Savage looked over her smarty-pants glasses. "You know I don't discuss my personal life, Celia."

"Yeah, well, okay, but see, I want to have sex with Ian, but I'm afraid I might break him." She curled her fingers into knots but didn't move because she was in no mood for a couch fart. "And he needs to have sex. Soon."

"What makes you say that, Celia?"

She thought back to the time Ian said he was dating a girl solely for the sex because he needed a "fix." Then, she thought about how he'd been working a lot, broken pinkie and all. She thought about the way he seemed tense the past couple days—a lot of weird finger-tapping and knee-shaking.

"Celia?"

"Look, I just know he needs to get laid. He deserves to get laid, but what if I break his hip or something? That's why Imogene said I should turn him."

"Celia Merkin!" Dr. Savage yelled at her. She actually yelled, and she looked murderous.

"I'm not going to." Celia shook her head. "It never even occurred to me. I don't even really know how, and I wouldn't do that to Ian—unless he asked, I guess."

Dr. Savage uncrossed and recrossed her legs. "Let's get something clear."

Celia nodded.

"Turning a human is much easier than you think, which is why we practice safe blood use."

"Safe blood use?"

"If a human has been bitten by a vampire in the span of up to two to three days and then ingests the blood of a vampire, that human has a very good chance of turning. If the blood exchange is immediate, there's no question, but it's that two-to-three day period that can be dangerous."

"But I don't, like, bleed on him."

Dr. Savage blinked her long lashes at her, slowly. "I'm just trying to make things clear so that you and Ian don't make a mistake."

"So you're not...you've never thought about turning your boyfriend?"

"My boyfriend is not relevant to your treatment, Celia, but maybe someday when he reaches my own human age. It's not necessary, though. I truly believe humans and vampires can have fulfilling and happy relationships."

"Yeah," Celia said, "until your human dies. Don't you want to spend the rest of your life with the guy you love?"

She pointed her pen at Celia. "You and Ian are still in the honeymoon phase. You have no right to make those kinds of calls yet, for him or you."

Celia slouched; the couch farted. "So what about sex? How am I supposed to have sex with Ian and not shatter his spine?"

"Are you still using the Ralph technique?"

"I don't want to use it in bed with Ian!"

Dr. Savage gave her the gift of an annoyed sigh. "Not to its full extent, but you might have to a little, just to calm yourself down." She paused. "And try not to hold onto anything when you orgasm."

"No shit."

Celia went home irritated and decided a swim in the ocean was just the ticket.

She found Ian in his apartment working overtime on some big gaming project for some big nerd company in New York.

When Ian talked to Celia about his job, she usually just stared at him and daydreamed about his pecs because when he talked about his job, he spoke a different language: gamer language, which was almost as bad as the surfer lingo he tossed at Ralph when he visited Happy Gas. Almost.

She stood in his bedroom door and watched his non-broken right ring finger do the work of his metal-wrapped pinkie. "Hey."

"Hey." He didn't look up at her.

"I'm going to go swimming." She paused. "Will you come make sure I don't drown?"

He smiled at his computer screen. "Yeah, gimme a second, okay?"

"Okay." She sat in his living room. A blank space lingered where a normal person would have a TV, because apparently the video games Ian mastered for work were all computer-based. Bike magazines were on the table by her knee, and the fresh, piney scent of good weed and woodsy BO embraced her.

Ian held her hand as they walked down to the beach, and she peeled down to her bra and undies. She took his hand and pulled him toward the crashing, black waves, but as usual, he stopped as soon as his toes hit water.

She smiled up at him. "I could protect you from monsters, you know."

He smiled back but shook his head.

The water was getting warmer by the day. Sweltering Florida summer would arrive soon, along with nights that never cooled and the smell of citronella. More tourists. More traffic. She could worry about that mess later. For the time being, Celia was in the ocean, and the ocean never disappointed her. She was surprised to run into some dolphins. They poked and prodded at her like she was a beach ball. She pet their rubbery skin until they realized she wasn't food and went spinning, scattering away. Celia glanced back at the beach and caught Ian grinning full bore, his eyes trailing after the silver, moonlit tails of their neighborhood porpoises.

When she got back to the beach, she wrapped him in her wet embrace.

"Now, I'm gonna be sticky," he said into her hair.

"We'll take a shower."

He looked down at her with his hands on her lower back. "Yeah?"

She wasn't nervous as she walked Ian back to his apartment; she just wasn't sure what the hell she was going to do with him once she got him in the shower. Her experience with man parts was admittedly limited, but she'd seen Ian's and felt it through fabric before, so…yeah, she was still totally clueless. If Ian was as laid back about sex as he was about everything else—even his vampire girlfriend—she felt she would be fine, especially when she thought about that "nuh" sound he made in the restaurant bathroom on their first date. That noise alone was enough to make her want to grab him and do whatever women did to make men happy.

They got to Ian's bathroom, and Celia turned on the water, which was when she decided to come clean. "I have no idea what I'm doing."

"Like, in regards to life, or…?"

Celia didn't know how to answer that question, so she put her hand on the front of his shorts. "I'm talking about this."

He closed his eyes for a second and sighed through his mouth. "Oh. Really?"

"Remember? Sex twice. Just had my first orgasm a couple days ago. Yeah, no clue."

"I'm not very concerned." He pulled his t-shirt over his head and threw it on the floor.

Celia watched him take off his shorts. "You're not?"

"No." He turned her around and unclasped her bra. He basically lifted her into the shower, and once there, both of them totally nude, he pressed her against the cold tile beneath the showerhead and kissed her.

"Wait, I'm sticky," she muttered into his mouth.

"Don't care." He put his hand in the place Celia liked, which made her knees shake and her eyes wiggle in her head.

"Wait!" She pushed his hand away. "This is about you." She held onto him and turned them both around so his back was against tile. Then, Celia experimented.

She quickly learned there was a distinct advantage to being a vampire in human/vampire sexual situations. She heard things humans could not, like increased heartbeats, for instance, or more importantly, where the blood was pumping.

It was pumping in her hand.

The soap helped, as did Ian's "nuh" noises, which turned into an echoing barrage of "oh my gods" and "Celias" as the minutes passed. In the end, Ian crushed the shower curtain in one hand and held her face to his with the other. He opened his mouth, but no sound came out. Celia watched all of this in rapture. Her fangs went boing.

Talk about a light bulb moment! Celia realized, watching Ian try to catch his breath and remain upright, that she immediately wanted to touch him some more, which made him twitch and stop breathing altogether.

"Sensitive," he muttered.

It took all her resolve to not attack him all over again, just to hear his noises and see the way his face changed. Celia's orgasm had been great, but making Ian happy felt like the best thing she'd ever done in her whole life. It was like living every happy part in every rom-com eighties movie ever. That was how she felt, watching Ian recover—all naked, shark-bitten, lanky six-feet of him.

Celia had her second orgasm about ten minutes later.

Dry and wearing loose pajama pants, Ian made popcorn while Celia went to her place to prep the TV. She was going to show him *When Harry Met Sally*. When he arrived, he laid his head in her lap while balancing a bowl of buttery fluff on his stomach. She put her hand in his hair.

Between kernels, he said, "Imogene says that I love you."

"Huh?"

"I love you."

"Imogene says?"

"Well. I say."

She leaned forward on the couch, forcing him from her lap and into a seated position. "I'm confused."

He tossed a piece of popcorn in the air and caught it in his mouth. "The other night, she said I was talking about you too much and obsessing over the cute things you do."

She leaned back a little. "I do cute things?"

"All the time. Anyway, she said people only talk like that about their significant other when they're in love."

Celia's brow furrowed. "You think Imogene knows about love?"

He shrugged. "She knows about lots of things."

Celia was so distracted by the mere idea of Imogene being in love, she didn't notice Ian's hand on her hip.

"Celia."

She looked at him.

"I love you. Really."

"But…why?"

He paused. "You need an explanation?"

"I don't know," she said. Not even Celia's parents used the "L" word. If she thought being a vampire was foreign territory, this was like being on Mars.

Ian leaned forward. "You're sweet and funny and…weird. And you seem to have no idea how beautiful you are. I'm childish and annoying and kind of an idiot, but that doesn't seem to bother you." He scratched his chin. "You don't like me because of the surfing or the way I look. You just…" He chuckled. "You just like *me*—for everything I am, and I've never had that before with anyone."

Celia had trouble swallowing. "Okay."

He nodded, speech finished, and laid back down in her lap.

She put her fingers in his hair and thought back to the time when he puked right in front of her and she still thought he was cute. She considered the way his touch made her fall apart—in a good way—and how it felt to be in his arms, so maybe, just maybe…

"I think I love you, too," she said.

"Good," he whispered.

He fell asleep halfway through the movie. Celia sucked adoringly on his shoulder.

CHAPTER FIFTEEN

Celia left Ian and Imogene in her apartment where they somehow played Scrabble while watching *Jeopardy!*. Needless to say, she was impressed. She rode her bicycle to Happy Gas, where her huge, bald boss, Omar, was still standing around. He gave her the eye, but not the one she was used to—not the "you're late" or "why aren't you wearing your ugly orange apron" eye. No, he gave her *the eye*.

"You look different," he said.

She walked past him maybe a little too fast.

Ralph made obscene gestures toward the cash register. "It's because of all the world-class champion surfer sperm she's been—"

She smacked him on the back with accidental vampire strength. His skinny, teenage chest almost knocked the register off the counter, and he was left gasping for breath, choking.

Omar rubbed his shiny head. "You got a boyfriend, Celia?"

She shoved her bag under the counter. By then, Ralph was in a groaning ball on the filthy floor. "Yes," she said.

"Well." Omar wagged his fat finger. "Don't let him get in the way of your work."

Because being a gas station attendant takes such mental acuity.

"Sayonara," he said as he left, and Celia wondered when he'd gone from Mafioso lingo to ninja.

She picked Ralph up off the floor by the back of his shirt and smacked him a couple times in the chest.

"Sorry, sorry," he choked.

"Don't ever say something like that again, you little twerp, or you will never hang out with Ian for the rest of your idiotic little life!"

Ralph looked at her like a frightened child, and she realized being with Ian was totally making her more assertive.

She'd changed her reading material. She'd stopped reading vampire books. Now, she was nose-deep in self-help. Tonight's feature, which she hid whenever she heard an unexpected noise, was called *How to Be Awesome in Bed*. She was leaning back behind the Happy Gas counter practicing something called the "Cowgirl Shimmy" when her phone rang in her purse.

"Hello?"

"You're out of blood." It was Imogene.

Celia smacked herself in the forehead. "I completely forgot about my weekly pick-up."

"Well, now what the fuck are we supposed to do?"

"I can text Steve. Schedule a pick-up for tomorrow night."

"I need some tonight." Imogene paused.

Which made Celia realize…"Do not bite my boyfriend, Imogene."

"Come on," she whined. "Just a little? I'll glamour him. He won't even know it was me."

"No, we do not glamour Ian—and you do not bite him."

She sighed. "Fine. We're rolling your way."

Imogene hung up as Celia said, "Whu-wha—"

Imogene's black convertible screeched into the Happy Gas parking lot three minutes later. Her purple hair was in windblown knots, but because she was kind of insane, the look suited her. Ian looked surfer boy extreme in khaki shorts and a forest green hoodie. His hair was tossed from an afternoon walk along the beach (progress for him), and his late spring golden skin was deepening to a warm, sexy bronze.

He jumped the counter and gave her a big, wet smack on the lips. "I want to go with you to meet Steve."

"What?" Imogene pushed her sunglasses onto her head. "I'm going with her."

"Who says?"

"I say," she replied.

"Does not compute."

"Wait, stop." Celia put her hands on his chest and pushed him sideways so she could get a better look at Imogene. "Who said anything about going to see Steve?"

"We need blood." She shrugged. She glanced around the empty gas station. "It's not like you're doing anything right now."

"I'm at work."

Ian kissed her neck. "Imogene's gonna stay and watch the place."

"Bullshit," Imogene said. "You're staying and watching the place."

"Rock-paper-scissors?"

"You're on." She pushed her glasses down over her dark eyes.

"Hey!" Celia yelled. "Both of you. Calm down!"

They both went silent until Imogene said, "Huh. Is she the dominant one in bed?"

"No," Ian and Celia said in unison.

"Look," Celia continued, "before we do anything, I have to get in touch with Steve. Plus, I don't even have my big red cooler."

"It's in the back of my car."

"Oh." Celia looked to the convertible outside. "Well…"

Ian smiled down at her. His eyes glowed like fluorescent blue fireflies.

"Hang on. Let me just…text him."

Ian and Imogene cheered.

As Celia waited for a response, her friends played football down the aisle with a loaf of stale bread. She sometimes thought it was kind of weird that they got along so well. Imogene was the grumpiest, meanest, most bloodthirsty person Celia knew; Ian was like a tall teddy bear on 'shrooms. She guessed they complemented each other. Then, she thought about she and Ian, and it was kind of the same thing; they complemented each other, too.

Steve was his usual terse self via text, responding to her inquiry with "K."

What followed was an epic rock-paper-scissor battle that began with Ian's announcement: "If you glamour me, this doesn't count."

"She's not allowed to glamour you," Celia said pointedly with her hand on his shoulder.

After three rounds, her boyfriend emerged victorious. As he did a victory dance somewhere between the robot and general flailing, Imogene ripped Celia's orange apron off and pointed at the exit. "Blood. Go, bitch."

Ian drove them both to Lazaret, which gave Celia the opportunity to ask, "Why do you want to meet Steve anyway?"

"He sounds angry."

"And that makes you want to meet him?"

"Uh-huh." He nodded as they crossed the bridge. "I like trying to make angry people uncomfortable with cheerfulness. It's my thing."

She chuckled and then grabbed him by the side of the neck and licked his face.

As usual, no one paid attention as they entered Lazaret Memorial Hospital. Nurses scurried around in shades of pastel scrubs, and Celia wondered if sometimes she subconsciously glamoured people. How else did two people who closely resembled beach bums just waltz into a hospital with a bright red cooler? Hopefully, she wasn't accidentally glamouring Ian into loving her.

They took the elevator up to see Steve and found him alone, curled over a microscope. Before she could speak, his tiny head shot up, and he started sniffing the air...*sniff-sniff-sniff*...until he turned around and noticed them, noticed Ian.

Suddenly, bringing Ian seemed like a really bad idea.

In his plastic-wrapped shoes, Steve made it to them in vampire time, which made Ian almost fall over—until Steve caught him by the wrist. "I'm Steve."

"Ian." He had to clear his throat twice to find his voice, probably because Steve's fangs (way bigger than Celia's) were out, and his black eyes were totally black, as in no whites left.

Steve's shark eyes darted to her. "What are you doing here?"

"I told you I was making a pick-up." She tried to insert herself between her dealer and her boyfriend, but Steve kept tugging on Ian's arm, keeping him close.

"The blood's in the cooler." Steve gestured with his head, his black eyes never once leaving Ian's neck.

Celia stuttered. "But you-you usually…"

"Ian, huh?" Steve licked his lips. "Wanna make some extra cash, pretty boy?"

"No, thanks, creepy blood dealer guy."

Steve smirked and looked at Celia. "He yours?"

"Yuh-yeah."

"The way he smells, you know how much money you could make off his blood? I could sell his for double my going rate—triple maybe—especially if vamps got a look at him."

"Could I have my wrist back?" Ian pulled at his arm.

Steve didn't let go. "You'd get a cut, obviously," he told Ian. "I'd make it worth your while."

"Celia?" Ian glared at her.

Then, she noticed his heartbeat sounded funny. Her human was terrified. Screw boing; her fangs went Ba-BOOM! She shoved the angry Hispanic midget backwards and stepped in front of the man she loved, fangs out, hissing.

"All right, all right." Steve held his hands in the air. His eyes went back to normal, but his fangs still hung over his lower lip. "Just saying. Shit." He tore the cooler from her arms and headed for blood storage.

Celia turned to Ian. "Are you okay?"

She didn't expect him to be smiling. "That was hot."

"Huh?"

"You going all fangs-out for me."

"Oh." She covered her mouth. "I didn't mean to. You were just…scared."

He put his hand on her face. "I shouldn't be, with you around."

She smiled, but inside, Celia was worried.

When Steve returned with her weekly batch (some extra for Imogene, of course), she grabbed Ian and headed right for the door. From behind them, she heard, "Let me know if you change your mind, Ian." She didn't look back.

They found Imogene sulking behind the counter of Happy Gas upon their return, reading Celia's self-help sex book. She'd gone through three bottles of peach juice, which Celia would have to pay for.

Despite being seemingly clueless as to the feelings of others, Celia must have looked tense. "Everything okay?" Imogene asked.

Celia nodded and shoved the cooler at her. "Take Ian home, and don't leave him alone."

"Celia…" He put his hand on her arm.

She put her hands on his shoulders. "I'm serious. Stay with Imogene until I get home, okay?"

"What the fuck happened?"

"Steve took a particular liking to the smell of Ian's blood," Celia said.

"Who wouldn't?" Imogene snorted. "He's like Thanksgiving and Christmas wrapped up in bacon."

Celia buried her face in her hands. "Imogene."

"What? That was a compliment."

"Thank you?" Ian said.

"Imogene, wait in the car."

She spat a raspberry as she left.

"Sleep at my place," Celia told him.

He nodded.

"I should never have let you go with me."

"I'm fine."

"For now."

"I have you. I have nothing to worry about."

If only she had as much faith in herself.

The hours at work passed like days, weeks, years. All she wanted was to be home with Ian, wrapped around him, listening to the sound of his breath. Plus, she was starving. She should have kept a bag of blood for herself.

When Celia got home, her apartment was quiet. Imogene looked like a broken rag doll on the couch, sunglasses snug on her head, mouth wide open as she snored quietly. Celia glanced into her bedroom, where Ian was tangled in her sheets. Then, she headed to the kitchen for a quick snack, but as she reached the fridge, Ian stopped her.

She gasped. "I thought you were asleep."

He nodded. The hair on the right side of his head was flat, and his light eyes were puffy. "Come to bed."

"I'm starving."

"I know." He took her by the hand, and she followed behind. He let go of her long enough to take off his t-shirt and lay down on his back in the center of Celia's bed.

She eyed his slightly freckled chest with the smattering of dark hair.

"Come on." He pet the bed at his side. "It helps me sleep."

Celia took off her orange apron and crawled in next to him. They were used to feeding by now, so he didn't tense under the tug of her teeth. He sighed and pulled the ponytail holder out of her hair. Ian tasted better than pizza, even New York style, with the thick crust and fresh garlic. She pulled out her fangs and licked a little. She knew he liked when she did that.

His fingers were in her hair when he said, "My parents are coming Saturday."

Celia wiped a drop of blood from her chin. "What?"

"For someone so intelligent, you sure have a hard time understanding what I say."

She chuckled and bit back into his pec.

"Ow!"

She licked the fresh wound, which made him hum.

"So I'm meeting your parents Saturday night," she said.

"Yeah."

She absentmindedly tongued his nipple. "Huh."

"What?"

"Say what again," she quoted.

"They speak English in what?" Ian laughed. They'd watched *Pulp Fiction* the week before; Ian had picked it, and even though it wasn't eighties, Celia actually enjoyed it.

"I've never met someone's parents before," she said.

"We should make a list of all the firsts I am for you." He rolled onto his side and pulled her to him.

"Tonight was the first time I considered ripping someone's throat out."

"Is that how you kill a vampire?"

She shrugged in his arms. "I'm not sure."

"Sunshine. Stakes," he muttered against her forehead.

"Sunshine for sure. The rest could just be mythology. I'll have to ask Dr. Savage."

"Later." The venom coursed through Ian's system. She could hear his heart slow down, his body calm. He was right; he did sleep better after she bit him. She slept better just knowing he was there.

CHAPTER SIXTEEN

In her head, Celia kept a countdown clock: two days until the arrival of Ian's parents.

She figured they would hate her and think she wasn't cute enough for their son and/or think she was an idiot. She went through every negative scenario possible, from her fanging out at the dinner table to her tripping on a curb. Every embarrassing outcome possible, she pictured, and she didn't even have time to see Dr. Savage for advice.

That night, Ian and Imogene sat on her couch watching *Jeopardy!* and Ian kept shouting questions before Imogene could even read the answers.

"Cut it out." She elbowed him.

"Read faster. You're a vampire." Ian had a race Saturday morning (the official reason for his parents' visit), so he ate some strange-looking whole grain cereal with apple juice—not milk—apple juice. He was almost fully assimilated to Celia's schedule, considering he now ate cereal for dinner.

"Why are you pacing?" Imogene asked.

"What am I going to say to your parents? How am I going to talk to them?"

"Vishnu," Ian said.

"Huh?"

He looked up from the TV. "What?"

Celia rolled her eyes. He was impossible to talk to during *Jeopardy!*.

"You know, at least you don't have real person problems. Meeting Ian's parents is cake compared to the possibility of losing your house."

Celia paused. "You're losing your house?"

Imogene shrugged. "It's been a slow pick-pocketing month. Plus all the dudes I've been biting lately haven't been carrying cash."

"I can lend you some money," Celia said.

"From your part-time Happy Gas paycheck. *Dude.*" She looked over her glasses at her.

"No, I got something like two million bucks from my parents' life insurance policy."

Ian dropped his cereal bowl, which Imogene caught before it hit the carpet. She handed it back to him, her mouth wide open.

"Thank you." Ian's voice sounded two octaves higher than usual.

Then, they just sat there, gaping at Celia. *Jeopardy!* was forgotten.

Celia stopped pacing. "Did I say something wrong?"

"You have, like, two million dollars just…sitting around?"

Celia shrugged at Imogene. "Well, most of it's in a bank. I don't keep it all in my mattress."

Imogene glanced at Ian. "I don't think she gets what I'm saying."

He cleared his throat. "Sweetie. You're a millionaire?"

"Yeah. So?"

"And yet she wears yoga pants every day and lives in this shit hole." Imogene gestured to her David Bowie poster and collection of VHS tapes.

"Hey, it's beach front. How much do you need to borrow, Imogene?"

She looked sort of mopey. "I don't know. Like four hundred?"

"Okay." Celia headed to her bedroom but smelled Ian behind her. She reached for her stash, and he laughed.

"You actually do keep money in your mattress."

"Only a couple thousand." She glanced back at him.

One of his eyebrows was super high, and he had a smirk on the mouth she loved to bite. "I have an idea," he said.

"Does it involve *Jeopardy!*?"

"No." He was silent.

"I will kiss that smirk right off your face."

"Funny, that doesn't sound like a threat."

Celia kissed him to make her point. "What's this idea?"

"Well, it's your money," he said, "but you know that scene in *Pretty Woman* that you like so much?"

She stood on her tiptoes. "The one where she gets to go shopping and have salespeople fawn over her and she buys all those pretty dresses?"

He smiled. "Yeah, that one. The shops at St. Arthur's Circle don't close until eleven, which gives us a little under two hours. What if I went and put on my suit and played Richard Gere for you?"

She put the hand not holding cash on his chest. "You'd go shopping with me?"

"I would be honored to go shopping with you, Vivian."

She hopped around in her stocking feet. "Oh, my gosh, you remember her name from the movie?"

"Celia, we've watched it three times."

"Right." She winced. "Go put on your suit!"

They took Imogene's car. Ian said she wasn't invited; this was "a couple's thing." Celia thought Ian looked totally dashing in his one and only suit. Plus, he'd somehow managed to gel his hair back over his forehead, which made him look about ten years older and very respectable. Celia had on her muumuu dress, but she thought it wasn't as bad as Vivian in her hooker gear.

They arrived in busy St. Arthur's Circle. Celia waved at Dr.

Savage's office as they drove past. She wanted to scream at her therapist, tell her, "My boyfriend is taking me shopping!"

She felt like she was in a movie...

Zoom in on St. Arthur's Circle, Florida. Palm trees are everywhere, and hidden between them, nude marble statues. There are fountains and rich tourists on every corner. The shop fronts are lit with golden light— beacons of glutinous American over-spending.

Enter the happy young couple. He looks delicious. He looks like he could be on the cover of GQ. *She has red hair, curves, and a huge smile. Their hands are clasped as he drags her through expensive parked cars and to their first shop: Shoe Heaven.*

"Every woman needs a good pair of heels."

"How do you know that?" Celia asked.

"My mom told me."

The shoes were indeed first. Ian made Celia try on a dozen pumps, and since the owners of the shop were these two gay guys, they scurried around like horny rats—if rats got horny; Celia wasn't sure. Anyway, whenever Ian spoke, they jumped...and drooled. The gay boys finally talked her into three-inch red pumps that Ian said matched her hair and a pair of sensible black open-toed heels that Celia thought Imogene would really like.

After that, they went to a place called World Fashion that had sitar music playing and smelled kind of like incense. The women were really nice. They helped Celia find the right sizes and the right styles that suited her over-size-eight physique. Ian would give her a thumbs-up or thumbs-down on outfit options. When no one was looking, she even snuck him into the dressing room, where they made out like a pair of teens.

Next was To Be Yours, a more romantic place filled with dresses reminiscent of a Disney princess. Celia bought some jewelry there and a hat with feathers.

They hit fashion gold in a shop called All Woman. It was retro but in that eight-hundred-dollars-a-dress sort of way. There was another gay dude watching the racks, who first offered them a glass of wine. Then, he went to work. He was like a color guru. Every dress he brought made Celia's vamp skin glow like moonlight—and everything was a perfect fit!

Nothing was ever a perfect fit for Celia. Either the butt was too tight or the waist was too big or the pants were too long. But this gay dude was a magician. When they left, Celia kissed him on the nose. She even wore one of her new dresses out into the St. Arthur's night. She left the muumuu in the dressing room, curled into an embarrassing ball against the mirror. No more muumuus for Celia Merkin!

Ian carried all her goodies back to the car, and she finally realized she felt good standing next to him. She didn't feel like an imposter. She felt like a hot girl with a hot boyfriend. She felt like she was going to impress the hell out of his parents Saturday night. She also felt frisky.

On the car ride home, she started by just sucking on Ian's ear. Then, she went for it. She put her hand on his upper thigh, and the car almost lurched off the road.

"Celia."

She giggled and moved her hand around a little. "Want me to stop?"

"No." He bit his bottom lip.

"Can we tonight?"

Ian glanced from her and back to the road. She assumed he knew what she meant, because he smiled and increased the speed of the car by about twenty miles an hour. They didn't need to explain their intentions to Imogene when they got back, because she just huffed and said, "Finally! I have a fucking date." She grabbed the keys from Ian but did spare a moment to say, "Nice dress, Merk," before disappearing into the night—as she so often did.

Ian put Celia's newly acquired clothing on her living room floor.

Celia felt like she might be losing her nerve—maybe because Ian wasn't carrying her to the bedroom and ripping off her new dress. Or maybe because he wouldn't look at her.

She spoke, just to say something. "Did you want to do it here or your place?"

"I have condoms," he said.

"We don't need them. I can't get pregnant."

That made him look at her.

"I was gonna tell you. I know you want kids, but—"

"Celia." He gave her a half-smile. "It's okay."

"Then what's wrong?" She wrung her fingers. "Do you not want to?"

"Of course I want to." He put his hands on his hips and toed at the carpet.

She looked at his pinkie. "You're scared I'm going to break another bone, aren't you?"

He chuckled, thank God. "No." He paused. "Okay, let's sit down." He took her hand and led her to the couch. He sighed. "Celia, I've had sex a lot."

"I kind of figured."

"But you haven't."

She nodded.

"I need to make sure you're doing this for you and not because you think it's what I need."

"Oh."

"I just don't want this to feel like an obligation because you think I'm some kind of nympho. Because what we have already is great. I don't want you rushing into anything."

She leaned back against the couch. "I've never had an adult conversation about sex before."

"That's kind of what I'm getting at." He smiled and brushed some of her hair off her neck. "Is sex tonight really what you want or is it just for me?"

Celia thought about it. She looked at Ian. Then, she looked

beyond his utter adorableness and thought about the way he made her feel—which made her stand up and say, "Nope, I really want to bang your brains out."

"Okey-doke." He stood up, put his hands on her hips, and threw her straight up so that her legs wrapped around his waist.

Celia giggled into the collar of his shirt.

There were three things she learned during what will forever be known as "Life-Altering Sex with Ian Hasselback:"

1. Celia thoroughly enjoyed removing Ian's suit—so many layers and so much fun.

2. Large things really did fit in small places.

3. There was nothing more beautiful than Ian. Not sunsets. Not pizza. Not even David Bowie in *Labyrinth*. Not A-positive blood. Nothing, nothing, nothing...

Afterward, sweat glued her face to his chest. Ian's breath still hadn't slowed. He twitched when she rubbed her naked skin against his side.

"I love sex," Celia announced.

"Yeah, you do," he muttered.

Her cheek made a *squelch* noise when she pulled away from him. "And look, no broken bones."

"Yay!"

"What do we do now?"

"Huhm?" Ian's eyes were still shut.

"Can we do it again? Right now?" She made the whole bed bounce.

"Celia. Lie down."

She circled his left nipple with her fingertip. "What do people do after sex?"

"Go to sleep?"

"It's too early to go to sleep."

He winked one eye open and looked at her. "Come 'ere."

She laid down as instructed, and he wrapped her in his arms. Her nose was in the sweet-smelling spot where his neck met shoulder.

"So what do we do?" she asked.

He made a nondescript noise in the back of his throat. "Play twenty questions?"

She laughed against his collarbone. "Am I being annoying? I'm being annoying."

"You're fine."

She reached her hand around and played with the shaggy hair on the back of his neck. "I'm sorry I can't have kids."

"Celia, you're a vampire. I probably should have seen that coming."

"I guess. I just know you want them."

"I want you more," he said.

She buried her nose against his chest because her fangs were out. She hadn't known they popped out due to the sensation of pure happiness.

He was silent for a second. "You know you don't have a heartbeat, right?"

"Yeah, it's creepy, isn't it?"

"Something else I'll get used to," he said.

She licked his throat until his breath hitched.

"I really do have to get some sleep, Mermaid. I gotta get up early Saturday."

"I know." She ran her fangs over his skin but didn't bite down.

He twitched again. "That tickles."

Celia leaned up and looked at him. He was already half to la-la land. "Maybe I'll go for a swim," she said, although she was really hesitant to wash him from her body.

"Mm."

"Will you ever get in the ocean again?"

"No," he said.

"Why not?"

"I'm scared."

170

She brushed pieces of sweaty hair off his forehead. "You always say what you mean, don't you?"

"To my detriment." He opened his eyes and touched her lips. "You've never looked more gorgeous."

"I don't really have to go for a swim," she said.

"Good. I think I'm ready for round two." With that, he swooped an arm around her waist and pulled her hard against him.

"Wait, I thought you said you needed to sleep."

He pulled her closer with his hand on her ass. "I'll sleep when I'm dead."

CHAPTER SEVENTEEN

When Celia woke up, Ian was gone. She knew how he was the day before a race: he did an endurance ride—long on distance and low on speed. Then, he ate a huge plate of pasta with lean meat sauce, side salad, and water—lots of water—and for dessert, a kale smoothie.

Celia allowed herself an extra hour of sleep, because she'd just had tons of sex. She knew Ian had joked about needing his "fix," but Celia now understood. After rolling out of bed, she popped open a bag of blood, sat on her kitchen counter, and considered how much she wanted sex again already. She wanted sex on the couch, on the beach, on the very countertop on which she sat.

She slurped her bag of A-positive, but it didn't taste as good anymore, because it wasn't Ian's blood. This was possible cause for concern, because she knew damn well one human could not sustain a vampire without ending up deaded—and they were not allowed to do that. Dr. Savage said so, and even Imogene agreed with her.

Celia sniffed. Ian was home from his ride! She went old school and leaned against the kitchen wall. She put her fingers in the marks she'd left more than a month before when she'd tried clawing through the plaster to get to him. But she didn't have to do that anymore, did she? She made a little happy noise.

Then, she heard the *clomp-clomp* outside and wondered what Imogene was doing up so early. Her friend kicked the front door open; Celia didn't think it even locked anymore.

"Merk!"

"Kitchen."

Imogene appeared in the doorway from the living room but paused, mid-step. Her boot hung in the air like a suspended anvil. "It smells like sex in here."

Celia wrapped her robe tighter around her waist. "It does?"

Imogene pointed at her. "You fucked like bunnies last night."

"Imogene." She rolled her eyes.

"What? You totally did. Ha!" She smacked her slim upper thigh. "Was he as good as he looks? 'Cause I bet he was as good as he looks."

Celia looked at the ceiling but couldn't press her lips together hard enough to suppress a smile.

Imogene cackled. "Yeah, I got laid last night, too!" She held her hand up, and Celia gave her a high five. Imogene reached into her tight jeans and pulled out a wad of cash. "Oh, and thanks, but I don't need this anymore." She handed Celia's money back to her.

"Imogene, what did you do?"

"Bachelor party, baby. They were loaded. With booze and cash."

Celia shoved the four hundred bucks in a kitchen drawer. "Who'd you have sex with?"

"A lady doesn't kiss and tell."

"You're not a lady," Celia said.

Imogene wandered back to the living room (after filching a bag of B-negative), and Celia followed her. "That's not why I'm here anyway. Another human got killed last night. Jugular, just..." She made a croaking noise. "Torn out. One of us did it. Probably the same asshole newbie who did the first one." She slurped thick, sweet red.

Celia sat down on the arm of her couch. "Damn."

"Shit happens. I just wanted to drop in and check on you and hottie over there." She nodded toward Ian's apartment and plugged an earbud into her head. She pushed a button on the cassette player attached to the side of her jeans and nodded her head to music Celia couldn't hear.

"Imogene?"

She glanced at Celia.

"Were you…worried about me?"

She squawked. "No. I don't worry about anything."

Celia smiled a little, because naïve as she was, even she knew when someone was lying.

Imogene nodded toward the wall. "What's walking wang doing over there anyway?"

"Imogene, don't call him that!"

"What? I saw it the day we put him in the bathtub. No wonder he struts." She wrinkled her nose. "But where does he put it when he bikes?"

Celia rolled her eyes. "Speaking of, he has a race tomorrow. You know how he has to prepare."

"Oh, early night for him, then. Me and you should go out."

"Maybe."

"Let's go bug him." Imogene stood, and of course, Celia followed. She couldn't wait to see Ian, not after last night. She couldn't wait to give him a sloppy kiss.

Imogene stepped out into the night and stopped, which made Celia smack into her back. Imogene dropped her bag of blood on the porch and kicked it backwards into Celia's apartment.

"Imogene, what the—"

Celia glanced around her and noticed two people on the porch right outside Ian's apartment. She saw the girl first and thought of a phrase from *When Harry Met Sally*: "your basic nightmare." She was everything Celia wasn't. She was everything even Imogene wasn't.

She was at least Ian's height with silky red hair, big tits, big lips, long legs, and a dress that would have covered one of Celia's arms. Her lips were the color of red paint.

Then, Celia saw *him* and started screaming. She wasn't sure why she was screaming. It wasn't her usual response to things, but under the circumstances, screaming felt right—very right—because Danny was on their front porch.

"Celia?" he said, and she imagined she looked all a mess with sexed up hair and unshaved legs in nothing but a damn robe.

Of course, Danny looked picture-perfect, just like when they met at Tequila Sunrise. He was in a different suit, more summery this time: pastel and made of some sort of cotton mix, maybe even linen. He had on an equally summery sweet grass hat, which he removed when he saw Imogene. Celia thought he even bowed to her a little— to Imogene, not Celia.

Ideal timing for Heidi to come out, screaming over *True Crime*, and Ian to open his front door in nothing but a towel and run right into Basic Nightmare. Thankfully, he held onto the towel, but the bitch put her hand on his chest and her newbie fangs audibly went Boing, capital B.

"What in the Sam hill is going on out here?" Heidi said.

"Heidi, go back inside." Imogene's voice sounded different and kind of scary. She stared at Danny, and Heidi went back to her apartment without question.

Ian backed away from Basic Nightmare. "Celia, you okay?"

"Uh…" she said.

"Ian, get dressed."

"Imogene, what's—"

"Get. Inside. Now."

Celia caught his gaze for a second before he did as he was told. Celia guessed when a vampire gave commands, it was a good idea to listen.

Imogene latched onto Celia's wrist and pulled her along as they took a stand between their new arrivals and Ian's front door. "You smell like a hospital," Imogene said.

Basic Nightmare glared down at them. "You ain't no fresh daisy yourself, sweetheart."

"You like where your fake tits are right now? I can rearrange them for you."

"Whoa, ladies. Everything's jake." Danny pushed Basic Nightmare back and stood a half-foot from Imogene—whose hand was honestly cutting off all feeling in Celia's arm. Danny smiled that dazzling smile of his. His chocolate eyes shined. "I can see you're a bearcat."

"You must be Danny. What the fuck are you doing on this porch?"

Danny paused. "Looking for Celia, of course. I missed you, baby."

Imogene kept Celia behind her. "Bullshit, you did. You bailed on her."

He shrugged, and Celia remembered what his body looked like under that suit: broader and with bigger muscles than Ian, plus more hair, like a wolf. "I'm not into commitment," Danny said.

"Me neither, bucko. That's why I don't turn people. I think you should probably leave and never come back."

He put his hat back on his head, covering his perfectly coifed swish of dark brown hair. "Look, we just need a place to stay for a little bit."

"Oh, yeah?"

Danny looked over Imogene and right at Celia. "Hey, baby, I had some trouble up north. I'm just trying to lay low for a while. You won't even know we're here."

Celia finally found her voice. "You're not staying at my place."

"Just for a little while." He pointed at Ian's front door. "Tall drink of water your man? You could stay with him for a couple days while we stay at your apartment."

"No way," Imogene said.

"I don't think he was talkin' to you," Basic Nightmare said.

"Put a muzzle on her, fancy pants, or I'll rip her fuckin' face off."

Celia had never heard Imogene talk like that, and she hoped never to again. Even she wanted to run, and Imogene was her best friend.

"Vixen, calm down," Danny said.

"You're Vixen? Stripper name much?" Imogene snickered.

"Exotic dancer."

Imogene guffawed just as Ian's front door opened again. Celia looked up at him. She must have looked totally freaked, because he stood up even taller. "I'm Ian. Why are you on my porch?"

"They were just leaving," Imogene said.

"Ian. I'm Danny."

"The Danny who left her?" Ian nodded down at Celia.

Danny held his hands up in front of him—a symbol of surrender. "Hey, man, I got cold feet."

Ian took a quick breath through his nose. "Why don't you walk those cold feet back to wherever you came from." It wasn't a question.

Danny's pretty dark eyes found Celia, crushed between the people she cared about most. "Does he know what you are?"

"Yes," Ian said.

"Ain't that cozy?" Danny smiled at Ian. Celia wanted to pluck every straight, white tooth out of his head—and she thought Imogene might actually do it. "Ian. Man to man, could you give me a second with your girl?"

Ian looked to Celia for a response. Imogene was either consciously or subconsciously shaking her head no. Celia took initiative. "Guys, go into Ian's apartment."

"Merk—"

"Just gimme a second, okay?"

Imogene finally let go of her arm, which was now just a limp piece of flesh, and Ian kissed Celia's forehead before they both disappeared inside.

Vixen gave her a hard look, and Celia could tell every inch of her was being analyzed. "How'd an ugly girl like you land a piece like that?"

"Vixen," Danny hissed.

She gave him an angry face.

All it took to calm her was a hand to her arm and Danny's warm brown eyes staring her down. "Baby, would you give us a second?"

"Yeah." She pouted, but at least she walked away.

Danny turned back to Celia and put his hands in his pockets. "So. Ian?"

"What do you want, Danny?"

"I told you. I need a place to stay."

"Get a hotel."

He shrugged. "I'm a little short on cash. Come on, baby."

"Don't call me that."

He smirked. God, he was gorgeous…like a rattlesnake or a Great White. "Let me stay at your place or I'll tell Steve not to deal to you anymore."

Celia felt her mouth open in a shocked "O." After all Danny had done to her, he would take away one of the only gifts he'd given? "You can't do that," she said.

"Yeah, I can. I own him. I own half the dealers in the American South." He leaned closer and licked his lips. "Your pretty boyfriend probably gives you, what, two bags a week? You can't live on that. How do you think he'd feel if you started feeding on other guys, huh?"

Just like that, Celia felt things pulling away like the tide: her blood, her Ian, and her unexpectedly happy life. Danny once said he could make her better; this was the second time he was just making things worse.

"Fine," Celia said. "You can stay."

Danny tried to take her face in his hands, but she batted him away. He laughed—a high-pitched, unpleasant noise. "See? We can all get along." He turned toward the beach. "Vixen!" Then, he turned to Celia. "Got any blood in your fridge, baby?"

"Just get away from me." Celia backed into Ian's apartment as she heard Vixen's stiletto heels on the porch.

Imogene was on Celia like a vamp to a fresh vein. "You get rid of them?"

She shook her head. "He threatened my supply. He said he would cut me off from Steve if I didn't let them stay."

Imogene's eyes went to the ceiling.

Ian sat in a chair wearing jeans and a wrinkled Bonnaroo t-shirt. "Danny seems like a dick."

"Totally," Celia agreed. "How did he find me?" She fell into Ian's lap.

"Find *you*?"

Celia looked up at Imogene who looked down at her like she was dumber than a dung beetle.

"It was mere coincidence that you live here, Celia," she said.

Ian stood and almost knocked Celia over. "What are you talking about?"

Imogene, whose hair was growing bigger the more irritated she became, put her hands on her hips. "What did they smell like, Celia?"

She shrugged. "I don't know. Gauze. Sick people."

"A hospital?"

Celia nodded.

"They came here after they saw angry Steve. Who else saw Steve this week?"

"Ian."

Imogene gaped at her.

Celia stood up, too. "You're saying they're here for Ian?"

"Not as dumb as you look, Merk."

"Imogene," Ian said warningly. "What the hell are you talking about?"

Imogene sighed. "Both of you, sit your asses down. You need to understand the world we live in."

Ian glanced at Celia. She felt fidgety, nervous, but when he took her hand, they sat together on his couch. He put his arm around her shoulders, and she felt a little bit better.

Imogene didn't sit. She paced. "Where do you think Steve's blood bank comes from?"

"Blood donors," Celia said.

"Right." She pointed at her. "But some blood costs more than other blood, right?"

"I guess," Celia said. "Steve's offered, but I'm fine with just...whatever."

Imogene stopped pacing. "Are you? Lately?"

"I don't understand," Celia said.

"Ian, where's the best weed in the country come from?"

"Southern California."

Imogene smiled something sinister and covered her eyes with the red sunglasses she'd stashed in her back pocket. "Well, right now, the best blood in the country apparently comes from Admiral Key."

Celia was silent, and so was Ian until he finally blurted, "Wait. Me?"

Imogene crossed her arms.

"No, no, no," Celia said. "You're saying Danny is really here because of Steve—because of Ian's blood?"

"I'll ask again: how's the bagged stuff taste after Ian?"

Celia shook her head.

"It tastes like shit, doesn't it," Imogene said, "now that you've had top shelf." She nodded at Ian and sat down. Celia was squeezed between them. "I blame myself for letting you take Ian to meet Steve the other night. I never should have done that." Imogene sighed. "Look, I didn't want to ever have to tell you this, but there are enterprising vampires who hunt for people who smell like Ian. They kidnap them and make them blood slaves. Bleed 'em until they die, and it can take years. That's where the expensive shit comes from."

Shakily, Celia muttered, "And Danny wants to do that to Ian."

Imogene nodded.

"Oh my God." She waved her hands in front of her face.

Meanwhile, Ian put his head between his knees. "I don't feel good."

"You have to turn him," Imogene said.

Ian's head popped up just as Celia said, "What?"

"Turn him before he's dead."

"I feel sick…"

Celia looked at Ian, who looked literally green. "Are you gonna puke?"

"I don't know. Why don't you get me a whiskey? Imogene, can you get me a whiskey?"

"Yeah, dude." She moved at vamp speed to the kitchen.

"Ian?" Celia put her hand on the back of his neck. He felt about a-hundred-and-ten degrees.

"I'm okay," he said.

"I'm not."

He looked up at Celia, and his blue eyes were smiling. "You'll keep me safe."

She didn't know if he was right.

Imogene returned with a big bottle of whiskey, no glasses, and took a drag. She then handed the bottle to Ian who took enough sips to make his Adam's apple jump.

Celia ran her fingers through his hair. "Should you be drinking? You have a race tomorrow."

"Shit," he said. "My parents."

"Huh?" Imogene looked up.

"My parents are coming tomorrow morning."

"No, they are fucking not," she said.

They both gawked at Imogene.

"Ian, do you know where babies come from?"

"I think so," he said.

She dragged the bottle away from him. "If you smell like liquid gold, what do you suppose your parents smell like?"

"A lot like me," he said.

From behind her sunglasses, Imogene looked around his apartment. "And you better take down any evidence of your brothers. If Danny finds out there are four of you, your whole family is fucked."

Ian took the bottle back. "I need to call my parents."

"What are you going to tell them?" Celia asked.

He took a chug. "Yellow fever outbreak?"

Celia looked back to Imogene. "So what do we do now?"

She looked at Ian. "Keep an eye on him. 'Til they leave."

"How do we get them to leave?"

She shrugged. "I'm sure we'll think of something. We're all moderately intelligent." She stole the bottle back from Celia's boyfriend.

Celia put her hand on his shoulder. "I'm sorry. I'm so sorry."

"It's not your fault," he said.

"What are you talking about? None of this would have happened if you hadn't met me. Before me, you only had the ocean to be afraid of, and you can avoid that unless there's a tsunami, which doesn't happen on the Gulf Coast anyway, so why am I even talking about tsunamis?"

"Wow," Imogene said. "That's the first time I've heard her go Rain Man in a while."

Ian shushed her. "I love you. I wouldn't have found love if I hadn't found you."

"I love you, too."

Imogene groaned. "Just turn him already."

"No," Celia said. "I like him just the way he is."

"Fragile. Breakable. Delicious. Yeah, I like him, too, until he's dead."

"I really think I'm gonna be sick," Ian said.

"We're going to get through this."

"Listen to that," Imogene said. "I almost believe her."

"How do you turn someone anyway?" Ian asked.

"Easy," Imogene said. "If you've been bitten recently, all I have to do is slip some of my blood in your food."

Ian looked up at her. "Imogene, that sounds like a threat."

"Is it really, though?"

"If you turn him," Celia said, "I will tie you to a picnic table and wait for sunrise."

Imogene smiled. "I swear she's the dominant one."

CHAPTER EIGHTEEN

They were in lock down. Imogene thought if Danny didn't know that they knew about the hunt for Ian, then he and Vixen would go away whenever they got bored of Admiral Key—which shouldn't take long because Admiral Key sucked (Imogene's words).

Celia moved into Ian's apartment. He put tin foil on his bedroom window, so now they didn't have a hydroponic apartment; they had a hydroponics *farm* where three vampires lived and two fridges were filled with blood. (Ian had to move all his kale.) If the cops showed up, they were going to have to just kill all of them—if Danny and Vixen ever took a break from constant shagging.

Ian and Celia heard them all night and sometimes in the middle of the day—shagging. It wasn't like in the movies where you heard the bedframe shake. No, this sounded more like someone being murdered and liking it.

Celia was just glad she'd already gone over there and collected all her new clothes, but she was now without a television. She couldn't hide behind her cheerful eighties films, and Ian had to work, so he couldn't even keep her occupied.

Imogene would leave to sleep but be back at 8:30 sharp every night. She would just sit there and stare at Ian. She hadn't mentioned turning him again, but Celia couldn't help but think the thought was on repeat in her deviant brain, like a scrolling headline: "Must turn Ian. Must turn Ian. Must turn…"

Maybe that was why Celia hadn't bitten him lately. If he hadn't been bitten, Imogene couldn't sneak blood into his food, and he wouldn't turn. Then again, maybe Celia shouldn't have given herself that level of pre-planning. She really hadn't bitten him because they hadn't been alone, and even when they were, they had to listen to Danny and Vixen *murdering each other.*

Even worse, Celia hadn't gotten laid since their first time together. She finally found a guy she wanted to fuck (Imogene's voice in her head again), and they were in crisis mode.

Celia told Omar at Happy Gas she needed to go on sabbatical. Apparently due to her use of a big word, he agreed and gave her two weeks off. Celia just hoped that was enough time to get her vamp daddy and his whore the hell away from her boyfriend.

Celia and Ian sat in Dr. Savage's waiting room, and Ian read *Psychology Today.*

He had missed his big race Saturday morning because he'd accidentally gotten drunk the night before and couldn't stop puking—not from the alcohol, more from his nerves. He told his parents he had the flu, which made his mother threaten to drive down immediately to take care of her son. At that point, Celia had been coerced onto the phone and forced to talk Ian's mom off a cliff.

His mom sounded nice. She had one of those indiscriminate Southern accents that made Celia picture a beauty queen. Based on the looks of all four of her sons, Celia guessed she wasn't far from the truth. Celia said she would take care of her little boy. Yes, his mother still called him "little boy," Ian being the youngest son and all.

Next to Celia in the office, Ian said, "Did you know that one in twenty men admit to sleeping with a teddy bear?"

He wasn't really talking to her. He sometimes just announced things he found amazing. She turned and looked at him. She smiled and pushed some black curls from his forehead.

So far, Ian had taken the whole possible blood slave thing very well. Celia wasn't surprised. He was like a shallow pool—relaxing, soothing, but not much going on under there. She didn't think her boyfriend was stupid. He was smart, in a way (*Jeopardy!*, anyone?). He also had a keen understanding of mortality due to a hungry Great White in Hawaii. Despite this, his range of emotions was lacking. He was either happy, horny, or kind of happy.

Celia had to face it: her boyfriend was being prepped for slow slaughter by two vampires currently living in her apartment, and he still wanted to cuddle. It was Celia's idea that he come with her to therapy, only because Imogene couldn't keep an eye on him that night. She said she needed a night off for some "real man blood." Celia understood. Even sitting in Dr. Savage's office, if she looked at Ian too long, her gums burned. Fangs threatened. She wanted to feed constantly when she was around Ian—or get laid.

The feelings were now infuriatingly interchangeable.

The door to Dr. Savage's office opened, and she led out a tall, gorgeous vampire with long, blonde hair and bright green eyes. The girl wore a dress that looked like it came from Imogene's extensive closet—in other words, mouse-sized. She had legs that closely resembled unblemished ivory. She was another example of what vampires were supposed to look like. She dabbed at her catlike eyes as she nodded to Dr. Savage and whimpered, "Thank you, doctor."

"Of course, Katarina."

Of course her name was *Katarina*.

Ian didn't look up from his magazine until Katarina stopped dead in her tracks and started sniffing the air. Her teary eyes closed, then opened, and focused right on Celia's boyfriend.

"My, my," she said, "what expensive taste you have." She barely acknowledged Celia and took two quick steps toward Ian, who said something like "oh, shit," and reached for the nearest weapon, which turned out to be a statue of Buddha.

"Hey," Celia said, jumping to her feet, but Dr. Savage—somewhat out of character—latched onto the back of Katarina's head and sternly said, "NO."

Katarina seemed to wake from whatever trance Ian's blood had put her in and kept walking, straight for the exit and out the door.

Dr. Savage smiled like nothing weird had happened. "Good evening, Celia. You look beautiful." She sounded shocked, and rightfully so.

Celia had on one of her new outfits from the *Pretty Woman* shopping spree: a jean skirt and blue peasant blouse, fitted below her breasts. Ian said the color made her eyes pop and her tits look good. He had manifested this feeling earlier when he motor-boated her in the alley where they parked their bikes. Celia even had on little wedge heels, very beach chic.

"This must be Ian." Dr. Savage removed her black-rimmed glasses and reached her hand out. "I'm Rayna Savage."

"Uh..." He slowly returned the Buddha to its pedestal. "Are you gonna...?" He gestured to the exit.

"Attack you? No. I wasn't planning on it, although you do smell delicious."

"I get that a lot lately." Ian nodded and shook her hand. "Nice to meet you. Do you sleep with a teddy bear?"

"A small stuffed hippopotamus." Dr. Savage smiled at Ian—and not the patronizing smile she used on Celia—which made Celia cross her arms and stomp one foot. "Are we having a couple's session this evening?"

"No," Celia said. "I need to...we have a problem." She glanced up at Ian. Then, she glanced around Dr. Savage's office with the posters of trees and the ocean and the ever-present scent of lavender. "Is Ian safe in here?"

"I'm sorry?"

"Is he safe in your waiting room?"

"Of course?" Ian ended statements as questions sometimes; Celia wasn't used to her therapist doing the same.

"Okay." She turned and kissed his chin. "I won't be long."

Celia didn't sit down inside Dr. Savage's office. She was not in the mood for the farting couch, and she felt on edge.

"Celia, what is it?"

"Danny's back." She paced.

Dr. Savage sat down in her fancy, leather swivel chair. "Back in Lazaret?"

"No. In my apartment."

"Danny is in your apartment."

"With some newbie vamp hooker he met in New Orleans." Celia paused. "She's not really a hooker. Exotic dancer. I'm sorry."

"Why is he in your apartment?"

"Because, well, so here's what happened." Celia sat on the farty couch and told Dr. Savage about Steve, and Ian's blood, and how Imogene thought Danny and Vixen were only on Admiral Key to kidnap Ian and make him into a blood slave—which was why Ian was in the waiting room and why Imogene thought they needed to turn him immediately.

Dr. Savage was quiet, for a while, really.

"Dr. Savage?"

She stood and faced the windows overlooking St. Arthur's Circle. "I should have said something when I first smelled him on you, Celia, but your friend is right. There are circles of enterprising vampires who view human beings as cattle, bred to be slaughtered. There are porterhouses, New York strip, T-bone. Then, there is filet mignon. Your boyfriend is filet mignon."

"Oh-kay."

"I should have warned you to keep him away from other vampires. Not all vampires have moral qualms, like you or I. Some vampires want expensive blood, and some vampires want money. From what I've heard of your Danny, I suspect he likes both, so Ian would be of great interest to a vampire like Danny and his..." She waved her perfectly manicured hand.

"Exotic dancer."

"Yes."

"So what do we do?"

"Feign ignorance and politely ask Danny to leave."

Celia buried her face in her hands. "But I can't. He'll take away my blood connection if I make him leave—not that I'm even sure I could *make* him leave."

"He threatened your blood dealer?"

Celia nodded. "He said he owns him."

Dr. Savage slowly sat down. "Celia, why is Danny back in Florida? He's not local."

"No, he's from New York."

Dr. Savage's right eyebrow went all Vulcan. "New York?" She tapped her finger on the arm of her chair. "Right now, you need to stay calm. You need to stay close to Ian at all times. Do not let Imogene turn him. There's no need for that."

"I know," Celia said.

She smiled her simpering smile. "I'm glad you've been listening to me, Celia."

Celia rolled her eyes when Dr. Savage looked down to make some note on her therapist pad.

She tore the paper and reached across the table toward Celia. "Here is a number for my blood connection. She's not a dealer. She's a healer. Her blood is distilled with herbs and blessed by a shaman."

"You're fucking kidding me."

"What?"

"Nothing." She took the little piece of paper and smiled. "Thanks."

"Let me do some thinking on this Danny situation, and I'll get in touch. Come see me in two nights to check in."

Celia sighed and stood up. The good news seemed so anticlimactic after the bad. "We had sex."

Dr. Savage smiled—really smiled—probably because she was picturing Ian naked. She said, "Did you enjoy it?"

Celia felt her knees shake. "God, yes."

On the bike ride home, Ian did his usual thing and circled her so that she could keep up with his annoyingly breakneck pace. "So did you tell her how good I am in bed?"

She giggled and said, "Shut up, Ian."

"How I'm hung like a race horse?"

She stuck her tongue out at him, even though she knew it was true.

"Hey, let's not go home," he said.

Celia decided wearing a skirt on a bike was kind of a stupid idea as Ian continued.

"I'm sick of listening to your ex have sex all night long."

"Where do you want to go?"

"I have an idea." He smiled at her, and the wind ruffled his black hair until he looked semi-electrocuted, in a cute way.

She followed him past Happy Gas. She ducked, since she was on "sabbatical," as they continued farther along Admiral Key. They stopped in the parking lot of a 24-hour convenience store owned by an overly cheerful, overweight local named Shell.

"Wait here," Ian said. He parked his bike and ran inside.

Celia smelled the night. She smelled the sea and fishy fish. She smelled remnants of suntan lotion. From a parked car, she smelled beer and sweat. Above it all, though, even with him inside, she could smell Woodsy BO, the man she loved, mixed with the sweet richness of his blood. She was surrounded by blood, but Ian was still the only human for her. Who would have guessed she had expensive taste?

Ian came sprinting out of the store with a bottle in a paper bag and a big Mexican blanket. He tossed both in the basket of Celia's beach cruiser. "What are you up to?" she asked, smiling.

"Just follow me." He jumped onto his bike like a cowboy would jump on a horse. "And keep up!"

Yeah, she thought, *easy for him to say.*

He was nice enough to not go twenty miles per hour, but he had to be pushing fifteen. She moved her little legs at vampire speed and managed to keep his maniacal black hair in view. He made a sudden right hand turn, and poof! He disappeared into a bush. Celia put on the brakes.

"Ian?"

She squinted and noticed, ah, her boyfriend had not just nosedived into fresh foliage. There was actually a path. In fact, the path led into a park.

"It's illegal to be in the park after dark," she muttered, but she followed him anyway. Even though she couldn't see Ian, she traced his smell past flowering magnolia bushes with thick, leathery leaves. There were piles of hip-high hibiscus that probably glowed pink in the sun. She passed all that and almost wiped out when the path of small stones became a boardwalk.

"Ian!" she hissed.

She could still smell him, but she couldn't hear him or see him. She then realized they were in Poe's Park—a place where retirees walked their dogs in the mornings—and apparently crazed ex-surfers canoodled after dark. She assumed there were alligators, too, since they were right on the marshes. She was busy wondering if she could take down an alligator when she spotted Ian's bike and put on the brakes so hard, she was pretty sure she left skid marks.

Ian took hold of her handlebars before she could hurt herself, and in the dark, she saw the glint of white teeth. "Easy, Mermaid," he whispered. He leaned forward and kissed her forehead. He pulled the bagged bottle and Mexican blanket from her basket and took her hand. "Come on."

"We're not supposed to be here after dark," she said.

"Vampires aren't *supposed* to exist." He pulled her between two banyan trees. Lace-like edges of Spanish moss tickled her forehead.

Ian was good at navigating a path, even in the dark. Maybe he was onto something with all his kale smoothies. He led her to a clearing where they had a view of the water and far off lights of Lazaret. The moon was full and cast Ian's freckled skin blue.

Celia watched him unfold the colorful blanket and glance up at her. "I staked this place out weeks ago and thought of you."

"You did?"

"Sure." He sat down on the blanket and patted the fabric at his side. "I know you're embarrassed about it, but I've had a thing for you since I first saw you naked."

She giggled and parked herself at his hip, careful to avoid protruding roots and maybe alligators. "Nu-uh."

"Yeah-huh." He pulled a bottle of cheap sparkling wine from the paper bag. It reminded Celia of college in Miami when they used to buy the stuff for three bucks a pop. He used his long fingers to unfurl the bottle's foil. His pinkie was still encased in metal, but you'd never know it, the way he'd adapted to his injury, like Ian adapted to seemingly every circumstance.

"So are you just using me for my body?" she teased.

The edge of his lip turned up.

"Are you blushing?"

He smiled. "No."

Her fangs came out. "You are tho cute when you blush."

"You're so cute when you lisp." He used his thumb to pop the cork and only spilled about a thimbleful of budget bubbly before covering the spout with his mouth. He swallowed a big gulp. "I think you have an amazing body."

"Liar." She took the bottle from him and knocked one of her fangs when she took a sip.

"You do. You're..." He shook his head. "I don't understand who told women that protruding ribs and hipbones were a good idea. I don't get how a size two can be ideal."

She huffed at the mere idea of a size two. But then she poked him in the shoulder. "You can't tell me you haven't been dating size twos your whole life, Mr. Surfer USA."

He shrugged. "Yeah, well, the size twos never lasted." He took the bottle back but didn't drink from it. He set it down at the base of the nearest tree and turned to face her. "It's not just your curves, though." He put his hand on her cheek and kissed her, fangs and all. "I'm pretty damn fond of this mouth." His mouth moved to her neck. "And the way your skin tastes." He used his fingers to pull at the front of her shirt until his lips found the edge of her bra. "I really like these."

She closed her eyes and chuckle-choked.

She took off his shirt—basically just tore it over his head and threw it, they would later realize, into the marsh. Celia was still totally confused in regards to her physical responses. With Ian on top of her, roots beneath her, and the smell of sea mixed with the scent of blood, she didn't know if she wanted sex or food. That was when Celia had an idea.

Why not have both?

Ian made quick work of her skirt, and they made love. He kept his full weight off of her by resting on his elbows, and just like their first time, he watched her as he moved. She would have thought the scrutiny would make her uncomfortable—to have him staring at her while he was inside her—but it wasn't. She put her hand on his face.

Her fangs were out, which he could obviously see, which was why she felt comfortable when she asked, "Can I bite you?"

Ian seemed incapable of speech by then, but he nodded. She buried her fangs in his neck, and he made the "nuh" noise, louder than usual. His hand tightened in her hair, and for the first time in Celia's life, she understood the expression "banging." Ian and Celia were definitely *banging*, and she was an active participant. His blood gushed down her throat, and she was high, high, high!

Yes, yes, yes!

When the need-to-pee sensation started creeping, she pulled her teeth out of his neck and let go of his body in order to avoid breaking any other bones. He only held tighter to her as he twitched and spasmed and made a sound kind of like "guuuuahhhh." Celia had the presence of mind to watch, at least. She liked watching when Ian did *that.*

They laid on their backs on the itchy Mexican blanket holding hands. Celia rode out her incredible high, and Ian's body went half-comatose, pumped full of her venom but also drained in post-sexy-time bliss.

"Ian?"

"Mm?"

"I love you."

"I love you, too," he said.

"Do you want to be a vampire?"

"Not really," he slurred.

"I don't really want you to be one either." She rolled over and tickled the side of his stomach. "What'll happen when you get old?"

"I'll be the old guy with the hot girlfriend."

"And you're okay with not having kids?"

He licked his upper lip. "I don't feel capable of having this conversation right now."

"Sorry." She rested next to him.

"Tell me a story," he said.

Celia smiled. "What kind of story?"

"A happy one."

She leaned up on one elbow. "The first time I saw David Bowie I was five years old."

Ian laughed.

"And he had on a really bad blond wig and tight pants, singing with Muppets. And I remember wondering why the girl wanted to go home when she could live in a world with Muppets and David

Bowie." She watched Ian smile.

"That is a good point," he said. "Flaw in the film."

"Right?" She played with his hair. "I spent my childhood in front of a TV. You spent yours on a beach."

"Several beaches."

"Yet, we both ended up here."

"Meant to be," he said and yawned.

"Want to head back?"

"I guess I could use a nap," he said.

Only Ian napped at midnight.

Luckily, his neck had stopped bleeding, but the bite marks were kind of obvious. It didn't help that his shirt was covered in mud. He tied it on the back of his bike, unwilling to litter, and they piled the empty bottle of sparkling wine and the hideous Mexican blanket back in Celia's bike basket. Ian, post-bite, was okay to bike. He only weaved a little.

When they got back to the Sleeping Gull, Celia was less than pleased to find her front door open, and Danny on the front porch. He was in head to toe seersucker but no shoes. Apparently, he had acclimated some to beach life. His hair was hidden beneath a light blue newsboy hat, and he smoked a thin cigar.

There was no avoiding him. He stood up straight when they neared.

"Stop for a snack?" He winked at Celia after casting a glance at Ian's neck.

Celia heard the sound of pointed stilettos before she saw *her*. Vixen stuck her pointed nose in the air and sniffed. "Smells like sex out here." Her eyes found the shirtless love of Celia's life. "And Ian. Smells like Ian." She smiled at him in her itty-bitty red dress.

They had to walk past them on the porch to get to Ian's front door—that or jump the railing, and despite being immortal, Celia was still a damned klutz. She would never make it over the railing, so she held tight to Ian's hand and did her best to ignore the monsters that had usurped her living space.

"Excuse us," Celia said, but Danny threw his arm around her shoulders and steered her into her apartment. It smelled like blood in there, and she soon saw why. There was another couple inside—a human couple—with glazed eyes and drool on the sides of their mouths. They weren't dead but they were definitely dinner.

"We're having a little party," Danny whispered into her hair. His fingertips dug into the outside of her arm. "I know you just ate, but you want a nibble?"

Celia tried to look behind her, find Ian, but Danny's muscular upper body blocked her view.

"You should shut the front door, at least," she said. "What if someone saw?"

"Nobody's gonna see, baby, and if they did, what are they gonna do? We'll just tell 'em these two had too much giggle water."

Celia thought it wouldn't be a hard sell. There were empty liquor bottles everywhere. The obvious scent of smoke and sweaty sex permeated her apartment. They joked about the Sleeping Gull Apartments being a shithole, but Danny and Vixen were on their way to making it the God's honest truth.

She shoved her elbow into Danny's side to get away from him and turned just in time to see Vixen...licking Ian's open wound.

Ian was glamoured, and that alone was enough to freak Celia out, as she'd never seen him that way before and had never planned to. He looked like a zombie on his feet, his blue eyes unfocused and spooky. Vixen had him leaned against the doorframe, and her little pink tongue poked and prodded at the holes Celia had made in the park.

My holes. My blood. My boyfriend.

Celia unleashed a Hulk noise and sprinted at Vixen. There was no stopping her. She barreled into the bitch, and they went sprawling into the night, right over the porch ledge. They landed in a huge hibiscus bush, and since Celia didn't actually know how to punch, she just sort of flailed her arms at Vixen's face. She kept making these high-pitched cat noises, but it was obvious Vixen didn't know to fight either, considering she flailed her hands at Celia like cold, dead fish.

Celia didn't see red. She saw the whole fucking rainbow.

She barely heard Heidi screaming at her as the landlady arrived outside. Danny was laughing; Celia ignored that, too. Really the only thing that stopped her from clawing Vixen's eyes out was Ian, suddenly close, tugging at her shoulders.

"Celia."

She allowed him to pull her out of the bush and off Vixen's double-D implants. He wrapped his arms around her waist from behind, then pulled her to standing. For some reason, she felt the need to continue flailing at the air until she smacked her own boyfriend in the face. He said, "Ow," but didn't let go.

"Now, it's a party." Danny clapped his hands as his new creation stood in the center of Heidi's landscaping. One of her high heels was gone, and mulch stuck to her long, red hair. She pulled at her dress and glared at Danny.

"Why didn't you help me?"

"Baby, it was a hell of a show, let me tell you." He was bent over laughing with his hands on his knees.

"Speaking of which," Heidi said, "you're interrupting mine." Her blonde wig was on straight that night, and she was in ill-advised cutoff shorts and a bikini top that showed off her baseball mitt skin. "Celia, who are these people?"

"They're my...they're just staying for a couple days." Celia stared pointedly at Danny.

"Well." Heidi took a deep breath and blew her chest up like a balloon. "Keep it down. I gotta find out how the maid got away with killing the family cat." She turned and slammed her front door.

Ian still had his arms around Celia, but that didn't stop her from pointing a finger at Vixen. "Don't you ever, ever glamour my boyfriend again."

She stood there, crooked in only one shoe. "Or what?"

"I'll feed you your silicone," Imogene said. She arrived at Celia's side, arms crossed, white earbuds tossed over her shoulder. Based on the tone of her voice, Celia assumed she'd been listening to early Metallica.

"My bearcat has arrived!" Danny announced, opening his arms wide.

"You call me that again, and I'll feed you your own right testicle."

Celia felt Imogene's claw-like hand on her upper arm.

"Let's get inside, lovebirds."

They left Vixen cursing in the bushes as she searched for her lost shoe. Danny smiled as they passed and then gave Ian a once-over that was way more than friendly.

Imogene locked the door behind them, and Celia went to the kitchen to get Ian a washcloth for his neck. When she got back, her friends were on the couch. Ian looked stoned, and Imogene had her hands in his hair.

Celia must have looked murderous, because Imogene scooted away from him. "What? You know it calms him down."

"Forgive me for feeling a little territorial after tit bitch just glamoured him and licked his neck."

Imogene leaned forward on the couch. "She huh?"

Celia sat down next to Ian and held the damp cloth to his bite marks. He took the cloth from her hand and slouched.

"That stripper went after Ian?"

"Exotic dancer," he muttered sleepily.

Celia sighed. "She didn't bite him, but she might have if I hadn't turned around when I did."

"If he wasn't worth a shit ton of money, she might have done more than that," Imogene said.

Celia brushed Ian's hair with her fingers. "What do you mean?"

"I mean I've been poking around. Apparently, Danny and Vixen have been in Lazaret longer than we realized." She paused for dramatic effect. "They've been here since humans started getting deaded."

"You think Danny killed those humans?"

"No, even that idiot knows better. He's old. He obviously got turned in the twenties, right, what with his damn suits and calling everyone 'baby.' I'm surprised he hasn't called us 'dames' yet, for cripes' sake. No, a newbie vamp kills humans on accident because they're so hungry."

"But I didn't—"

Imogene held her hand up. "Yeah, Merk, I know, but you also vomit, and newbie vampires aren't supposed to be able to do that either. You're an exception, 'kay? But that Vixen fake-tit newborn, I wouldn't put it past her for a second."

"She's killing people?" Celia thought about the comatose humans on her couch next door.

"I can't be sure. I'm just saying, Danny is hiding something."

"Like wanting to use me as a blood bank?"

Imogene nodded at Ian. "More than that. I just don't know what it is yet." She stood. "Want a beer?"

Celia shook her head, no, but Ian nodded as Imogene disappeared into the kitchen.

"Are you okay?" Celia whispered.

"Yeah. Thanks for going psycho windmill on that girl."

"Did I really look like a windmill?"

Imogene came back with two cold ones and handed Ian his beer. Celia noticed his usual cheap Nattie Light smelled funny. At first, she thought it was skunked, but then it dawned on her.

"Do not drink that!" Celia grabbed the beer from Ian's hand. "Imogene!"

She snickered. "Whaaaaat?"

Celia glanced down at Ian. "She put her blood in your beer." She stomped into the kitchen and poured the can down the sink. "Imogene, we are not turning Ian!"

She shrugged. "It would solve all our problems."

"No, it wouldn't!" Celia smacked Imogene in the head.

Imogene batted her hand away and stood. "How so? If Ian was a vampire, we wouldn't have to worry about Danny and fake-tits kidnapping him and turning him into a blood slave. In fact, if Ian was a vampire, they would leave, and everything would go back to normal!"

"Normal? Normal! Ian ending up a vampire is not normal!"

"How long are you going to delude yourself, Merk? If you don't turn him, someday, he's gonna die—from natural causes or whatever, he will be dead, and you will be alone for eternity, missing him. You're a fucking vampire, Celia. Your boyfriend is human. How did you think this was going to end?"

Celia felt her eyes begin to burn.

"Enough!" Celia had never heard Ian yell before, and it made both the girls jump. He sounded commanding and really sexy. He stood and pushed them away from each other. "Sit down, both of you."

Celia fell back on the couch, and when Imogene huffed and hesitated, Ian grabbed her wrist and dragged her to a chair. He stood above them, shirtless with a washcloth against his neck, but his height alone gave him authority.

"First of all," he said, "my becoming a vampire is neither of your decisions."

"But—"

"Imogene." He pointed at her until she clapped her mouth shut. "Secondly, if I want to become a vampire—which I don't—it won't happen because some asshole next door wants to kidnap me. It'll be out of love." He gestured to Celia. "Thirdly..." He dropped the washcloth and raked his hands through his hair. "We gotta get Danny and Vixen the fuck out of here."

The f-word was not part of Ian's usual vernacular; therefore, he meant business.

"Duh," Imogene agreed, "but how?"

"Take back Celia's apartment. You have a new blood dealer, right?"

"What?" Imogene looked at her.

"My therapist gave me a connection, but the blood is, like, blessed by a shaman or something."

"Shit, it's probably pig's blood." Imogene buried her face in her hands.

"Look, it's good for now, right? Then, you don't need angry Steve, and that's what Danny is holding over you, anyway."

"So, what, I just go over there and ask them to leave?"

"I guess it won't be that easy, will it?" Ian fell down on the couch next to Celia.

Celia looked over at Imogene, who was biting her front lip hard enough to practically make herself bleed. She had her brows lowered. Then, she said, "I annoy you, right?"

"Huh?"

"I can be annoying," Imogene said.

Celia shrugged.

"I mean, I use you for your blood and never pay you back. I sit on your couch watching your TV and play with your boyfriend's hair even though I know it turns him on."

Ian nodded, expressionless.

"I drug you and make you go out when you don't want to. I make fun of you every chance I get. I'm everywhere you don't want me to be, even in your bed, so I'm annoying, right?"

"I always just thought of you as kind of mean," Celia said.

"What if I start annoying Danny and Vixen?"

"Meaning?"

"I invade your apartment. I drink all Danny's blood and watch your TV at Heidi's *True Crime* volume and interrupt them having sex. Oh, and borrow Vixen's clothes without asking."

"Hit on Danny," Ian muttered.

Imogene nodded. "Vixen would hate that."

"You hit on him, too." Ian gestured to Celia.

"Ew."

"Exactly. No man likes being hit on by an ex fling."

Celia paused. "So instead of threatening them to leave, we annoy them until they leave?"

"Yes," Ian said.

"Well, while we're over there fake seducing Danny, what are you going to do?"

"Get high."

"Typical," Imogene replied.

"Operation Burn Your Bed begins tomorrow night," Ian said.

"Burn my bed?"

"I'm not sleeping on that thing after what's been happening over there." He threw a thumb at the wall. "We'll burn your mattress once they're gone. A big beach bonfire."

Would it work?

She knew from personal experience Danny ran from anything that made his life difficult. Hell, he was in Florida, running from something in New York. He was a runner, and maybe, just maybe, if they could make him uncomfortable enough, he would leave.

CHAPTER NINETEEN

It all started when Imogene refused to go over to Celia's apartment due to what she termed "unnatural animal noises." Point of fact, Danny and Vixen were just *murdering each other* in Celia's bed. Celia was frankly surprised the entire complex had yet to call the police. You could hear their sexing from the beach, and on the beach, they were contending with the ocean—not a pond, but the life force of the entire world.

Imogene wouldn't go over because she said she didn't want to even consider the compromising, contortionist-esque positions she might walk in on. When Celia begged to differ (due to Imogene's earlier request to watch Celia have her first orgasm), she deflected by saying she just wanted to watch Ian use his tongue.

Point: Imogene.

While the girls argued in Ian's kitchen, they barely noticed him leave the room until the front door opened. Celia yelled after him when he turned left on the porch. By the time Imogene and Celia reached him, he had the front door to her apartment open.

The unnatural animal noises were suddenly louder.

The girls followed him inside, and thankfully, Danny and Vixen were not humping in the middle of her living room. They were actually in the bedroom, which made Celia cover her mouth and roll her eyes.

Ian, in true Ian fashion, stepped barefoot onto her living room table—covered in empty blood bags and a few roving flies—and started to sing.

"I want to..."

He screeched the opening lines of "Bicycle Race." It was the most annoying Queen song ever but oddly fitting for a competitive cyclist, especially a tone-deaf competitive cyclist. He went on for thirty seconds or so. With the final note, he extended his arms up over his head.

Celia's bedroom door popped open, and Danny came stomping out in nothing but a newsboy hat over his junk. "What the—" Celia watched his brown eyes take in the scene: Ian on the living room table, Imogene trying not to laugh, and Celia, staring at her boyfriend in awed adoration.

"Hey, man," Ian said. He stepped off the table. "Think I left some of my whiskey over here." He patted Danny's bare shoulder as he passed and walked into the kitchen.

"What in the tainted tit is goin' on out here?" Vixen stepped up next to Danny in a skirt...and nothing else. The hand covering Celia's mouth moved to cover her eyes. "Oh, hello, Ian," she heard Vixen say, which made Celia uncover her eyes.

Her boyfriend had, indeed, left some whiskey at her place, apparently hidden in the crisper drawer of the fridge. He drank straight from the bottle and eyed Vixen's stretched-skin double-Ds. Celia was about to feel bad about herself until Ian said, "Did you know your breasts aren't the same size?"

Vixen's red lips parted in a gaping hole. Then, she started smacking Danny hard in the shoulder blades. "You said they were perfect!" She retreated to Celia's bedroom, sobbing, followed by Danny's bare ass cheeks and his voice: "Baby..."

"He's a one man wrecking crew," Imogene whispered.

Ian stepped over the coffee table and sprawled out on Celia's couch. "There's some blood in the fridge, Imogene." He gestured to the kitchen. "Celia, why don't you pick out a movie?" He looked up at them both—and smiled.

Oh, what a wicked man.

Two minutes later, they could still hear Danny and Vixen yelling at each other in the bedroom. Imogene had her big boots on the coffee table and a bag of B-negative attached to her lips. Ian calmly consumed the dregs of a bottle of forgotten whiskey. Celia went through her VHS collection until they all agreed that *Dirty Dancing* was the best worst movie to watch.

Celia went to her kitchen and found it just about as destroyed as her living room. Again, empty blood bags were everywhere, along with dirty wine glasses, stained with blood—and Celia didn't even know she owned wine glasses. Flies circled the sink.

There was no A-positive left in the fridge, but she did find a bag of O-negative that would have to do. Other than that, Danny and Vixen were running low. Celia cozied up on the couch next to her brilliant, evil boyfriend just as her ex came strolling out of the bedroom in nothing but a pair of pants and striped suspenders. His copious chest hair was all a mess, like maybe Vixen had pulled on it to make a point. His dark eyebrows were lowered over his dark eyes.

Before Celia could even burp, Danny lifted Ian off the couch by the front of his t-shirt and then literally lifted her six-foot-tall boyfriend off the ground. Imogene and Celia both pounced, which wasn't actually in Ian's best interest, because as they tackled Danny, Ian fell sideways and smacked his head against the edge of Celia's coffee table.

Celia assumed they all smelled Ian's blood at once, because they all stopped wrestling and made a collective "hummm" noise.

Celia's legs were tangled around Danny's, her hands around his neck. Imogene had one hand twisted in his hair, and her fangs were out big time. Despite this, Danny sat up with both girls all jumbled around him, which made Imogene and Celia sit up, too.

Ian was across the coffee table from them, one of his legs over it. There was a small gash above his right eye, bleeding red, red, red...but Celia's fangs did not go boing, probably because she was suddenly panicked to realize Danny was way stronger than even Imogene. There was no way Celia could defend her now bleeding boyfriend from her maker, but she soon learned she didn't really have to.

Ian got this look on his face like Imogene got whenever Heidi called her Olive Oyl. Then, without moving, without blinking, he looked at Danny and said, "I dare you to come close to me right now."

It might have been the timbre of his voice or the way Ian wasn't afraid—at all. His heartbeat was Hannibal Lecter calm. He looked vicious.

Celia gulped.

"Get off me." Danny shoved Imogene and Celia to the side and stood up. He stomped to Celia's bedroom like a dejected ten-year-old.

Imogene sat up and pushed her crooked sunglasses off her face. "What the fuck was that?"

Ian dabbed at his head, but Celia crossed the table in time to lick the drops of blood before they made it into his eye.

"Since when are you Dirty Harry?" Imogene asked.

He leaned his head closer to Celia's tongue. "You think I've never been in a fight before?"

Imogene was silent for a moment. "Exactly. Yes. I think you've never been in a fight before."

Ian smiled. "You're right, I haven't, because I can do a scary voice."

"You really can," Imogene said. "You're totally full of awesome tonight."

Celia's bedroom door crashed open. Vixen stomped out. She was in full going out gear—silver tube dress and matching silver heels. Her red hair was wild and free around her shoulders. Her perfect pout was outlined in red, and despite his bleeding head, she cast an angry glare at Ian before strutting her stuff across the living room.

"We're going out," she shouted, which Celia felt wasn't strictly necessary, seeing as they were five feet away from her.

Danny came out in his seersucker suit. He looked dapper—and really pissed. "What are you doing here anyway?"

"What are *you* doing here?" Celia asked.

"Scatter before we get back." He gave Vixen a push toward the front door.

"She'll think about it," Imogene crooned.

Halfway across the living room, Danny paused, and his dark eyes found Ian. "I'll get you back."

Ian winked at him—the crazy man winked! "High noon. Tomorrow?"

Danny huffed, and he and his whore left Celia's apartment.

Imogene stood to get, Celia assumed, another bag of blood, but instead she went to the bathroom and returned with a fluorescent Band-Aid. "Here." She pushed the adhesive against Ian's skull. "It already stopped bleeding, but we don't need your scent floating around in the open air."

Celia nodded a surprised thanks. Then, she realized she felt very much not okay. She looked at the Band-Aid on Ian's head, the shade of a highlighter pen. He seemed to be acquiring quite a few impressive injuries thanks to her, shredded wipeout shin not withstanding.

Celia stood shakily and walked to the front door. As she stepped into the warm, sticky night, she heard Ian's voice behind her, calling her name.

She made her way to the beach, Ian close on her heels. He kept calling out to her, but Celia wouldn't turn back. She needed to go where he couldn't follow. She didn't bother taking off her clothes; Ian was too close and would be able to stop her. She just waded into the welcoming waves and didn't look back until she was in up to her waist.

"Celia!" he shouted over the sound of crashing water.

"Go away, Ian!"

She could see him, pacing along the waterline. "What did I do? Tell me what I did."

"You didn't do anything. You just…" It took all her resolve to say what she had to say and not start sobbing. "You need to get away from here. Get away from me."

Ian stopped moving. "What?"

"I can't protect you from Danny. You have to leave. Forever."

"Celia, what are you talking about?"

"If you live through this, there'll be another Danny someday. Someone else will want to hurt you. I can't…" She wrapped her arms around herself. "I can't deal with that." She took a deep breath. "We need to break up."

Ian was backlit by the Sleeping Gull glow. His crazy black hair glowed red around the edges. He had his hands on his hips, and the way he stood above her on the beach made him look like a giant. He didn't say anything, and Celia couldn't see the expression on his face. She was too far away. He was like a half-drawn cartoon.

"Shit, Celia," he announced.

She turned her back on him and stared into the darkness of the Gulf of Mexico. The sky was empty of stars, covered by a blanket of clouds. There were no boats on the horizon—no blinking green or red lights. Nothing. There was nothing out there, just like Celia felt there was nothing in her chest.

She could still feel him. Ian was still with her outside. She could smell his blood over the salty sea and beachy bird poo. Behind her, she heard the sound of a jumping fish. Then she realized it wasn't a jumping fish.

His arms wrapped around her.

"Ian!" She spun to face him.

His eyes were wide and looked almost as bright as his Band-Aid. His jaw was clenched tight. When she put her hand on his chest, she realized he was literally trembling.

"You're shaking."

"I'm scared shitless." His voice cracked, and he chuckled, once, eying the dark water that surrounded them on all sides.

Celia wrapped her arms around him and shoved her face between his pecs. As their clothes soaked up saltwater, she ran her hands up and down his shivering back. "Nothing's gonna hurt you out here." She wished she could say the same for on land.

"I'm not leaving you," he whispered over the tide.

"I can't lose you," she replied. "You're my white knight."

"Then, I guess we only have one option," he said, chin on the top of her head. "Danny has to die."

When they got back inside and explained, Imogene was fine with the idea. "Sure." She smiled.

"Of course you would say that." Celia rolled her eyes.

"What's that supposed to mean?"

She stood dripping on the carpet at Ian's place. "That you're a lunatic." Celia turned to face Ian. "And since when are you a lunatic? Aren't you all peace, love, and shit?"

He tilted his head, calmly. "I was a surfer. Not a hippie."

"We can't just—" She realized she was screaming. "Have people killed," she whispered.

"Danny's not people," Imogene said. "He's an evil son of a bitch."

"Plus, is it really killing someone if he's already undead?"

The girls turned to stare at Ian.

"I'm serious. Could you really, like, call someone in front of a jury for that?"

"I...don't know." Celia turned to Imogene.

She shrugged.

"I've never thought of myself as undead before," Celia said. "Uncool maybe." She nodded then shook her head. "We're not murderers!"

Ian took hold of both Celia's arms. "I don't know what else to do. Annoying him only seems to piss him off, and you can't follow me around forever. Frankly, it'll be a little embarrassing going to the bathroom."

Imogene took Celia's chin in her hand. "Vamps like Danny should be killed. Turning people and running off. Plus, I really do think Vixen is murdering humans. Eye for an eye."

Celia shoved her hand away. "You're sure?"

"Well, I'm not *sure*. I'm hoping, because I'd really like to slay that bitch."

Celia shook out of Ian's grasp and stepped out of her salty puddle. "Didn't you tell me once there are vampires who hunt vampires who kill humans?"

She shrugged. "It's what I've heard."

"Well, is it true?"

"I don't know. It's like the boogeyman."

Celia chewed on her fingernail. "The boogeyman does not exist."

"Okay." She fell down on Ian's furniture. "So it's not like the boogeyman. It's like the ghost of Elvis."

Celia gawked at her.

"What?" Imogene said. "You don't know if Elvis's ghost wanders Graceland."

"Ian!" Celia yelled.

He stepped between them. "All right, Imogene, can you not talk for a while?"

"Fine with me." She got up and clomped in her combat boots to Ian's kitchen.

Celia squeaked up at her boyfriend.

"Celia, say what you're thinking."

"I don't want you involved in a murder plot. You're sweet and innocent and you have a nice mouth." She shook her head. "I'm not okay with this."

He kissed her nose. "What about these hunters Imogene's talking about? This is what they do, right?"

"She doesn't even know if they're real!"

He touched his bottom lip, which was just what Celia needed to bring her back to Earth. The simple gesture reminded her of when they first met, before the first bite, the first orgasm, the life-altering sex. Before Vixen and Danny and, oh, *homicide.*

Celia pulled Ian into a hug that literally forced all the air from his lungs. "I love you."

He gasped until she let up a little. "I love you, too." With the influx of air, he gasped some more. He ran his open palm down the back of her hair and kissed the side of her head. He pulled back a couple inches so he could look at her. "Do you want to turn me?"

"No."

"Then we have to consider this."

Celia sighed.

"Would your shrink know anything about covert assassins?"

"I'm going to see her tomorrow night. Or I guess we're going to see her tomorrow night."

"Couple's therapy?" He raised an eyebrow.

His smirk made her smile. "What am I supposed to say? 'Excuse me, is there a rogue group of vampires good at execution?' Or better yet, 'How do I kill my jerk of an ex?'"

"That's right, we still don't know for sure about that." He turned to the kitchen. "Imogene, how do you kill a vampire?"

"Sunshine, bitch," she shouted from where Celia presumed she was perched on Ian's counter like a purple-haired gargoyle.

"We won't get Danny in the sun," Celia said. "He's old enough to know better."

"How old is he?"

"I don't know. Old. Have you seen the way he dresses?"

Ian glanced at the ceiling. "His vernacular is very antiquated."

"You use the weirdest words sometimes…"

Ian stuck his head around the corner to the kitchen. "Imogene, do you know another way to kill a vampire?"

"Dunno. It's not something we usually discuss, because, you know, it makes it sound like you want to kill somebody."

Celia glared at her pretzel-bent form on Ian's counter.

"What?" She looked at Celia over the top of her glasses. "It's like asking someone how to get blood stains out of car seats. Shit."

"We are not cut out for this," Celia muttered.

"Look, we'll go see Dr. Savage tomorrow night, and we'll go from there."

"Fine." She pointed her finger in his face. "But you're not killing anyone. If we can't find these mysterious vampire hunters, I'll kill Danny." She choked a little. "I guess."

"But I don't want you killing anyone."

"I don't want *you* killing anyone."

"Shut up, you pussies!"

They both turned their heads toward Imogene.

She pushed buttons on her hip-side cassette player. "I'll kill a bitch if I have to. Or two."

"Oh, God," Celia said. "Imogene, do you have a yellow pill?"

"Nope. Sorry, dude." She tucked her cassette player back in her jeans and hopped off the counter.

"Yellow pill?" Ian glanced at Imogene.

"Klonopin." She put her hands in her tight jean pockets. "I stole my last stash. Ran out. Might have some Xanax back at my place."

"It's fine," Celia said.

"Imogene, how about you let us have a date night, huh?"

"We just decided to have somebody killed, and you're in the mood for love?"

"Please." He gave her puppy dog eyes and a pouted bottom lip.

Imogene made a noise like a hiccup and gave him a hug. "God, you're cute. Hope your head feels okay in the morning."

Ian said his bathtub was maybe a little too dirty for an actual bath, but he had another idea. After cleaning a handful of his shaggy black hair from the drain, he started the shower and peeled off his damp clothes. "It'll be like sitting in a rainstorm." He smiled.

Celia followed him naked into the shower. He sat with his back against the tub, opposite the faucet side, and she laid with her back against him. His long, tan arms wrapped around her. He doused her shoulder in kisses as the lukewarm water rinsed the salt from their bodies. He was right; Celia thought it did feel like a rainstorm.

"You're not shaking anymore."

"Hunh?" He said into her hair.

"Like you were in the ocean."

He made a fractured happy noise. "I was terrified."

She rubbed her thumb over his forearm. "How did it feel?"

He paused. "Familiar."

"Will you do it again?"

He kissed the side of her head. "Only if you're with me."

Celia felt tingly. "That makes me very happy."

He held her tighter.

"I don't think I was ever very happy…until I met you."

"I'm sorry I took so long. But I'm glad you had David Bowie."

She chuckled. "I've hidden in movies all my life. Reality just sucked too much, so I watched all my movies and pretended the movies were my life. I was Vivian. I was Leia—"

"Especially in *Return of the Jedi*."

She hid her smile in his bicep. "Now, I realize I was just living other people's lives. And they weren't even real people."

Ian cleared his throat. "Why did you really quit school?"

She'd blamed it on her parents' death—that was what she told people, and they seemed to understand. Right after the funeral, she was so accustomed to "poor you" faces. When she said she was quitting the University of Miami, those faces turned to "we understand."

"I quit school because I didn't fit. Not with the other students. Not in the classrooms. It was just like high school all over again, except I was paying to be tortured."

"But you wanted to be a marine biologist."

"Maybe." She sighed. "Or maybe I just picked that because it meant I got to be close to the sea. I've never really wanted to be anything."

"Except loved."

She tilted her head up at Ian. "I didn't say that out loud."

"You didn't need to."

She rolled over on top of him. Their bodies squelched and smacked beneath their faux rainfall, and she kissed him.

CHAPTER TWENTY

Celia needed to focus. She needed to solve the Danny situation, and yet, her mind was filled with fantasies about her new favorite feature of Ian's.

Hint: it wasn't his bellybutton.

Following their makeshift shower rainstorm/make out session-turned sex, she barely slept all day. Neither did Ian, to the point where he finally said, "Celia, I can't feel my legs." Still, she couldn't sleep, so she just pet him and watched him sleep and considered all the additional things she wanted to do with his body. The girl had it bad.

That evening, they arrived at Dr. Savage's office a little early to give themselves time to regroup. Ian looked like a walking zombie due to not only Celia's daytime ministrations but also to a jumping that occurred right before they left his apartment.

The waiting room wasn't empty as usual. No, in fact, Dr. Savage's human was there, sitting cross-legged in a corner chair. He smiled up at them over a copy of *Garden and Gun*. He was probably late twenties and maybe a little young for a two-hundred-year-old vampire. Celia thought Dr. Savage's human was almost too good-looking—or maybe just boring good-looking, too traditional. He had nothing on her Ian.

The pretty boy didn't speak but went back to reading his magazine.

Ian and Celia sat on the couch opposite him. She put her hand on Ian's knee, and he jumped, having dozed off already.

"Hey," she whispered.

"Mm," he replied.

"I'm sorry."

"For what?" He rubbed his eyes and yawned.

"For keeping you awake all day."

"No, it was…" He smirked. "Yeah."

She squeezed his leg, hard. "See, you're not even coherent. I need you coherent."

"I'm coherent." He raised his voice to talk to the other human. "Excuse me. Do you know if there's any coffee around here?"

Pretty Boy chuckled. "Rayna doesn't believe in caffeine."

"Huh."

"She's got tea."

"That works," Ian said through a stifled yawn.

"No." The other human smiled. "It's, like, herbal."

"Oh."

"I'm Dean."

"Ian." He paused. "This is Celia."

"I know." Dean nodded at her and went back to reading.

Ian looked at Celia and shrugged.

A minute later, Dr. Savage's office door opened, and it was that hot chick, Katarina, crying…again. Celia wondered, what was with all the crying? What the hell did a girl who looked like her have to cry about anyway? Then again, with Celia's new clothes and Ian on her arm, she probably looked like she had it all together, too, when point of fact, she was planning to have someone murdered. Celia realized beauty didn't get you anywhere.

Katarina didn't lunge for Ian again, at least, although Celia did notice Dean in the corner. He put his magazine down and watched her pass and didn't start reading again until the pretty blonde vamp had left the building. Then, he whistled a little.

The doc smiled when she saw Ian and Celia on her couch. "How nice to see you both."

Ian stood up first and circled the table to shake her hand. Celia was impressed by the forcefulness of his movements, considering he'd been asleep three minutes prior.

Dr. Savage took his hand. They were the same height what with her five-inch-heel Louboutins. "Couple's session tonight?" She glanced at Celia.

"If that's all right." Celia stood in her light green baby doll dress and ran her hands over the fabric.

"Sure." She let go of Ian's hand. "Could I have a moment with you alone first, Celia?"

She nodded and followed Dr. Savage inside. She offered tea, which Celia declined. It was not a night for tea. Dr. Savage crossed her mile-long legs and put on an apparently new set of sexy specs, these in a shade of royal blue. "Ian looks tired. You haven't been feeding on him too much, have you?"

"No. I think I'm just a sex addict."

One of Dr. Savage's eyebrows lifted. "Oh."

"What did you want to talk to me about alone?"

"Has Danny left your apartment?"

"We're working on that," Celia said.

"So you have a plan?"

Celia folded her fingers into knots. "It's sort of Ian's plan."

"Good." She didn't reach for her leather bound book. "Do you think it'll work?"

From what she understood, murder was usually pretty effective, so she said, "Yes."

"Good." She nodded. "You said Danny was from New York."

"Yeah."

"How old do you think he is, Celia?"

She shrugged. "Old? I mean, not as old as you, but, well, he's a lot stronger than me and even Imogene, and he wears old clothes."

"As in holey?"

"Like a priest?"

"No. Like with holes in it?"

"Oh. No. I mean his style is from a swing-dancing flick. Dapper."

For a second, Celia thought Dr. Savage had turned to stone. She just sat there, staring at her, head tilted slightly left. She didn't move, didn't breathe, and didn't blink. The only sound was that of the doc's fountain tinkling beneath the shuttered window that overlooked St. Arthur's Circle. Beneath that, Celia heard a low rumbling to her right; she guessed Ian and Dean were chatting in the waiting room. She fidgeted until the couch farted, which woke Dr. Savage from her creep-tastic trance.

"I'm sorry." Dr. Savage cleared her throat. "I'm not feeling very well. Could we reschedule?"

Celia left the office dejected and heard sad music in her head.

In the waiting room, Dean had moved so he and Ian were sitting on opposite sides of the couch. They laughed about something. Celia stomped her foot to get her boyfriend's attention. Then, she sighed. "Dr. Savage isn't feeling well. We need to reschedule."

"Oh." Ian stood up. "Okay." He looked like he'd just won the Tour de France.

Dean stood up, too. "Hey, man, can I get your number?"

"Yeah, it'd be great to hang out sometime."

Celia gawked, but she shouldn't have been surprised. Ian could conceivably charm the habit off a nun. Of course he would make a new best friend in three minutes flat.

After the boys exchanged digits, Ian and Celia headed to the alley where their bikes were parked. As he unlocked his chain, he looked up at her. "Decapitation."

"Electric chair," she said.

"Hmm?"

"I thought we were just naming forms of execution."

"We are. It's how you kill a vampire. Decapitation and sunlight."
He kissed her nose.

"How do you know?"

He bent down to unlock her chain, too. "I asked Dean."

"Dean knew that?"

"Yeah."

"And he just told you?"

"I asked; he told." Ian put both their chains in Celia's bike basket.

"Huh. And I kind of thought tonight was a complete loss."

"You said Dr. Savage is sick?"

Celia shrugged. "She got all funny when I was talking about
Danny. Then, she booted me."

He nodded. "Dean said she has a really bad temper."

Celia's upper lip twitched. "He talked about her?"

"Sure, I mean, she's his girlfriend."

She didn't climb on her powder blue bike. Instead, she said,
"Want to get a drink?"

They ended up back at the Daiquiri Deck, where Celia ordered
what she considered her usual: Kryptonite. Ian ordered a Redbull and
vodka, tall. They sat on the balcony overlooking the glitzy shop
where Celia bought her first pair of pumps. Tourists milled about
below them like hordes of clicking deathwatch beetles.

"What else did he tell you about Dr. Savage?"

"She likes expensive shoes and went to Cornell." He yawned.

"That's all?"

"Sweetie, you were gone for, like, five seconds."

"And yet you found time to learn about decapitation?"

"It was the second thing I asked." He slurped on his drink, and
she was momentarily distracted by the pucker of his lips.

"Uh…" She shook her head to physically dislodge a couple choice images from earlier that day. "What was the first?"

"If there was a troupe of vampire assassins on call in Lazaret. He said he didn't know."

"Does Dean think you want to kill me now?"

"I wouldn't think so." He smiled sleepily.

"How does Dean know the answer to that question anyway?"

"Rayna probably told him."

"You're calling her Rayna now?"

He chuckled and glanced out into the street.

Celia put her hand on his cheek. "You have a huge hickie."

"Thanks." Even though he smiled, his bright eyes wandered.

"What is it, Ian?"

"We can't have someone killed, Celia."

She took his hand. "I know."

"So what are we going to do?"

She chewed her bottom lip. "Have another round?"

Two hours later, biking home was interesting. Despite years of training, Ian almost tumbled twice. Celia, on the other hand, bit it right into a hydrangea bush, which made her man laugh like a little girl.

She wasn't surprised to find Imogene's convertible in the Sleeping Gull parking lot. She was surely chewing on Ian's furniture by then, waiting for their "Kill Danny" report, which, sadly, was no longer "Kill Danny" but somewhere in the ballpark of "What the fuck are we going to do?" Celia felt like they were going in circles. Then, she realized Ian was actually circling her, showing off his speed. Was he sober already? The man's metabolism was more miraculous than immortality.

They locked their bikes up, and Ian lifted her, kicking and screaming, over his shoulder. He only paused and put her down when they noticed the front door to her apartment was wide open but silent inside. At least Danny and Vixen weren't *murdering each other*, but the silence was perhaps more off-putting. They stuck their heads around the corner.

Danny was on the couch, half-dressed, with a can of beer in his hand which he raised to them in salute. It was not a friendly salute. On the living room floor was Vixen. Her little pink dress rode up in the back so they could see the bottom of her ass cheeks. She straddled what appeared to be two barefoot male human legs, although Celia assumed an entire torso was also attached. A chick was on the floor, too, staring at the ceiling.

Celia didn't realize the girl was dead until Ian threw up over the side of the porch. Vixen's head popped up at the sound. She looked back at Celia. Her face was covered in blood. Her eyes were blown black, and she smiled a fanged-tooth grin.

Celia explained all this to Imogene as Ian continued to vomit in the privacy of his bathroom.

"Do you think he's bulimic?"

"No," Celia said.

"So they are killing people. And now, they're doing it in your house."

"With the door open."

"Right." Imogene nodded. She had half her frizzy hair up in a painted purple clip the size of Texas. She had her red sunglasses snug on her face. Her lips were black, as were her fingernails. Celia found the sight of her friend's familiar combat boots comforting. "Did you find out how to kill a vampire?"

"Ian doesn't think we should do it anymore."

She lowered her glasses to the tip of her skinny nose. "Ask him again now."

"He's busy," Celia said.

Imogene stood up. "Ian!" She opened the bathroom door without knocking.

Ian was on the floor with his head resting on the edge of the bathtub. His hickie-covered neck was fully exposed, and he was the color of moldy cheese.

"Hey, dude, how you feeling?"

"Redbull tastes worse coming back up," he said.

"How do you feel about Danny and Vixen?"

He lifted his head. "What tools do you need to decapitate someone?" He belched.

CHAPTER TWENTY-ONE

Imogene drove them to a garden center in Lazaret the following night. On the drive over, Celia asked, "Why a garden center?" As she stood in aisle eleven with Ian's hand clutched to her wrist, she didn't wonder anymore. Axes, saws, and pitchforks surrounded them. She didn't even look toward a row of expensive and multi-purposed chainsaws.

What a holy mess that would be.

Ian's hand was literally a claw on her forearm. "I'm out of weed," he said. She thought maybe the smell of fertilizer and mulch was like a pothead's Post-it?

He didn't look like a pothead that night. He looked preppy. He was in a navy blue polo and nice, dark jeans with flip-flops. Celia was just glad he wasn't barefoot, the way the man avoided shoes. He didn't have on cologne, so the smell of his blood wrapped around her like a poltergeist's hug.

To their left, Imogene made a karate noise—Bruce Lee on helium. She had a scythe the size of Chile's coastline in her hand, and she seemed to be doing a break dance battle with an invisible antagonist.

"Imogene."

She paused. "What?"

Ian made a sort of burp-choke noise. Celia really hoped he wasn't going to vomit in aisle eleven. He let go of her wrist and ran both shaking hands through his hair. "I'm going to go look at...uh..." He wandered away.

Celia crossed her arms at Imogene. "What are you, the grim reaper?"

"I wish. Wah!" She swung the scythe around over her head.

"You really think that's the most practical choice?"

"No, but it's cool." She did a high kick.

Celia looked around and picked up a big, red ax. She wondered if she could really do it—really kill someone. Could she honestly swing an ax and just chop Danny's head off? Would it feel justified or just...awful? Celia Merkin, who'd never done drugs in high school, never had sex until college, who'd really never done anything terrible in her whole life, was now considering bloody murder to save her boyfriend's life. She closed her eyes and shook the ax toward Imogene. "What about this?"

Imogene shrugged. "Sure. Whatever." She put the scythe down and moved in exactly the wrong direction. "Oooo, chainsaw!"

Celia found Ian sitting outside on the ground between two huge potted palms. He chewed his fingernails.

"You okay?"

"Yeah." He took her hand and pulled himself up. "So are we going with the scythe?"

"I was thinking ax."

He nodded.

"Ian, you're not all right, are you?"

He crossed his arms and touched his mouth. "I was thinking about my shark attack. Visualizing it. You know, movies try to make things look real, but..." He shook his head. "They don't quite...I didn't realize how much blood I had in my body until that day. This is going to be really messy."

"Oh."

"I was trying to think of a way for me to maybe wear a barf bag as a necklace?" He gestured to his throat and shoulders.

"Ian." Celia put her hands on his chest. "Vampires are dead, right? So maybe we don't have that much blood."

"Right. Uh-huh." He took a deep breath and closed his eyes. "So an ax?"

"Maybe."

"How about this?" Imogene shouted from down the aisle. She held a pair of garden shears that could have beheaded an elephant.

"Oh, God." Ian bent over and put his head between his knees.

They drove home empty-handed with Ian's head resting in Celia's lap in the back seat. She ran her fingers over his clammy forehead and touched his hair. Both motions seemed to calm him, as she knew they would.

The pads of Celia's fingers tickled the sides of his neck. She was starving. She knew she needed to feed, but this was not a good time for Ian. She had given Dr. Savage's blood connection a call, so they had some of what they referred to as "Shaman-Blessed Shit" because it tasted like blood mixed with sage and formaldehyde. Needless to say, Imogene threatened to go on a lot more of her "dates."

They pulled into the parking lot of the Sleeping Gull just as Ian's cell phone rang. He sat up and glanced at the caller ID. "It's my mom."

Celia nodded, and the three of them made their way to Ian's place as he said, "Hey, mom. Flu bug is almost gone…"

On the front porch, Celia watched Ian walk past them and head toward the beach. Then, she noticed that her apartment—for the first time since Danny's arrival—was dark.

"Huh." Celia stopped walking.

"What?"

She gestured to her closed front door.

Imogene smirked. "Do you think they left?"

"I don't know."

"Let's see." She reached for the doorknob, but Celia stopped her.

"Imogene, what if there are two dead bodies on the floor?"

"Well. Let's see." She pushed the door open.

There were no dead bodies, just darkness and the smell of stale blood. Imogene wandered further inside while Celia lingered over the place where, the night before, two humans were deaded.

She wondered what was done with the bodies.

"The assholes aren't here, but they're not gone for good," Imogene said. "Their clothes are still all over the bedroom. Along with," she lifted her lip in disgust, "evidence of their activities. Wonder if they have any real blood in the fridge." She *clomp-clomped,* and Celia followed.

The inside of her fridge was like El Dorado, except the gold was, well, blood.

"Holy shit."

"I thought Danny said they were low on cash," Celia said. She filched a bag of A-positive and stuck it under her shirt.

"Apparently not." Imogene grabbed two bags of B-negative.

Ian cleared his throat from the living room. Celia shuffled toward him, and he looked amused but in the way you're amused when you lose your house, your dog, and your favorite underwear all in one day.

He still held his cell phone in-hand. "There's something you should probably see on the beach," he said brightly. Celia felt like it had finally happened: dating a vampire had pushed his sanity off a cliff. He was sinking, like Artax in *The Neverending Story.*

"Ian?"

He just shook his head and turned toward the water.

Imogene and Celia followed. Imogene shamelessly slurped as they went, while Celia kept her blood supply carefully hidden. Ian's flip-flops were forgotten outside his front door. He trudged barefoot through the sand, lit gold by Heidi's cheap walkway spotlights. Then, beyond the light, he kept walking down the beach until he took a left and stopped.

He loudly cleared his throat.

"Oh, shit," Celia said.

Sure, it was possible some kids got bored and decided to construct huge piles of sand about three feet by six. Sure, maybe they decided to stop at two piles. Maybe one of the kids even cut off a manicured finger and left it poking out.

"I was wondering what they did with the bodies." Imogene slurped.

Ian fell on his ass in the sand. "We can't just leave them like this."

"What do you suggest? Viking funeral?"

He rested his head in his hands.

Despite Imogene's less than helpful comment, Ian was right. They couldn't leave two dead bodies hardly buried on the beach.

"We'll put them in my closet," Celia said.

They looked at her like she was a total nutter.

"What? Maybe Danny won't notice."

"He'll notice." Imogene sighed.

"Fine, then, we'll put them in Ian's closet."

Ian made a petite choking sound.

"Celia!" Imogene put her hand in his hair and started brushing his curls. If there was ever a way to calm a man...

"I'm sorry," Celia said. "I just want all of this to go away."

"I'll put them in my trunk."

"Really?" Celia watched Imogene continue to rake fingers through her boyfriend's hair.

"Just for a little while. I don't want my trunk to smell."

Celia ran up and hugged her, and she flailed. She pushed at Celia's shoulders until she realized Celia wasn't letting go. She felt like a fragile old man in Celia's arms, even though Celia knew better.

"Okay, okay, gross. Enough." She stepped back and adjusted her frizzy hair. "Ian, I need you to run interference."

"Okay."

"I need you to stand up first."

"Uh-huh." He didn't move.

Celia knelt down next to him and ran her hand down his cheek. "Ian?"

"She had nice fingernails," he muttered.

Celia glanced back at the lone fingertip that had escaped its shallow grave. "Is your brain going to explode?"

"Something's misfiring upstairs, yeah."

Celia went for the obvious move and continued Imogene's earlier ministrations of his black hair. "Sweetie, I love you."

"I love you, too."

"You want me to smack him?" Imogene said.

Celia looked up at her. "What do you mean by 'run interference'?"

"Well, we gotta drag these people past your sonar bat-hearing, bat-shit crazy landlady. We need a diversion." She nodded at Ian.

"How is he a diversion?"

Ian tilted his head into the palm of Celia's hand like a cat.

"Heidi thinks he's cute. Have him go talk to her."

"Do you see him right now? He can't talk to anyone."

"Ian." Imogene knelt on his other side. "What's the capital of Russia?"

"Moscow."

She paused. "I have no idea if that's right. What's, um…" She waved a hand at Celia. "Give me a fucking *Jeopardy!* question."

"Oh, uh, who's the Greek god of war?"

"Ares," he said. Finally, his eyes cleared. He looked at Celia. "Run interference?"

Imogene snapped her fingers. "And he's back! Okay, dude, go hang with Heidi. Watch some *True Crime*. Give us, like, twenty minutes, okay?"

"Okay." He stood and brushed sand from his jeans. The girls joined him as he said, "I'm sorry I lost my shit for a second."

"Don't apologize." Celia leaned up on her toes and kissed him. "I'm sorry I suggested putting corpses in your closet."

He shrugged. "Under the circumstances…"

"Get going." Imogene shoved him in the shoulder, and he walked slowly up the beach. They waited until they heard Heidi's high-pitched voice followed by a closed front door before beginning their archaeological dig. That was what Celia pretended it was, anyway. She pretended she was in Pompeii and she was some super cool character from *Indiana Jones*. She had to pretend, because the reality—she was digging up the dead bodies of two humans killed by her maker's whore—was way too much to contemplate without a nosebleed.

They successfully dragged the rotting corpses to Imogene's trunk without interruption. Sure, the bodies smelled like death. They left behind a trail of sand and maybe a few drops of stale blood. Other than that, mission successful, although Celia did hate to muss the back of such a nice car. Also, in the summer heat, those bodies wouldn't keep long.

Imogene and Celia returned to Ian's apartment, where they fell on the floor and reached for their hidden blood bags. Imogene slurped hers like a college kid hits a keg, while Celia was more mindful of the A-positive, considering they had only Shaman-Blessed Shit in Ian's fridge.

"He's a hell of a guy," Imogene said.

"I know."

"If we get through this, you'll live happily ever after."

Ian's door opened, and there he stood. For a skinny guy, he sure did fill a doorway—probably due to his height and the excessive expanse of his hair. His blue eyes glittered like fake diamonds at Kmart. He slowly lifted his arm, and there, between two long fingers, was a small, tightly wrapped joint.

"She gave me weed," he said.

"Hooray!" Imogene chanted. She clapped her bony fingers.

"Not all is lost." He kicked the door shut behind him with his bare foot. Celia smiled as she watched him head to the kitchen and return with a little blue lighter. He sat in the middle of his couch and invited them both to join, which they did. Celia cuddled closer than necessary, due to his smile: that massive grin that first made her fall in love, that and his smell and his neck and his…everything.

He took a short drag as he lit up, and Imogene leaned forward to swallow his exhale. "Wow, Heidi has good shit," she said, licking her lips.

Ian passed the joint to her. "She's got some local dude with good hookups."

"How does a senior citizen have good hookups?" Imogene took a pull and passed it to Celia.

She shook her head. "You guys share. I don't want to take it from you."

Ian leaned his head back on the couch. "Just have a hit."

She reached for the joint, and as she did, the front door pounded open. Celia thought, *This is it.* The cops had finally uncovered their nonexistent hydroponics operation.

Instead, it was Danny in a slick suit, perfect hair, and a fresh shave. He looked shiny and new.

"We just got home! I thought I smelled weed," he said, and with that, he plucked the joint from Celia's fingers, took a drag, winked at Ian, and left.

With the joint.

They all just sat there, staring. Something truly horrible had just happened. Celia was worried Ian was going to crack. Instead, he stood up and walked to his stereo. He pushed a couple buttons until Bob Marley started telling them "everything's gonna be all right." Ian stood there, taking deep breaths. Then, he turned around and smacked his huge hands together.

"I want to go swimming in the ocean," he said.

Oh my God, he really has lost it!

Of course, Imogene was on her feet in no time. "Just the ticket." She grabbed the bottom of his polo shirt and tugged upwards until she had him bare from the waist up. "Merk, this is what we need." She headed for the front door, peeling off layers as she went. By the time Imogene hit the porch, she was in nothing but panties.

Celia remained on the couch. "You want to go...swimming? Not just standing and shaking in the ocean?"

"It's time I went swimming, Mermaid." He extended his hand to her.

They walked down to the beach hand-in-hand. Once there, they discarded their clothes. Ian kept on his boxer briefs, and Celia kept on bra and underwear. They could already hear Imogene splashing and diving around amid the waves. She made the occasional hooting noise.

The water was warm on Celia's bare toes. Her hand in Ian's was even warmer. She looked up at him. He still seemed a little freaked, but he wasn't trembling. He was breathing a little fast for someone who'd just walked twenty feet. Then, he did something inexplicable. He winked at her, let go of her hand, and ran into the breaking waves. She laughed when he did a headfirst dive into a crush of white. He came up spitting saltwater, calling her name. She ran to him, and as usual, the waves momentarily eased her pain.

She had to swim fast to catch up, but when she did, she jumped on Ian's back and wrapped her arms around his neck. He paddled them out, past Imogene, past where they could touch, and together, they tread water.

"Holy shit," he said, laughing.

"You're a good swimmer."

"I damn well should be." His eyes looked out into the black of open water. "I can't believe I'm out here right now."

Celia went under water and came up against his chest. She kissed his salty chin. "Nothing will hurt you. Ever."

He crushed her mouth in a kiss and wrapped his arms around her until they both started to sink. They paddled back to where they could touch, where they found Imogene, floating on her back and staring at the stars.

"We need to talk strategy," she said.

"Strategy?" Celia wrapped Ian in her legs and arms and licked his neck.

"Well, we can't just go over there swinging axes," she continued. "I think we need to get them drunk. Really, really drunk."

"Drift Inn?" Celia suggested.

Imogene nodded. "Mm. Good call. Best place for blackouts."

"Okay." Ian paused. "So when?"

Imogene sat up, and her dark blue eyes were black. "Tomorrow. We get 'em drunk, bring them back here, and chop their heads off."

"Shit," Celia whispered.

CHAPTER TWENTY-TWO

It was a dark and stormy night.

Really, though, it was raining elephants and hippos. Thunderclaps shook the Sleeping Gull Apartments, and the electricity flickered.

During the day, while Celia slept, Ian went back to the garden shop and bought an ax, garden shears (for Imogene), and ponchos. Celia told him she really doubted they'd have time to put on ponchos before the decapitation, but he insisted because he was Ian and he vomited a lot. With the rainstorm, they at least had a viable excuse to wear them.

Celia stood in Ian's bathroom doorway and watched him get ready. She'd never seen him "get ready" before. He was freshly showered and naked with shaving cream like whipped dessert on his face.

"I was thinking." He ran the razor down his cheek. "Maybe they'll just turn to ash."

"Yeah?" She was surprised she could manage even one-word answers, what with her boyfriend standing there, clothes-free. She wanted to lick the V where his hips met...

Damn it, Celia! Get it under control!

They were preparing to kill people, and Celia still wanted to jump Ian's bones.

"Like, in *Buffy*," he continued, "when she would stake vampires, they would just go up in a cloud of ash, right?"

"I have no idea," Celia said.

He rinsed the razor in the sink. "I think it was *Buffy*."

Thunder rolled.

The door to Ian's apartment opened, and Celia took a step back to see Imogene under the shelter of a slick, black umbrella. She stepped inside and whistled. Celia sighed and closed her naked boyfriend in his bathroom.

She tossed her soaking wet umbrella on Ian's couch. "I'm telling you, Merk, I don't know how you keep your fangs out of his neck every five seconds."

"I prefer his chest."

Imogene leaned over in a dress the size of a teacup: strapless, gold, with dark purple leather pumps. "Whoa, cool." She went for the grotesquely oversized garden shears still in a huge garden center bag. She snapped them open and closed, twice, in the air. "I call these."

Ian came out of the bathroom cleanly shaved and in boxer briefs. Imogene dropped the shears and gave him an indecent hug.

"Imogene," he muttered into her hair.

"Cut it out," Celia said.

She stepped back. "Hey, if things go tits up, I just wanted to have one more feel of man flesh."

He nodded. "That makes sense."

Both girls watched his cute, muscular ass head to the bedroom.

"They're not home, by the way," Imogene said.

"Huh?"

"Wipe the drool off your chin."

Celia did.

"Danny and Vixen. They're not home."

"Oh."

The light above them flickered and then went out. The rain on the roof sounded like goblins with little hands and feet trying to get inside.

"Shit," Imogene whispered.

From the bedroom came a blinding flash of light.

"Ian." Celia covered her face.

"What? It's dark," he said.

"So you harnessed the power of the sun?"

Celia glanced out from behind her hands. "It's his *X-Files* flash light."

"Huh?"

"Mulder and Scully always had these huge flashlights."

Imogene shook her head, lost.

Celia sighed. "How are we even friends?"

Imogene smiled. "I ask myself that every day."

"I don't take this as a good sign," Ian said. He was, at least, almost fully dressed: dark jeans and a black button-down, half buttoned. Apparently, he thought murder was a dress up occasion.

"I don't believe in signs," Imogene said.

Then, with a flash of lightning and a roll of thunder, Ian's front door swung open. A horrendous figure stood in the doorway—tall, in a space helmet. Its skin was like beef jerky, and it had hands like claws.

They all screamed.

Then Heidi stepped in the line of Ian's flashlight. "What the hell is the matter with y'all?"

"Jesus, Heidi," Imogene gasped. "I thought the damn aliens had landed."

Their landlady made a disgusted face, but truly, in the dark, with The Wig and over-tan flesh, she did look like a mix between "Take me to your leader" and a zombie corpse.

"My TV just shut down," she said. "What am I gonna do now?"

Heidi without *True Crime*? The world might not survive.

"Hang with Ian." Imogene was already making her way to the front door.

"What?" he said.

"Just stay here for a minute. Merk. Move it." Celia noticed Imogene took the garden shears with her.

She leaned up on her toes and kissed Ian's cheek. He smelled like spicy aftershave. "Be right back. Stay here."

Outside, they inched beneath the overhang to avoid getting soaked through and through. As usual, the door to Celia's apartment wasn't locked, and it was silent inside—as far as she could tell. The rain now sounded like a hammer pounding stakes through the ceiling.

"Imogene, what are we doing?"

"Investigating." She leaned the shears by the front door and walked to the kitchen.

"You're not investigating. You're drinking their blood."

"So? The electricity is out. It's just gonna go bad."

Celia couldn't argue there. She followed Imogene into the darkened kitchen and caught a bag of flying A-positive right in the face.

Imogene jumped on the counter and slurped. Celia was impressed her friend could be so acrobatic in stilettos. "Wonder where they are," she said.

"Probably killing a bunch of people."

"Mm." She nodded. "This is some seriously good shit. Danny must have paid extra."

"Again, how?" Celia unscrewed the top of her blood bag. "They don't have any money."

She shrugged, and thunder shook the apartment. Over the sound of the storm, Celia heard her front door open and smelled Ian.

Imogene leapt from the counter. "You told him to stay put."

They stepped around the corner, and Ian stood in the doorway. Outside, the rain came in sideways and soaked his jeans. He took

236

rapid, stuttering steps to keep from tripping as he was shoved through the doorframe. Only then did Celia realize he wasn't alone. In fact, there was a whole mini-mob on her front porch.

Danny was behind Ian in a black suit, similarly sodden, with one of Ian's kitchen knives in his hand. He shoved Ian's back hard against Celia's entertainment center, which sent a half-dozen VHS tapes skittering across the stained floor. Celia went to move, but Imogene's hand stopped her, because blood dealer Steve came in next, wearing hospital scrubs. He held their ax in one hand, Ian's *X-Files* flashlight in the other. Vixen followed the midget, who placed Ian's flashlight on Celia's coffee table.

"Bitch is wearing one of our ponchos," Imogene said, but Vixen didn't look like she heard. In fact, Vixen looked like she'd popped sixteen acid pills and called it a day—and she was covered in blood. They were all covered in blood, except Ian and Heidi, who weaved inside in her cat puke robe, obviously glamoured, and sat on Celia's couch. Her blond wig was sideways and, due to the rain, closely resembled a dead animal with a bad perm.

"Hey, Red." Danny used one hand to push the wet, dark hair off his forehead. He kept his other hand wrapped tightly around the kitchen knife pressed to Ian's throat.

"Don't call me that," Celia said.

"You must be the angry midget," Imogene snarled. "Steve."

The light from the flashlight reflected off the ceiling and made him glow. Steve looked at her with black eyes and blood on his chin. "You must be the purple-haired glamour goddess. Heard you can glamour people from ten feet away."

"I can do a lot more than that…"

"Enough!" Danny shouted over the storm.

Vixen walked barefoot on shaky ankles to Celia's chair and sat down. She hugged her knees and rocked forward and back.

Celia stared at her. "How much blood has she had?"

"Gee, I don't know, baby. How many neighbors did you have?"

"You killed all my neighbors?"

Danny's fangs were stained red. "Except her. Since you're so buddy-buddy with the landlady, thought you'd want to watch us do her."

Celia glanced at Heidi, then at Ian, who despite the knife at his neck, seemed incredibly calm.

"Sit." Danny nodded to the couch, and when the girls didn't move, he pushed the knife against Ian's throat until Ian pressed his lips together and closed his eyes.

"Okay!" Celia grabbed onto Imogene's arm and pulled her along. They sat on either side of Heidi, who didn't acknowledge their presence but just stared straight ahead with glazed, drunken eyes.

Steve kept his black eyes trained on them as he said, "Let's taste the goods."

God, no. Celia knew what that meant. "Wait—"

"Relax, baby." Danny winked. "Just a little sample. And I wouldn't make any sudden moves or I'll cut his throat."

"If you bite me," Ian said, "I will tear your teeth out with my bare hands."

Danny smacked Ian's cheek teasingly.

Steve smirked. "I like your pretty human. Hopefully, he'll stay alive long enough for us to have some fun." He took hold of the front of Ian's shirt and tugged until all the buttons flew loose. Celia's usual feeding spot was revealed, and Steve pushed his thumb against the remnants of an old bite mark, to the left of Ian's nipple. "I'd go for his chest, too." Steve sneered.

Celia felt rage like she'd never felt before. Sure, she'd once beat the shit out of Vixen. But in that moment, she literally thought she might be able to decapitate Danny and Steve in one fell swoop, with mind power alone, especially when Danny slashed the knife across Ian's chest.

It was a small seam, maybe two inches from left to right, but Ian winced, which made Celia call his name. A drop of blood dribbled between his pecs, and midget Steve leaned forward, licked. Danny licked the knife in his hand, and they nodded.

"That is the berries."

"I don't even know what that means," Steve said.

Meanwhile, at the smell of fresh, expensive, human blood, Vixen covered her ears and shook her head.

Imogene leaned against the opposite arm of Celia's couch. "Dude, what's wrong with your girl?"

Danny looked at her. "She's just OD-ing a little. She'll be fine."

Celia kept her eyes trained on Ian, whose eyes found hers. In the tint of the flashlight, his cheekbones looked like jagged cliffs. His eyebrows wrinkled together, but he smiled softly, as if reassuring her everything was all right—except everything was not all right.

"What are you going to do?" Celia said.

"Well, we're going to kill you and the bearcat and make your boyfriend a blood slave." Danny nodded to the ax in Steve's short-fingered hands. "Thanks for buying an ax. It'll make it easier to chop off your heads."

"You will never get close enough to touch my head," Imogene said.

Danny handed the knife to Steve who happily pressed it against Ian's Adam's apple. "I don't know if you've noticed, bearcat, but I'm older, stronger, and faster than you."

"Bring it, old man."

"Wait! Just stop." Celia tried to sound commanding. "Money. You want money, right? I have money."

"*Had* money, baby." Danny used his hands to style his hair. "Vixen and I spent all of it on blood and booze."

"No, you didn't."

"The four hundred in your kitchen." He gestured with his arms. "The couple thousand clams under your mattress. We spent it. It's gone."

Celia shook her head and continued. "There's more. Lots more. A little less than two million."

Danny put his hands on his slim hips, and although she couldn't hear him over the thunder, she saw him mouth the words, "Bullshit."

"Really. I inherited it from my parents' life insurance."

Danny stood there, considering. He glanced back at Steve. "How much can we make off tall drink of water?"

"Depends on how long he stays alive." Steve licked Ian's chest again.

"Your best guess."

"However long he stays alive, it takes work to sell blood, right?" Celia shouted. "I can just give you the money, free and clear. And you can let Ian go."

Danny started to pace. He had his hand on his chin. "Two mill," he muttered.

Celia looked at Imogene and noticed her eyes danced back and forth between Ian and the wall by the front door—Ian, wall, Ian, wall. Then, Celia saw what she was looking at, the garden shears. Celia wanted to say no—*hell, no*—not with a knife against Ian's skin, but Steve didn't have the knife on Ian's skin anymore. Steve was too busy licking Celia's boyfriend to remember the knife. She sort of shuddered, but Ian was the one whose long fingers clawed at the wall behind him. Maybe if Imogene took care of Steve, Celia could at least tackle Danny, cause a diversion, get the ax, and chop-chop. She thought it would probably be just two against two; Vixen didn't look like she would put up a fight. Yes, it could work, but then Danny kicked the bedroom door open playfully and spun around.

"You know, I think I'll take Ian."

There was no way Celia was going to let that happen. She no longer wondered whether or not she could kill someone; nope, Celia Merkin knew with certainty that murder was the order of the night, and she was willing to lose a limb if only to save Ian's life.

She nodded at Imogene and exploded. She let out a frightful battle cry and shot forward from her seat. Her body literally left the ground, and she soared like Superman, arms extended, in the direction of her shocked maker, who took several steps back to escape her vicious clutches.

But before she could reach him, there was a voice, a familiar voice, from the darkness of Celia's bedroom. "Skipper," the voice said, which made an already unsteady Danny spin around and catch a samurai sword to the throat. Celia landed on her stomach on the stained carpet and watched with glee as Danny's head flew through the air and landed like a rain-soaked beanbag on her coffee table.

She heard a loud snip to her left and turned. A shower of blood covered Ian's face as Steve's little midget noggin went the way of a dandelion head, followed by a fountain of blood that covered her boyfriend, their newly purchased garden shears, and Imogene. Blood even spurted up and hit the ceiling.

Once Steve's corpse joined Danny's on the floor, Imogene wiped her face with the back of her arm and said, "That was way messier than I expected."

Surprisingly, Ian didn't vomit. He just stood there with his eyes closed.

Celia sprung up, pointed her finger right in Danny's dead face, and shouted, "Big mistake! Big! Huge!" Then she puked.

Heidi sat up straight, looked around, and said, "You're never getting your deposit back."

Then, Dr. Rayna Savage and Dean the human stepped out of Celia's bedroom and joined their party.

"What...the...fuck..." Celia muttered through dry heaves.

As the storm calmed outside, Celia's therapist rearranged them on pieces of furniture. She put Vixen in Celia's bedroom, because the girl was so far gone, she didn't even notice Danny was dead. Heidi took her seat, and Dean handed Ian a towel and guided him to the couch next to Celia. Dean was also thoughtful enough to cover both decapitated heads with additional towels from Celia's bathroom, which was nice, since Danny staring at Celia without his body was kind of disconcerting, especially in the dark.

Ian put his hand on Celia's knee. "How bad do I look?"

He looked like he'd just gutted a grizzly bear. "Not bad," she said.

Imogene refused to let go of her garden shears. Blood coated her face, neck, and even tinted the edges of her hair. "Who the hell are you people?"

"Imogene." Celia cleared her throat. "This is my therapist, Dr. Rayna Savage."

"It's so nice to meet you, Imogene."

Imogene didn't take Dr. Savage's outstretched hand. "Is that a samurai sword?"

"Yes, it's my weapon of choice."

Imogene looked at the headless bodies on the floor, and then at Celia. "What the fuck is going on here, Merk?"

"I really have no idea."

"I do," Heidi hissed. "You're making a damn mess of my property."

Celia sighed.

Imogene gestured with the garden shears. "Why the fuck does your therapist look like Trinity from *The Matrix*?"

She really did. Her hair was pulled back in a brutal bun, and she was in head-to-toe skintight leather. Dean didn't look much different. He was Keanu Reeves to her Carrie-Ann Moss. All they were missing were the Ray-Bans.

"Imogene, will you please sit down?" Dr. Savage said. "I'd like to explain."

Imogene huffed and stomped to the kitchen, almost knocking both Dean and Dr. Savage over in the process. She came back with two bags full of blood and sat on the arm of Celia's couch to slurp.

"How can you eat right now?" Celia asked.

"How can you not?"

That was when Dr. Savage—if that was her real name—started talking. Apparently, Danny's real name was Skipper Penrod.

Imogene snickered. "I would have changed my name, too." *Slurp, slurp.*

"I was born to darkness in the early 1800s after having lost my husband to tuberculosis. I was nothing but a naïve young woman, so when I was turned, I went a little…" Dr. Savage frowned. "Crazy. I killed a lot of people." Dean put his hand on her shoulder. "Then, I met an older vampire, Monroe, who taught me how to control my tendencies. I only turned one human, ever."

"Danny," Ian said.

"I met Skipper in New York City in 1925," she explained. "He was a young man from a poor family near Tin Pan Alley; I was a psychology student at Cornell. We met at a jazz club, and well, one thing led to another…He really liked red hair."

"You don't have red hair," Celia said.

"I do. I dye it." Dr. Savage smiled.

Celia stared at her.

"I feel the dark hair makes me look more professional." She pressed her lips together. "Skipper and I had a true connection. He was very dependent on me, loving, sweet."

"Huh?" Celia gawked at the well-dressed headless corpse at her feet.

"Well, he changed. I was very wealthy, and he became obsessed with money. He swore he would never be poor again. He also had infidelity issues."

"No way." Imogene slurped.

"Skipper and I grew apart and eventually lost touch. I hadn't thought about him in decades. Then the word came that humans were ending up dead. It started in New Orleans, then New York, Vegas. Then, here, in Lazaret, of all places."

"You knew it was Danny," Celia said. "Skipper."

"I suspected as much, as most of the victims were redheads."

Celia gulped.

"Then, in our session, Celia, you started talking about Danny, and…" She shrugged. Celia would have felt so much better if she'd had on her wire rims so she could give her the "probing therapist look."

"What's with the samurai sword?" Imogene tossed her empty bag on Steve's dead body.

"Oh, I'm a hunter." Dr. Savage looked at Dean. "We both are. We met at a conference."

"What the hell kind of conference?"

"For slayers. There's one every year in Miami."

"You kill vampires?" Ian put his arm around Celia. "But, Dr. Savage, you *are* a vampire."

"We kill bad vampires," Dean said. "And sorry I couldn't be straight with you when you asked about assassins, man. We like to keep a low profile."

Ian nodded. "No hard feelings," he muttered.

"Vampires are not allowed to kill humans anymore, Ian," Dr. Savage said. "It's the modern age. We consider ourselves to be civilized."

"Uh-huh," he said. "Be honest, how much blood do I have on my face?"

"A bit."

Ian excused himself and headed for the bathroom, where Celia promptly heard him hurl.

"So part of your job," Celia said, "when you're not being a therapist…you hunt bad vampires?"

"Yes, although I do believe in therapy. I don't want you to think you should stop your sessions."

Imogene chuckled.

Celia eyed the mess on her floor. "What do we do with the bodies?"

Heidi spoke. "Oh, honey." Celia had forgotten she was even there. She pulled off her blond wig to reveal short, spikey, brown hair. "It's not hard to get rid of a body."

Dr. Savage extended her manicured hand. "I'm sorry, you are?"

Heidi shook her hand, twice. "The landlady. I ran into one of your kind over in Texas once. Had a hell of a time in the sack."

Imogene laughed like Butthead but stopped abruptly. "Shit, I have two dead humans in my trunk." Before Dr. Savage could reach for her sword, Imogene continued, "Danny and Vixen's mess. They left the bodies on the beach."

"Oh," Celia said, "and they murdered all my neighbors."

Heidi rolled her eyes. "There goes the neighborhood."

"Literally," Imogene said.

Dean nodded. "That could be a problem."

"Which part?" Celia asked. She really had no idea.

"Well, vampires are easy to get rid of. We just leave them on a roof and wait for sunrise. They'll burn up like firewood."

Celia was glad Ian wasn't back to hear that.

"I'll take care of it," Heidi said.

They all turned to stare at her landlady.

She sighed. "Go get that handsome, sensitive boy from the bathroom and buy him a drink. Drift Inn should be hopping about now."

Celia stood. "But Heidi—"

"No buts, young lady. Or whatever you are. Don't worry about me; I can handle myself." She kicked her slipper against Danny's shoulder. "Are you taking care of them, doc?"

"Gladly." Dr. Savage smiled. "It's been very nice to meet you, Heidi."

Heidi grumbled.

Celia sent Dean to the bathroom to take care of Ian as Imogene and Celia went to her car and dragged the now rotten bodies from her trunk and up to the apartments. They didn't have to worry about neighbors, because all Celia's neighbors were dead. The smell of fresh meat spun over the Sleeping Gull Apartments like a hurricane. The literal storm had passed, though. The sky was already clear, littered with silver stars.

As they walked back up on the porch, Imogene grabbed Celia's arm. "What the hell is Heidi gonna do?"

"Do you really want to ask her?"

Imogene stuck out her bottom lip and wrinkled one eye. "No, I guess not. Drift Inn?"

The group parted ways. Dean and Dr. Savage tossed all remnants of dead vampire into the back of their SUV. The trunk was covered in thick plastic. They were obviously professionals. They took Vixen with them—not to kill her; Dr. Savage said she wanted to "rehabilitate" the newbie vamp, just like Monroe had done for her all those years ago. Celia was all too happy to see the stripper go.

Ian went to his place and changed his shirt. He'd managed to wash all the blood from his face, but honestly, the last thing he looked like he needed was a drink. He was green as a mint sprig, which made Celia hug him until he couldn't breathe. He finally gasped "Celia," and she let go.

As they pulled away in Imogene's convertible, Heidi stood in the darkness and waved.

The Drift Inn was packed with stinky-smelling beach goers, half-homeless beach bums, and alcoholics. The usual bartender, angry Santa Claus, was there with a shirt that read "Poop," in white letters. Imogene used her powers of persuasion to get them three double pours of Jameson's. She had on one of Celia's t-shirts (way too big) to cover her blood-soaked dress. Although she'd washed her face, Celia could still smell blood in her friend's purple hair.

"Well," Imogene said.

Ian did the full double shot. "Problem solved."

Celia giggled, but then covered her mouth. It was not the time for laughter. Or was it?

Imogene did her usual Butthead chortle, and Ian was soon laughing so hard, salty tears pooled beneath his bright blue eyes. He laughed until he went silent, and the silent laugh meant he was hysterical, unable to stop. Celia put her arm around him and soon felt Imogene's arm over hers. They leaned together in a three-way hug until their collective laughter shook the barstools and earned them a suspicious glare from angry Santa.

They rolled like tumbleweed down the rabbit hole of inebriation.

Hours later, Imogene drove them back to the Sleeping Gull Apartments on Admiral Key. They were about a block away when they noticed the light. If Imogene's car clock hadn't read 2:30, Celia might have thought the sun was coming up. Then, they pulled into the parking lot and realized both rows of apartments were on fire.

They all climbed out and stood, staring. There was no fire truck yet, although they heard sirens in the distance. Imogene weaved on her feet, and Ian's mouth hung open.

Then Celia remembered. "Your *Star Wars* action figures…"

Ian blinked and looked down at her. He looked at her for a long time before he reached out and put his arm around her shoulders. He kissed her forehead and held her tight.

They had to step back when the fire truck arrived. The fire was fought, but the fire won. Their apartments were heaps of black, smoking rubble. There were cops there, too, who asked them questions. Ian explained they were tenants but had been out for the night. That was when they got the bad news—Bloody Betty had murdered all their neighbors. They didn't have to feign shock, because *who the hell was Bloody Betty?*

"Don't you ever watch *True Crime?*" the detective asked. He looked like an extra from *Miami Vice*. "Bloody Betty is one of the most prolific Black Widows in history. She's killed at least four husbands. A few others have gone missing, but she's never pulled anything like this. She's obviously escalating, and now, she's on the move again. She wears a wig to hide her identity." He leaned in close. "You're all very lucky you weren't home this evening, let me tell you."

Ian threw up a bottle of whiskey in the nearest bush.

CHAPTER TWENTY-THREE

She licked her name across Ian's lower abdomen and listened to him eat a slice of cold pizza. They were in the most expensive hotel in Lazaret—because they could. They were also on the floor, because the king-sized bed just hadn't been enough space for their sexing.

After getting the nod from the cops that they could leave the Sleeping Gull, they requested Imogene drive them to the Chantelle: a rich bitch hotel with crystal chandeliers, marble floors, and signed pictures of famous people in the bar—plus really heavy-duty velvet curtains in all the rooms. It would be such a bummer to go up in flames after all they'd gone through with Danny.

First, though, they picked up pizza at a twenty-four-hour joint near the beach, because Ian was starving and because Celia liked the smell of pizza.

Following a delicious bath in a swimming pool-sized basin in their suite, Celia attacked her boyfriend sexually. Through all the chaos and fear of losing him forever, she'd gotten all kinds of horny. They did it in the bathroom and on the couch. They did it in bed until they fell out of bed and kept doing it on the floor. They did it until Ian couldn't do it anymore. Even then, Celia kept touching him and licking him.

God, she loved her Ian.

Celia's fangs never once went boing. Somehow, she'd transcended the blood lust without a *Ralph*. She could smell the fresh knife wound on Ian's chest. She could hear his heartbeat. But it was just about love, intimacy, and orgasms. It was all about Ian being alive.

She licked his left nipple, salty from sex sweat. She heard him swallow another bite of pizza with pepperoni and black olives. She took a deep breath of pizza, Ian, and sex. She moaned.

He put his hand in her hair. For a guy with two fingers taped together (his pinkie still wasn't fully healed), he could still do amazing things with his digits. "Do you want to move in together?"

She lifted her head and looked at him. His black hair was soaked with sweat. His blue eyes were turning red around the edges from leftover alcohol and exhaustion. He was freckly and tan, despite his newly realized nocturnal tendencies. He was her Ian, and she smiled like a fool when she caught the scent of woodsy BO.

"Really?" she asked.

"I mean we already kind of were."

She touched his lips. "Yeah."

"Can we find another place on the beach?"

"I would accept nothing less." She smiled and ran her fingertips over his cheekbones.

His eyes slid shut. "Celia, can we go to bed soon?"

"Yeah." She leaned down and kissed his forehead.

He started snoring, piece of pizza still in-hand.

Celia got up and turned off the chandelier. She removed the pizza from Ian's hand and curled against his body like a cat. In his sleep, he put his arm around her and pulled her tight against his chest. As she was about to nod off, Celia heard his slurred whisper. "Mermaid."

CHAPTER TWENTY-FOUR

When Ian's parents heard about the fire, they threatened to rush to their son's aid and bring him anything and everything he'd ever left at his childhood home in Panama City. He told them to hold off until he and Celia found a place.

That wasn't helpful at all, because once Ian announced they were moving in together, his parents went psycho and said awkward things like "Are you getting married?" and "Does she want children?" really loudly so that Celia could hear their voices pumped through Ian's cell phone from across the hotel suite.

They soon found a cabana on Admiral Key. It wasn't far from the charred remains of the Sleeping Gull Apartments, and it was about double the size. Also, the landlady didn't wear a wig. Celia had come to be suspicious of all people who wore wigs.

Their home was a cozy little place with small windows and efficient air conditioning. It was about thirty feet from the beach, and they were hidden from neighbors by some insane Old World Climbing Fern bushes that basically overtook anything in their path.

Mr. and Mrs. Hasselback were exactly what Celia expected. Ian's mother, Char, was an ex-Florida beauty queen and retired flight attendant with bleached blonde hair and beautiful skin. Ian's dad, Douglas, Sr., looked exactly like Ian, except thirty years older and with brown eyes. Ian had his mom's eyes.

Not only were they what she expected, but they were what Ian had warned—overbearing, nosey, and sweet as pecan pie. They didn't understand why Celia and Ian had to move at night, but Ian explained Celia was a night shift worker, and they couldn't mess with her routine.

His parents wanted to know all about Happy Gas, Celia's dead parents, her future plans (she didn't have any yet), and how much she loved their son (about a ton). To Celia, it felt like they stayed forever. It was cute how they doted over their youngest. He was obviously the favorite. It did suck having to keep her blood in a cooler in the bedroom closet, though. Plus, Celia had to hide Imogene from the Hasselbacks because they *could not* meet Imogene. Celia knew her best friend was not for general consumption.

Imogene took over midget Steve's clientele. She didn't operate out of the hospital like he did, though. With a personal loan from Celia, she moved away from Mizzenmast and onto Barkentine Beach, within walking distance of the Drift Inn. She had a nice little place where she dealt, and she was super popular with the local vamps because she was hot and liked to have fun. She was on her cell phone a lot, but other than that, not much had changed. Imogene was back to carrying her cassette player everywhere and hiding behind her red plastic sunglasses. She licked Ian's cheek every chance she got.

Celia stopped seeing Dr. Savage professionally, although she did see her sometimes, socially. Dean and Ian hung out often since Dr. Savage was busy with her new protégé, Vixen. Celia had only seen the former exotic dancer once since Danny went down, but she looked nice. She didn't dress like a whore anymore, and she wasn't murdering people, so that was good. Despite Celia's suspicions, she still insisted "Vixen" was her real name.

Celia was back working at Happy Gas, and Omar kept

threatening to make her a manager. Ralph treated her with the utmost respect now that she was living with Ian. Sometimes, Ian even let Ralph come over, and they would talk about surfing and get high.

Ian bought a surfboard. He hadn't used it yet, but it sat against the wall of their place, and he pet it like a dog. He did continue going out with Celia when she swam in the ocean. She found her swim time much improved with Ian there, which was funny, since her night swims used to be solitary, just Celia and the slimy sea. With Ian there, it felt like something they shared together. Celia wanted to share everything with Ian.

When she started trying to rebuild her movie collection, she realized it was super hard to find anything on VHS anymore, so she got with the times and actually bought a DVD player.

Ian bought her first DVD: *Labyrinth.* Celia did have one surprising realization—she didn't want to buy *Pretty Woman.* She felt like she didn't need it anymore. Instead, Ian bought the special anniversary DVD, because he said it was now one of his favorite movies. Go figure.

———◆———

They met Imogene for a round of drinks at the Drift Inn. It was pretty packed, considering it was a Thursday night during tourist season. Celia still didn't know how tourists even found the place. It looked like a shoebox by the side of the road.

Celia only had two drinks. (She didn't count shots.) Despite this, she got sick when she and Ian got home. He held her hair back as she hurled, which was very gentlemanly. Then, they fell asleep wrapped around each other.

She didn't know what time it was when Ian's heartbeat woke her, but it sounded like a steel drum in her brain. She put her hands on either side of her head and curled into a little ball, groaning. She didn't want to wake Ian, so she went to the bathroom, just in case she was going to spew again—but she didn't feel sick. Celia just felt weird.

She swore she could still hear Ian's heartbeat from the bedroom, but then she realized, over the sound of their ever-running air conditioner, that just wasn't possible. She leaned her hands on the sink and stared at herself in the mirror. She didn't look like she was going nuts, so what the hell was that noise?

Then she noticed the noise was coming from inside of her. Considering vampires were dead and didn't have heartbeats, this realization was somewhat off-putting. She wondered what the hell was in those drinks at the Drift Inn? She had a momentary *Spaceballs* moment where she thought maybe some little creature was about to pop out of her stomach, covered in blood, and tap dance in the bathtub.

Little creature.

Holy shit, little creature!

Celia covered her mouth with her hand to stifle a scream.

Ian always said he wanted kids.

ABOUT THE AUTHOR

Sara Dobie Bauer is a writer, model, and mental health advocate with a creative writing degree from Ohio University. She spends most days at home in her pajamas as a book nerd and sex-pert for SheKnows.com. Her short story, "Don't Ball the Boss," was nominated for the 2015 Pushcart Prize, inspired by her shameless crush on Benedict Cumberbatch. She lives with her hottie husband and two precious pups in Northeast Ohio, although she would really like to live in a Tim Burton film. She is also the author of *Wolf Among Sheep, Life without Harry,* and *Forever Dead.* Read more at SaraDobieBauer.com or find her on Twitter @SaraDobie.

Want more Celia and Imogene?

Turn the page for suggested discussion questions, and to find out about *Bite Somebody Else*,
available June 20, 2017!

Thank you for reading!

We hope you'll leave an honest review at Amazon, Goodreads, or wherever you discuss books online.

Leaving a review means a lot for the author and editors who worked so hard to create this book.

Please sign up for our newsletter for news about upcoming titles, submission opportunities, special discounts, & more.

WorldWeaverPress.com/newsletter-signup

BOOK CLUB DISCUSSION QUESTIONS

1. Celia is about as awkward as a giraffe on skis. Are there certain situations in your life that make you more nervous than others? What are they?

2. Bite Somebody takes place on the beaches of Florida, Celia's favorite location for night swimming! What's your favorite place to visit, and why?

3. Obsessed with Pretty Woman, Celia dreams of being "better." If there was one thing you could change about yourself, what would it be?

4. Imogene is pretty much shameless and without regret, and yet, Celia loves her. Do you think Imogene would make a good friend? Why or why not?

5. Celia's attraction to her neighbor, Ian, is immediate—and sort of weird since she falls in lust with the scent of his blood. Have you ever felt an instant connection to someone, blood type notwithstanding? What made that person so special?

6. Ian refuses to go into the ocean thanks to a Great White attack. (The shark apparently thought Ian smelled like bacon.) Is there a fear in your life that you refuse to face? Do you think you'll ever move past it?

7. (Insert ominous music here.) Celia's dreaded ex comes back and almost ruins everything. Do you still hold resentment toward any of your exes? How can we move beyond the past—preferably without using a pair of garden shears?

8. Ian loves Celia just the way she is, awkward vampire and all. Is there a couple in your life that reminds you of Celia and Ian (even if

it's you and your significant other)? Talk about what makes their relationship so special.

9. Ian and Celia experience some speed bumps in the bedroom. (Breaking Ian's finger, for instance, is a bit not good.) Have you had an awkward bedroom mishap? Do tell!

10. Imogene tells Celia about a song a boy once sung to her about how true love is easy. Do you think that's true … or is true love actually a lot of work?

11. If you could be more like a character in this book, which would you choose: Celia, Imogene, Ian, Dr. Savage, Heidi, or someone else? Why?

Need ten or more copies of Bite Somebody or Bite Somebody Else for a book club or other discussion group? Contact publisher@worldweaverpress.com to order at a discount!

MORE SPECULATIVE ROMANCE FROM WORLD WEAVER PRESS

BITE SOMEBODY ELSE
Immortality is being a horrible influence on your best friends. Forever.
by Sara Dobie Bauer

Imogene helped her newbie vampire friend Celia hook up with an adorable human, but now Celia has dropped an atomic bomb of surprise: she has a possibly blood-sucking baby on the way. Imogene is not pleased, especially when a mysterious, ancient, and annoyingly gorgeous vampire historian shows up to monitor Celia's unprecedented pregnancy.

Lord Nicholas Christopher Cuthbert III is everything Imogene hates: posh, mannerly, and totally uninterested in her. Plus, she thinks he's hiding something. So what if he smells like a fresh garden and looks like a rich boarding school kid just begging to be debauched? Imogene has self-control. Or something.

As Celia's pregnancy progresses at a freakishly fast pace, Imogene and Nicholas play an ever-escalating game of will they or won't they, until his sexy maker shows up on Admiral Key, forcing Nicholas to reveal his true intentions toward Celia's soon-to-arrive infant.

"In *Bite Somebody Else*, Bauer concocts a devilish brew that's one part *What We Do In the Shadows* and one part *She's Having a Baby*. If you loved the charm and wit of *Bite Somebody*, its sequel is sure to intoxicate!"
—E. Catherine Tobler, author of the *Folley & Mallory* series

"Raunchy and irreverent, *Bite Somebody Else* is a vampire romp oozing with sexual tension and laugh-out-loud surprises. Crank up some '80s music, sip a rum punch, and start reading!"
—Beth Cato, author of the *Clockwork Dagger* and *Blood of Earth* series

MORE SPECULATIVE ROMANCE FROM WORLD WEAVER PRESS

A reluctant vampire hunter, stalking New York City as only a scorned bride can.

LEGALLY UNDEAD
Vampirarchy Book 1
by Margo Bond Collins

Elle Dupree has her life all figured out: first a wedding, then her Ph.D., then swank faculty parties where she'll serve wine and cheese and introduce people to her husband the lawyer.

But those plans disintegrate when she walks in on a vampire sucking the blood from her fiancé, Greg. Horrified, she screams and runs—not away from the vampire, but toward it, brandishing a wooden letter opener.

As she slams the improvised stake into the vampire's heart, a team of black-clad men bursts into the apartment. Turning to face them, Elle realizes Greg's body is gone—and her perfect life falls apart.

"Ms. Collins delivered tenfold with her debut of theVampirarchy series, I've found my new favorite vampire hunter in Elle Dupree! In a word…FANGTASTIC!!!"
— Romancing the Dark Side

"Manages to take typical features of urban fantasy and make them its own. Left me desperate for the next chapter in Elle's story. I'll be curious to see where Collins takes the Vampirarchy series next!"
— All Things Urban Fantasy

"I LOVED this book!! This book has it all: humor, romance, suspense and vampires…what more can you ask for!"
—Reading Is A Way of Life

MORE SPECULATIVE ROMANCE FROM
WORLD WEAVER PRESS

OPAL
Fae of Fire and Stone, Book 1
by Kristina Wojtaszek

White as snow, stained with blood, her talons black as ebony...

In this retwisting of the classic Snow White tale, the daughter of an owl is forced into human shape by a wizard who's come to guide her from her wintry tundra home down to the colorful world of men and Fae, and the father she's never known. She struggles with her human shape and grieves for her dead mother—a mother whose past she must unravel if men and Fae are to live peacefully together.

Trapped in a Fae-made spell, Androw waits for the one who can free him. A boy raised to be king, he sought refuge from his abusive father in the Fae tales his mother spun. When it was too much to bear, he ran away, dragging his anger and guilt with him, pursuing shadowy trails deep within the Dark Woods of the Fae, seeking the truth in tales, and salvation in the eyes of a snowy hare. But many years have passed since the snowy hare turned to woman and the woman winged away on the winds of a winter storm leaving Androw prisoner behind walls of his own making—a prison that will hold him forever unless the daughter of an owl can save him.

CHAR
Fae of Fire and Stone, Book 2
by Kristina Wojtaszek

Fire is never tame—least of all the flames of our own kindling.

Raised in isolation by the secretive Circle of Seven, Luna is one of the few powerful beings left in a world dominated by man. Versed in ancient fairy tales and the language of plants, Luna struggles to control her powers over fire. When her mentor dies in Luna's arms, she is forced into a centuries-long struggle against the gravest enemy of all Fae-kind—the very enemy that left her orphaned. In order to save her people, Luna must rewrite their history by entering a door in the mountain and passing back through time. But when the lives of those she loves come under threat, her rage destroys a forest, and everything in it. Now called The Char Witch, she is cursed to live alone, her name and the name of her people forgotten.

Until she hears a knock upon her long-sealed door.

MORE SPECULATIVE ROMANCE FROM WORLD WEAVER PRESS

DEMONS, IMPS, AND INCUBI
Edited by Laura Harvey

Demons, Imps, Incubi: dark, powerful, and forbidden. Only the foolish would seek one out for seduction, and yet . . . deals are struck. Souls are ensnared.

But must a demon's agenda always be demonic? Can he be redeemed? Or does being bad feel too good to bother with redemption? Long ago, imps were more mischievous and playful—*naughty*, perhaps?—and perceptions of them have only grown more sinister over the centuries. The incubus craves sex, but what makes us crave him?

Explore dark and sensual worlds with eight brand new stories of magic and seduction that will set you aflame by Cori Vidae, Alexa Piper, Erzabet Bishop, Mark Greenmill, Nicole Blackwood, J. C. G. Goelz, Jeffery Armadillo, and M. Arbroath.

COVALENT BONDS
Edited by Trysh Thompson

Covalent bonds aren't just about atoms sharing electron pairs anymore—it's about the electricity that happens when you pair two geeks together. This anthology celebrates geeks of all kinds (enthusiasts, be it for comics, Dr. Who, movies, gaming, computers, or even grammar), and allows them to step out of their traditional supporting roles and into the shoes of the romantic lead. Forget the old stereotypes: geeks are sexy.

Featuring nine stories ranging from sweet to hot, by authors G.G. Andrew, Laura VanArendonk Baugh, Tellulah Darling, Mara Malins, Jeremiah Murphy, Marie Piper, Charlotte M. Ray, Wendy Sparrow, and Cori Vidae, *Covalent Bonds* is a chance for geeks get their noses *out* of the books, and instead to *be* the book.

MORE SPECULATIVE ROMANCE FROM WORLD WEAVER PRESS

OMEGA RISING
The Wolf King, Book 1
by Anna Kyle

Cass Nolan has been forced to avoid the burn of human touch for her whole life, drawing comfort instead from her dreams of a silver wolf—her protector, her friend. When her stalking nightmares return, her imaginary dead sister's ghost tells her to run, Cass knows she should listen, but the sinfully hot stranger she just hired to work on her ranch has her mind buzzing with possibilities. Not only does her skin accept Nathan's touch, it demands it. Cass must make a decision—run again and hope she saves the people who have become her family, or stand and fight. Question is, will it be with Nathan or against him?

Nathan Rivers' life is consumed by his quest to find the Omega wolf responsible for killing his brother, but when the trail leads him to Cass and her merry band of shapeshifters, his wolf wants only to claim her for himself. When evidence begins piling up that Cass is the Omega he's been seeking, things become complicated—especially since someone else wants her dead. Saving her life might mean sacrificing his own, but it may be worth it to save the woman he can't keep from reaching for.

SKYE FALLING
The Wolf King, Book 2
by Anna Kyle

Skye, a Fae-shapeshifter halfing, could die if she doesn't find out how to wake her dormant wolf, so mere rumors of the Wolf King's return are enough to convince her to sneak through the portal between Faerie and Chicago in search of his aid. But the dizzyingly bright lights and sounds of the human realm are too tempting to ignore. So is the sexy shapeshifter wolf intent on capturing her—the one who stirs her sleeping wolf just long enough to bind the handsome stranger in a mate-bond.

World Weaver Press, LLC

Publishing fantasy, paranormal, and science fiction.

We believe in great storytelling.

worldweaverpress.com